NEST

NEST

28 Tales of Pulp Fiction

Francis DiPietro

Writers Club Press
San Jose New York Lincoln Shanghai

Nest
28 Tales of Pulp Fiction

Writers Club Press
an imprint of iUniverse.com, Inc.

For information address:
iUniverse.com, Inc.
5220 S 16th, Ste. 200
Lincoln, NE 68512
www.iuniverse.com

ISBN: 0-595-14065-3

Printed in the United States of America

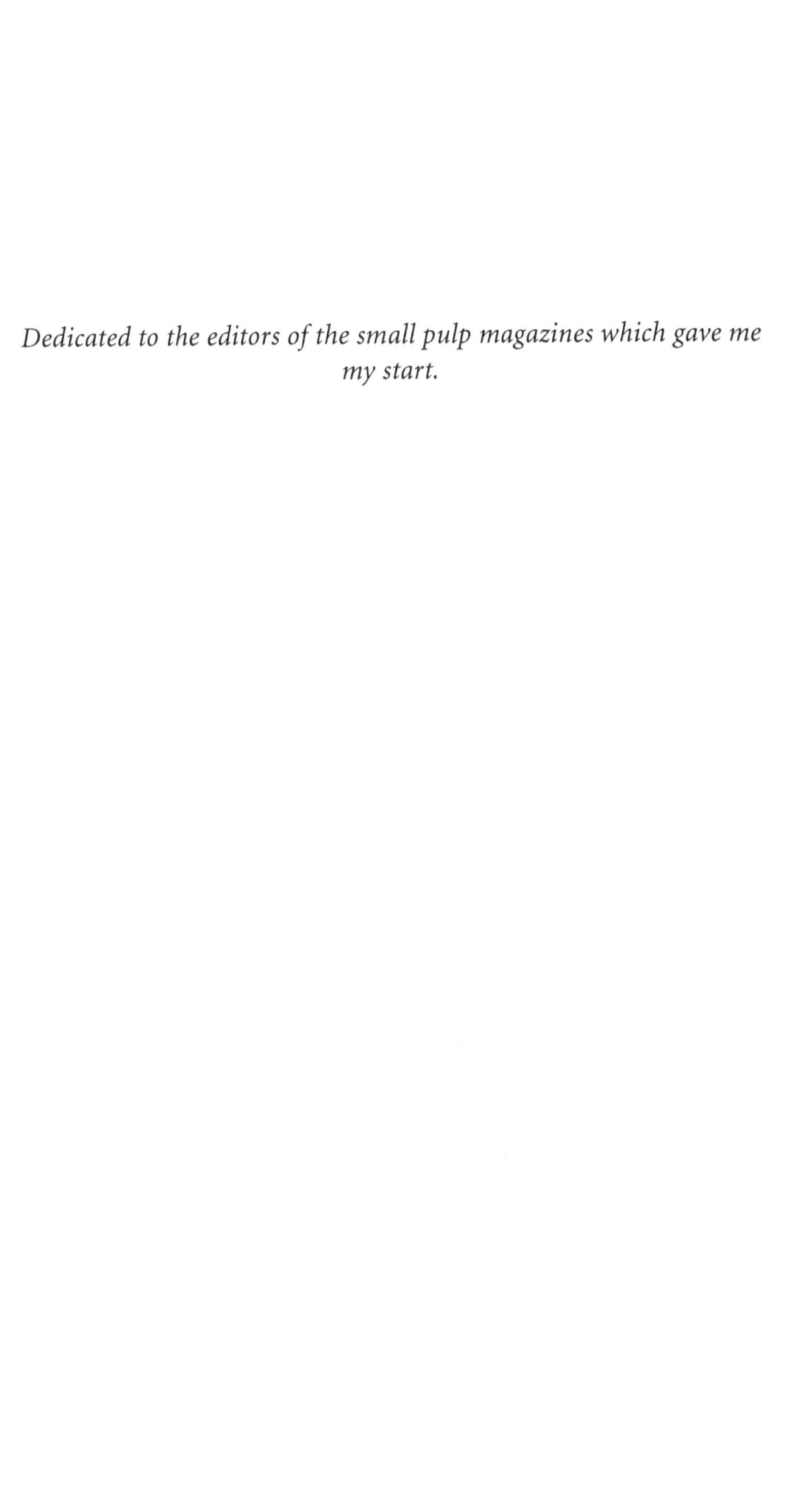

Dedicated to the editors of the small pulp magazines which gave me my start.

Epigraph

I hope readers will continue to enjoy these stories, written mostly from 1991-95, when I focused on enhancing my publication credits with small to mid-sized magazines. For writers today the road is different, and I still clearly recall Harlan Ellison's words that there are no proving grounds for writers of today—no vast sea of pulp magazines to test one's talents and hone one's skills. But I think an answer has finally arrived in the form of digital publishing (either alone or in conjunction with print). It's lovely for an old non-mainstream writer like myself to know that my stories are no longer subject to the whims and fancies of a single, deskbound editor, but answer to the higher mandates of their intended audience.

With digital publishing we can all be like Neo at the end of The Matrix: free to propagate a remarkable revolution.

Acknowledgements

A Pose for the Lady first appeared in **Midnight Zoo** magazine

Pork Chop's Last Stand first appeared in **Outlaw Biker** magazine

Fraidy Katz first appeared in **The Fractal,** George Mason University

Nineteen first appeared in **Zoiks!** magazine

The Keechelus Incident and *The Thousand Injuries* first appeared in **Eldritch Tales** magazine

Old Harry's Grave first appeared in **The Pinehurst Journal**

All the Trimmings first appeared in **The Bahlasti Papers**

Scorched Mercy first appeared in **Hyperbole Studios**

The Coffee Nuts first appeared in **Aberations** magazine

Contents

A Death of Honor

The circus, lovely and with gleaming promise, came to Martinsville early in the spring. Massive tent stakes were driven into Hadley Memorial Park by burly manchildren with Thor-like hammers. Thick velvet drapes veiled the secret wonders of each cage, car and trailer. No one would see anything without paying their admission.

Yoshio Rusker had recently moved to Martinsville. At age nine, his greatest transportation worry was that his model airplanes might get damaged. His dad and mom, Tashimoto and Helen, were each teachers. Four months ago they were nestled in Osaka, but now things were different.

"You weren't even here for the Fall Foliage Festival," one of Yoshio's teachers told him. "How could you possibly know anything about Martinsville?"

"Father taught me," said Yoshio simply.

The rest of the class giggled. Girls pointed and put their hands over their faces. Boys laughed openly and wildly.

"Oh," said the teacher, "*Papa San.*"

Tashimoto Rusker was a town oddity. A Japanese teacher with an American father and a Japanese mother, who married an American and moved to America, Tashimoto didn't feel at home in either country.

Today he completed his first semester as a teaching assistant to an American History professor. It was the first time Tashimoto had been reduced to an assistant since he was in his twenties. But it was temporary, and he would work hard.

His wife Helen knew this.

"That's why I married him," she told her friend Marcia playfully. They sat in the Rusker's wide kitchen, sipping French vanilla coffee, their hands occasionally magnetized to a pastry. "Tash is all the man I want him to be."

Marcia lowered her eyes and sipped. "Is he…built like an American man?" she asked tentatively. "Because I've heard all sorts of stories about Oriental men and how small—"

Yoshio arrived home from school just as his mother smashed her coffee cup against the wall and screamed to Marcia, "It's a lie! It's a lie! Every woman asks me this and it's a filthy fat-assed lie!"

When Marcia saw the slanty-eyed kid standing in the doorway behind Helen, she decided to hone her possible retorts down to one: "You need a nice big vibrator, hon." She whispered it to Helen then stood and patted Yoshio's head as she left.

Mother and son looked at each other.

The mid afternoon sun played tricks upon the windows, and patches of light and shadow measured across the floor. Coffee ran down the far wall, snaking to the linoleum, joining broken pieces of the cup that Helen threw.

"What does 'vibrator' mean?" asked Yoshio.

Helen took the boy in her arms, hugging him with her lips to his hair, smelling the Johnson's shampoo. "It means that your father tries very, very hard," she whispered.

At supper that night, Tashimoto did indeed try very, very hard not to get upset. He ate peas angrily, clinking his chopsticks against the plate. "I don't want you seeing Marcia so much," he said into the dish. "She doesn't behave well in front of Yoshio."

"Yes, dear," was all that Helen said. She wanted her husband to feel the respect he deserved. His sleek crop of obsidian hair and straight white collar did little to hide his feelings.

"Can we go to the circus, dad?" Yoshio asked suddenly. It was a question he had planned carefully, and he waited the whole day for this quiet stretch during supper.

"There's a circus in town?" Tashimoto asked Helen.

She nodded. "All the kids know about it, and it only pulled in this morning. It looks big."

Tashimoto eased his attack on the peas. "I have never been to an American circus," he said.

Yoshio smiled.

The next night, after the Rusker family ate at Burger Villa. Tashimoto drove their Dodge Caravan to Hadley Memorial Park, which was already quite full of cars. Yoshio watched the big tent and Ferris wheel and animal cages with awe. This was the kind of America he had pictured in his mind, many months past in Osaka.

Tashimoto ushered his family down to the field. The air was heavy with a cotton candy and butter caramel scent, and crazy music played from inside the tent.

They approached from the rear, and had to round a dark corner where the animal cages were. A small alley had been formed by the rows of equipment, and the circus helpers—big manchildren who worked for little more than food and slept in foldaway cots—mulled through the shadows, chuckling and swearing and drinking. They congregated near the ape cages, their jobs essentially done until it was time to pack.

"Who are those men?" Yoshio asked.

"They help with the circus," Helen told him, but Yoshio didn't see them doing anything helpful. The apes were even acting dubious in their company.

"Leave them alone," said Tashimoto, "and they won't bother you." He patted the nape of Yoshio's neck. "Now let's have fun."

Inside the big white tent was gathered most of Martinsville, their wholesome whitebread faces all thronged together and chattering. The mayor sat with his three daughters and sipped gin from an unmarked plastic cup. The town barber let his two boys run through the aisles and spit at younger children. The chief of police kept eyeing the elephants.

After paying admission to the show, which started in moments, the Ruskers found an available strip of bench and sat together. Tashimoto excused himself for a minute, and as the lights went down he returned with three ice cream cones.

A snake man, a cowboy, a fat lady, dancing lions, a tattooed bald man, prancing horses, and a dozen clowns performed. A thin woman did a handstand on the trapeze. An elephant rolled over. A crazy magician pulled flowers out of his pants.

"How do you like the circus?" asked Helen.

"It's wonderful!" Yoshio replied.

"I like it too," said Tashimoto. He leaned sideways and whispered to his wife, "I've got to find the bathroom."

Tashimoto made his way across the aisle and down a platform. He saw no restroom signs, but he was able to locate an attendant.

"Do you have a restroom?" he asked.

The man nodded. "Around the corner, outside, by the animal cages," he said.

Upon exiting the big tent, Tashimoto was greeted by a sky full of stars. Crickets chirped at the base of the treeline and the grass was combed by a gentle breeze. With so many people inside the tent, being outside alone made him feel like an astronaut leaving the ship. But it was lovely and haunting.

Locating the cages again, there in the alley of equipment, Tashimoto proceeded humbly. Long shadows combined with a dim moon—dark enough so that only the eyes of the animals in the cages could be seen. They were so, so quiet.

Deeper into the tight alley went Tashimoto, until near the end, where crates were stacked to form a wall, he saw a pair of porta-johns. Selecting the one that looked cleaner, he went inside and did his business by the light of an overhead green Cyalume lightstick. He finished and opened the door.

A massive man in dirty clothes stood directly in his path. His hair was cut unevenly and he gave off the sweet odor of spilled brandy. He smiled at Tashimoto, revealing many missing teeth.

"You need a friend?" asked the big man drunkenly. Behind him was only the blank void of the long alley both men had traversed, one following the other.

"Excuse me," said Tashimoto, trying to pass.

The large stranger bumped his chest into Tashimoto. "I've got a better circus for you than that tent," he said.

"Leave me alone," Tashimoto said firmly, with honor.

The muscular man smiled playfully as he shook his head, no, and in an instant his large hand covered Tashimoto's mouth. The stranger's big arms pressed Tashimoto against the man's torso, so that Tashimoto's greatest struggle only kicked dirt. Up close, the stranger smelled like old cabbage.

Not wanting to alarm others, the burly man dragged Tashimoto away from the porta-johns. With his face and body pinned, Tashimoto heard the rattle of keys. "I'll hurt you if you move," said the stranger. He opened one of the cages.

A filthy handkerchief constricted around Tashimoto's mouth.

The stranger threw him to the floor of the cage and locked the heavy bars. The big man giggled.

A family of four apes watched from the far corner. Tashimoto tried to stand but the big man held him face-down. "Don't struggle and I won't hurt you," he said angrily. He worked at Tashimoto's belt violently, then the zipper, until the pants finally peeled off with a great heave.

Excited now, the big man unzipped his fly and tore off Tashimoto's underwear. His enormous hands pinned the smaller man's torso down. He leaned forward and pushed.

A horrible pain consumed Tashimoto. The big man started to pump, slow at first but then with great force. He held the Japanese teacher under him like a rag doll. He drooled on Tashimoto's back as, with a heaving rush, he came.

The apes were utterly aghast.

And in an instant, the big man dismounted, opened the cage and was gone. Tashimoto did not move. He could feel his own blood. His hands untied the gag.

The night was sweet and somber. Crickets still chirped in the distance and the breeze was still gentle. Tashimoto cleaned himself up as best he could and returned to the tent.

"We were getting worried," said Helen.

Tashimoto sat timidly. The pain still lingered, but he had faced this thing with honor. No police station would have a file on this incident, and the only one he would tell would be his doctor, early the next morning.

He didn't care if it was a crime. Some things should not be reported.

"This is it!" said Yoshio happily. "The big ending!"

A cage containing four apes was wheeled into the center of the ring. As Tashimoto could now clearly see, there was something very special about these apes. A sign on the side of the cage proclaimed, "These apes are able to communicate through sign language."

The bars opened, and Tashimoto watched dumbfounded as the apes emerged and told their trainer what they had seen.

One of them produced Tashimoto's torn underwear.

A Pose for the Lady

My old office was just down the hall from a budding dental clinic, and each day I was forced to deal with the screaming children and terrified adults who would shoot nervous glances at my own clients and ruffle their newspapers in uneasy anticipation. When my business started to slump because of this, I still tried to remain the perfect neighbor, never playing my office elevator music too loudly and always closing my door before I got into an argument with a Customer. In spite of these numerous precautions, I soon realized that the battle was hopeless, and late in November of my first year in business, I relocated.

A lady by the name of Sally Kellerman (no relation to the actress), who worked with an importing company one floor above mine, was the only person in the entire building to say goodbye to me. I recall her being on the pretty side, mid thirties. That day she was wearing a lovely dress with a floral pattern and lipstick that was dangerously close to fire engine red. She approached me as I was lugging a couple of boxes out the door, sweating rather profusely in the pre-winter cold.

"Mr. Trevis, you're bound to catch pneumonia if you keep this up! Why, just look at you. You're head's already steaming!"

I stopped, turning my eyes upward. "So it is," I said, feeling rather silly. Sally giggled.

"Why didn't you just get a couple of movers? Let *them* worry about getting pneumonia."

"Movers cost money, and that's something I don't have a heck of a lot of. Besides," I said, in a somewhat lower and more embarrassed tone, "I sent out notes to all the other offices asking if anyone would help me move, and…"

"No one?" she asked. "Not one volunteer?"

"'Fraid so." I sat on one of the large boxes and wiped my brow with the back of my hand. "I at least figured Harold Murphy up on the fourth floor would give me a hand. I used to buy him lunch almost every day."

Sally inhaled quickly and rolled her eyes. "What a bastard! All of them; they suck. It's like they left you out here to die." And without another word she came to my side and started pushing a carton toward the front door.

I couldn't help but notice the low cut of that floral dress and how Sally's breasts would bulge and threaten to literally break out every time she bent over, due mostly to the fact that she wasn't wearing a bra. Office politics?

"You know, if you had sent me a note I would have been glad to help—and I really mean that, too, Mr. Trevis," she said in response to my discovered stare.

"My friends call me Al, not Mr. Trevis."

A smile broke out, followed by another giggle. "I never would've figured you for an Alex."

"I'm not. My name is Allston. Does that sound better? Allston Townsend Trevis." Now it was my turn to smile.

"Holy shit! What a fucking name! 'Allston Townsend Trevis'. Really? Were your folks twisted?"

"No, just eminently corruptible…*I'm kidding.*"

Between the two of us we managed to knock off the rest of the boxes in pretty decent time—way before Sally's rotund boss came pounding down the stairs looking for her, and we were able to establish a time for a dinner date. Her place, just after eight. She gave me the address and phone number and I looked smartly at her and nodded, but as soon as she rounded the corner I scrambled for a pen and paper. I was like that, and I suppose I would have had a lot more customers if my ego didn't get in the way when a name was quickly dropped at a party or luncheon. Lord knows those guys who whip out a crayon and write on their napkins are far richer than I am.

My car started begrudgingly in the nippy air, and the coldness of the steering wheel made me wish I had brought some gloves along with me. The warm-up time would be long, and my breath had already clouded the windshield when I turned the defogger on. And then I noticed something. It was very odd that I didn't remember putting it there, but right in front of me on the windshield, plain as day, was the single, finger-scrawled word:

"Soon."

I peered at it stupidly and was on the verge of determining whether it was in my handwriting or not when the mist on the windshield cleared and the word temporarily vanished. I suppose I could have turned off the defogger and waited for the word to reappear, but it didn't seem of much importance to me at the time. It was only later that it occurred to me the word had been drawn from the inside of the car, in a style of writing that came close, but was not my own.

Too many things were on my agenda for the morning to afford me time to stop and think, so I didn't. Instead I passed away the hours by completing some minor errands, such as picking up some new stationary, checking my post office box, allowing The Grumbling One a ten dollar feed on gas, etc. Nothing special, although I did stop by a floral shop to buy some nice pretty weeds for my date—and don't think I underrate them. When begonias aren't even in your league and roses aren't even in your galaxy, you buy some nice pretty weeds (preferably ones with a "Sale!" tag on them).

The rest of the day blurred like the downward plunge of some great rollercoaster, and when my head stopped spinning I found myself wiping my feet on Sally Kellerman's doormat, finger poised to ring the bell.

The flowers were under my arm, nice and snug, but a little voice was asking me how I would like it if somebody knocked on my door and handed me a gift direct from under their armpit. Yuk. I quickly shifted the flowers to a "present arms" position before I rang, feeling like some half-assed version of the FTD Florist.

Sally took a long time to answer, and the cold wind took the opportunity to whip right through the suit I wore, chilling me in all the wrong places. I survived, though, and was treated to a very nice sight indeed when the door finally did open. Sally was wearing a delicate blue kimono with a liberally low cut, and I immediately felt like a Manhattan chauffeur who had been hired by a nudist colony.

"Oh! You brought flowers! How lovely." She pecked me on the cheek but my eyes weren't quite high enough to meet hers. "I'll have to put these in water. Come in, come in!" And without further prompting I shut the door behind me and flicked a mental finger at the coldness outside.

Sally had shuffled off to my right, calling back, "Make yourself at home, sailor." I grinned, found her closet, and peeled off the layers a bit. "Don't mind if I do," I said in a tone too low for all but my own ears.

We had a monster pot roast for dinner and washed it down with some very good port wine. Between munchings we made the usual rounds of small talk, followed by those awkward, *let's-get-to-know-each- other-better* glances that can only be mellowed by doubling the dosage of good port wine. We followed this prescription religiously for a while until our "good port wine" had developed an attitude and our livers told us that they had thrown up (so to speak) the white flag in the battle against inebriation. Then all we could do was exchange glassy-eyed, slack-jawed smirks and secretly wonder to ourselves if we were sober enough to fool around properly and with a modicum of effectiveness.

That question was soon answered and our doubts expelled, and it was like a jump-frame to the next scene: me and Sally supine on the bed, weakly smoking cigarettes and lamely holding hands. Our eyes were fixed on the blank ceiling and our minds drifted in limbo. After a while, I got dressed.

I think I was entertaining some fanciful thoughts about lobster bisque when I heard the front door smash open and heavy footsteps pound into the little house. We were both too numb to scream, but I quickly motioned for Sally to hide under the bed and I ducked into a nearby closet. It was then that I saw the telephone on her nightstand, and my nerves and my brains were battling to see whether I would make a run for it. Secretly, I think I rooted for my brains.

And then they were upon us; three, four, five men pouring into the room. They discovered Sally first, and I silently swore at myself for instructing her to hide under the damn bed. By the time the closet was opened and a large pair of gloved hands was pulling me out they already had a gun to Sally's head. I had just enough time to hear the "*ssswwkk!*" of the silencer do its job, then it felt like a Louisville Slugger had just sent my head on a home run blast, and the world went away.

*   *   *

Lights…very faint…blurred…a shadow, moving around, watching me. When consciousness finally decided to pay me a sales call I was very slow in answering, but eventually I got around to it. My head felt as if it was still careening out of the ballpark, and I would have traded my left nut for a couple of Tylenol. Such was the state of things.

A little fat guy with a crescent moon bald spot on his head was smiling at me, and I felt like slugging him.

"Have a nice rest, Cinderella?" he asked me with mock kindness. Then he turned and shouted into the next room, "He's awake and fairly responsive!"

Next thing I know a bunch of guys in suits are jamming around trying to get the first dance with me. At length a big guy with even bigger hands won out. His immense fingers started poking me in the ribs and he was mumbling "Well, well, well…"

At that moment I think I did something artful, like puke into his massive palm. Before the blackness washed over me again I could hear him adamantly swearing, and the shuffleshuffle of many feet hurrying to leave the room. Apparently the port wine had grown fangs and horns for its early reappearance.

Unpleasant dreams about what they did to Sally Kellerman haunted my disturbed sleep, and when my eyes opened yet again they encountered cold-looking tiles. A stream of water was jetting out at me from high above, and only then did I realize that I had been plopped into a shower, puke-stained clothes and all. Not wanting to reveal myself as being all chipper and ready for an interrogation, I feigned sleep…dreamland…lights out—whatever you want to call it.

Pretty soon I heard a rustling as the stall door opened. I could sense a presence there, just looking at me. Carefully, I cracked an eyelid and saw old fat boy himself, his jaws working out of habit, like a cow chewing cud. He was leaning over, and the path behind him looked clear enough, so, as quickly and quietly as possible I shot out my hand, grabbed him by the collar, and sent his face smashing forward into the tiled wall. He slumped on top of me with a fading groan then checked-out of reality for a while.

I got up with some difficulty, made a quick scan around the bathroom, and found a nice dry robe tucked into a hamper. I put it on over my sopping clothes. If I had any luck, The Corpulent One had come into the bathroom to actually use the bathroom, not just to check on me, and his buddies wouldn't be missing him for a little while longer.

Some peeking through the keyhole told me the hallway was empty, and I did some mighty fine tip-toeing across its old wooden floorboards. From what I could tell the house appeared to be one of those Victorian jobbers, complete with Oriental rugs and an oak staircase, which told me I was on at least the second floor. Open doors off to my left and right led to unoccupied bedrooms, and a big brass mirror was at the end of the hall.

I could hear voices in the distance below, and although I could have made my way out a window, I just had to know what the bastards were talking about.

"Hee-hee!" someone laughed. "They paid for just one but we took two instead! Not bad."

A loud, gruff voice broke in. "You can't do much with a fucking corpse, Chester."

"Unless you're into necrophelia! Hee-hee!"

"Not funny," he snarled. "The take was successful but it was too damn messy. They won't be pleased with that."

Chester the jester stopped laughing. "B-But we took care of the body real well, Hank. They can't fault us on that one, you know."

"The body itself isn't the problem, it's the other people who are bound to miss the body. Sonner or later a big stink is gonna be raised, and we've gotta cover ourselves. That Trevis character upstairs might be able to give us what we want or he might not. You see, he has this awful memory. Either way, we can't let him escape from the zoo, if you know what I mean."

"Sure, sure...", Chester replied. "I understand all that. Don't you worry. Mrs. Pheney is going to do justice to Adolf."

A third man spoke up just then, and I din't care much for what he asked.

"Hey, where's Elmo? He's been up there pretty long."

There was a pause.

"Pretty fucking long..." Hank repeated, and by the time he said "Check it out," I was halfway out the window.

Two hours later a police lieutenant was listening to my story rather skeptically, lifting his bushy eyebrows at regular intervals. When all was said and done he steepled his fingers together and leaned back in his chair, whistling.

"Murder with a silencer…an old Victorian house…Hank, Chester and Elmo…What are you fucking kidding me?"

So much for police support.

"It's true, officer," I said lamely.

From out of nowhere, a doughnut appeared in his hand. He leaned back in his chair and said, "Loose ends always give your type away. For instance, who the hell are Mrs. Pheney and Adolf?"

I swallowed hard, forcing my brain to think.

"I…don't know," I said at length. "I have this real bad memory sometimes, but I swear all this is true."

The lieutenant leaned forward, picked his nose, and gave me his best man-to-man face. "Look, why don't you go home, take something for that hangover of yours, and get some sleep. I'm sure you'll feel like a real asshole in the morning; and if you think up any new murder mysteries, write a book."

Smiling with pseudo-sympathy, he sent me on my way.

But the ironic thing was, I couldn't go home. They would be looking for me. Hell, I couldn't even go back to Sally's to pick up my car. In short, I was really screwed, and the latenight cold was getting its revenge on me as I walked through the empty streets with clothes that were far from dry. I had to dump the robe in a garbage can before I went to the cops, but it didn't help me in hiding my hangover.

I got a bright idea and called myself a cab. Luckily, the men who captured me weren't interested in the small amount of cash I had in my wallet. Either that or they were going to wait until after they killed me to steal it. The thought wasn't pleasant.

"Where to?"

Now that was the question of the night, and my options were looking anemic. Oh, what the hell, if they were going to get me then so be it. There's an old saying that goes "It is far, far better to die pissing in the face of your enemy than waiting for him to piss in yours"—or something like that. I told the guy how to get to Sally's place.

Either Zeus was on my side or Pluto was in the crapper and couldn't check on me just then, because there was no trace of a living soul anyway near, or, thankfully, inside the house. These guys must have missed the day they covered surveillance in crook school.

Well, one of the first things I did was take a good, long look at that damn "Soon" on my windshield. I cursed lustily when I had determined little about it and suppressed the desire to write "*Almost*" in defiant response.

Thirty minutes and several bracing cups of coffee later I had managed to draw up a few conclusions. One: the writing on the windshield was meant to get me nervous, maybe even to do something stupid, like go looking for trouble. Two: they seemed fairly confident in the fact that they would get me. This coupled with the "they" they kept referring to in their kitchen conversation led me to believe they had a good amount of outside support. Three: at the present time they had to be scrambling like the proverbial blind mice to find me again, or else their boss would chop off something more vital than just their tails. Four: all this didn't amount to a horse's hairy ass in practical terms, and it certainly wouldn't have won me any votes for the Sherlock Holmes award. But still, something somewhere had to give, and if the fistful of shit that I blindly threw in the air just happened to hit the fan, I wouldn't complain.

Of course, good old Mrs. Pheney and the infamous Adolf were the big mysteries here. I was now sure that these names sounded familiar to me, and all I could do was give my termite-infested mind more time to work things out.

*   *   *

I managed to get a little sleep before the horrible lonliness of morning met my eyes. The bad guys, I concluded, had to be resting as well, because Lord knows how long they were awake planning this thing. It was a very saddening thought that I would never see Sally Kellerman again—at least not on this side of the white picket fence—and the total sobriety of a dead-calm morning had me warily weighing my options.

Except for a busted front door, the bad guys left no trace of their presence. No blood stains, no muddy footprints, no bullet shells. Nada.

Obviously, the police weren't interested in doing my sleuthing for me, but that was okay. That lazy lieutenant would soon be knee deep in *merde* once some hard evidence started turning up. My business was one possible line of defense, but to the crooks it probably looked more like a jugular vein. That could prove to be an advantage.

And, you may ask, what exactly do I do for a living?

That's the best part.

I'm a taxidermist.

Yes, a taxidermist. I stuff dead things.

I'm sure that you can now understand why I had to relocate my office. After all, how would you feel if your pet schnauzer just kicked the bucket and the only taxidermy man in six cities just happened to have his office next to the Bloody Drill of Horrors Dental Asylum? That wouldn't make you feel too comfortable, would it?

I made myself some toast and was about to scratch my balls when I suddenly realized who Mrs. Pheney and Adolf were. Damned if I couldn't put my finger on it before, but Mrs. Pheney was a former client of mine. A brooding old hag; and that was on her good days. Adolf, her prized pooch, was the patient. He had kicked the bucket while humping a nice young purebred, and the old lady wanted me to immortalize him.

Well, as it turned out, she didn't like the job I did. In fact, she absolutely hated the job I did, but it really wasn't my fault. You see, she told me that she wanted his "final pose" to be gratifying and yet realistic. I told her I would come up with something. A couple days later she comes into my shop, and I unveil my masterpiece: Adolf, with a generous hardon, permanently frozen in his final, fatal humping position.

Right away the old bag starts gasping and a few seconds later she keels over and faints right in front of her stuffed dog. For that one instant in time it looked for all the world like little Adolf was still alive, getting ready to wildly hump his elderly owner. But when Mrs. Pheney recovered, she failed to see the humor of it all. That's when she decided to call the hit men, I guess.

All things considered, I had one up on them, and I had to make damn sure that in the next twenty-four hours they would only see my shadow and grasp at air.

Later that morning I hauled ass out of Sally's house and, after a preliminary check under the hood, took to my car. I spent a great deal of time driving around looking for an old Victorian house, and when I finally found something that fit the bill I parked a safe distance away from it and waited. Sure enough, I saw good old Elmo himself come out to get the mail. A big white bandage was on his nose and he didn't look too pleased with life in general.

Now that I had a confirmed sighting, the first thing I wanted to do was disappear. When the time came, I would know how to get to them.

I drove to a picnic field with trees on all sides of it and started opening the packing boxes that Sally had helped me load into the car. Everything I needed was there, and I set up shop in the middle of the meadow, using my rear bumper as my office chair and the floor of my trunk as the work area. Naturally, a taxidermist needs to use many chemicals to do the job properly, and I was the kind of guy who developed an affection for the little bottles of liquid and vials of powder. My collection of the potent suckers outcompassed my need for some of them, but I suppose that deep down I had secretly prayed for an opportunity like this.

After some tough evaluating and coin flipping, I concluded that the drug Haloperidol, or Haldol, was just the kind of neat little time bomb I was looking for. Used mostly in the treating of total psychotics, Haldol does a number on the central nervous system and some of its more adverse reactions can include slurred speech, drooling, hypotension, collapse, grand mal seizures, coma, and a quick death if enough is given. There is no known antidote for it.

The drug comes in neat little tablets, syrup, injectables, and even suppositories. I only had the tablets, so I took a fistful of them and crushed them in a bowl until the resulting product was a fine powder. Carefully, I poured the contents of the bowl into a long vial, put the cap on and pocketed it. With something just short of haste I repacked the boxes and closed the trunk. As an afterthought, I fished around in one of the boxes and pulled out a scalpel. For an instant my eyes were mesmerized as I watched the sun glint off its polished steel, then I put it in my shirt pocket, like a deadly little pen. Too bad I didn't have the time to kick off my shoes and take a nap with the dandelions.

More planning and scheming took up the rest of my day, but when the sun finally ducked behind the horizon and night once again engulfed the city, I was ready.

*   *   *

The guise of a pizza delivery man is anything but new. However, in this particular case it fit in well. A few stops at a salon and a theatrical shop early in the day gave me all I needed in the way of a disguise. At first the shop owners couldn't understand what I wanted, and although I'll admit there's a great deal of humor in delivering two large sausage and pepperonis when you're dressed like MacBeth or Beowulf (just think of it: "*Eat on, MacDuff; and damn be he who first reaches for Rolaids!*"), I wasn't feeling quite so adventurous.

At first I thought fat Elmo would turn me and my steaming hot pizzas away when I apologized for the mix-up, but sure enough, just as I was getting ready to give them to him for free he dug out a wad of bills and flipped a couple at me. I thanked him for his patronage as he greedily took the poisoned pizzas off my hands.

As the door shut behind me I couldn't help but mumble the catch-word of the day, "Soon…"

* * *

It seems funny to reflect upon that night now, for the intervening time has caused me to realize that what I did later that evening was definitely an evil act. Previously during the telling of this story I had entertained thoughts of simply ending it with the pizza delivery, but now I understand that insatiable and morbid curiosity which grips your very intestines and doesn't stop until it's squeezed all the, ahem, you know what I mean.

I suppose that lazy lieutenant got quite a scare when he went to work the next morning, for standing right in front of the stairs to the police station were several rather odd-looking characters, each with their hands up in the air in a classic "I surrender" pose. I can just imagine the look on his face when he gazed down at their feet and saw the wooden planks…

You see, they were all stuffed and mounted, just like a row of schnauzers, posing for the lady.

God rest your avenged soul, Sally Kellerman.

Pork Chop's Last Stand

"I don't give two Spanish farts!" said Rufus "Pork Chop" Mallone to his old lady. "A man's woman is supposed to stick by him and support him, no matter what."

The trailer in which they dwelt was filthy. A velvet Elvis hung over a food-stained couch, and their cat, Trickles, lived up to her name by peeing in the sink.

"Now you listen to me, Pork Chop," said his old lady Jenna. "A woman can only take so much. In the past six months you've lost your job, lost three teeth, lost your sex drive, and lost your marbles. Shit, the only thing you've gained is weight!"

Ouch. Words like that hurt the tender Pork Chop, who was a sensitive guy despite his skull tattoos. He looked down at his gut helplessly. Was it his fault that barbecued chicken tasted so good?

"Get off my ass," Pork Chop told Jenna. "I'm just in a slump right now." He went to the fridge and got himself a Miller. "The only time you're quiet is when you've got a dick in your mouth…which reminds me—"

"Lay off it!" Jenna interrupted. "It was just the heat of the moment and all that Harlequin crap, that's all."

Pork Chop shook his head. "Roy's my best buddy. How could you blow him at my own birthday party?"

Jenna slammed the counter and raked her tangled hair. "You owed him four hundred, remember? Besides, you haven't had a boner since you lost your job."

"And I wonder why," Pork Chop challenged. "The thought of your empty head between Roy's hairy legs has scarred me for life!" He gulped down the beer and got another. Things didn't have to be this way, damn it; and today he was going to take charge.

Without saying another word, Pork Chop went to the bathroom and took out his ownership papers for the trailer, which he kept behind a bottle of unused Barbasol shave cream. Tucking the papers in the pocket of his overalls, Pork Chop belched heartily and scratched his balls and felt like a man.

Jenna didn't even ask why he left in such a hurry.

*   *   *

The Harley-Davidson dealership had more choppers than an Air Cavalry division, all gleamed chrome and toughness. Pork Chop wanted to pinch himself as soon as he stepped through the door.

"How can I help you?" a salesman asked. "Are you interested in any one in particular?"

"That depends," said Pork Chop shrewdly. He withdrew the ownership papers to the trailer and unfolded them. "How friendly would you boys be toward the idea of a trade?"

The salesman inspected the papers and talked to his manager. He returned with a smile.

"I think we can work something out…"

Twenty minutes later Pork Chop was sitting on the fattest, fastest hog he could buy…and it felt good. Jenna would be in for one helluva surprise when the claim people knocked on her door, but so what? Pork Chop wasn't going back.

At exactly twelve minutes past noon, Pork Chop's brand new Harley roared onto the boulevard. He sat proud in the saddle, his big gut bearing forward like a figurehead. In front of him the road was laid with barbecued chicken wings and freedom.

*   *   *

Back in the trailer, Jenna was getting madder by the minute. What had that crazy fat bastard gotten into now? The pay phone outside would probably ring soon, and Pork Chop would tell her he was in jail or something. She ate crackers furiously and flipped through the soaps.

Time passed.

Jenna swore to herself as she fixed dinner. Maybe Pork Chop had a heart attack. Maybe right now he was in some morgue, clumped on a cold marble slab, a tag on his toe. She had absolutely nothing to wear to a funeral, and worst of all, Pork Chop had no life insurance. Damn. If he was still alive, Jenna would make him regret it when he got back.

Time passed.

The next morning Jenna was awoken by representatives of the Harley-Davidson dealership. They showed her groggy eyes the papers Pork Chop had legally signed and relinquished, and at that precise moment, Jenna became filled with all the rage, fury, and righteous indignation a woman can hold.

"Look," she told one of the suits, "my old man really isn't sane. In fact, he's as crazy as a shithouse rat. So why don't you boys come in for a while and take your pants off. I promise to work hard if you tear-up that contract."

They looked at each other.

"No thanks," they replied. "You have twenty-four hours to vacate this trailer. If you're not out by then, the police will escort you out. Have a nice day."

The men left as unexpectedly as they came, and Jenna, faced with the end of life as she knew it, went to the pay phone to call her six brothers.

"Pork Chop left me high and dry," she told them. Deciding to lie, she added, "He beat me with a spatula and burned all my bras and let the neighbors have their way with me in exchange for beer! I want you to bring me his greasy head in a McDonald's bag! I want buzzards to pick at his bones! I want you to wrap his balls in a Tiffany bag and mail them to his mother! *I want revenge!*"

Jenna hung-up the phone.

*   *   *

The new chopper was just cherry. Pork Chop felt like a Bohemian king, riding where he pleased and eating what he wanted. His ears were even beginning to recover from Jenna's constant bitching.

All that changed when Pork Chop spotted six evil-looking dudes on Yamahas in his rearview mirror. These guys looked about as friendly as a canker sore.

Pork Chop reviewed his options. If there were only two or three, maybe he could take them…but six? And even though he rode a better bike, Pork Chop's extra weight made it unlikely he'd outrun them. Already they had gained much ground.

It was time to make a stand.

"Suck my dick!" Pork Chop swore. His beard ruffled in the wind and his wide face scowled. "These peckers want trouble, I'll show 'em trouble!"

The big man expertly did a 180 with his gleaming cycle. Dirt sprayed and rubber burned as Pork Chop headed on a collision course with his astounded pursuers. A fat, daring warcry burst from Pork Chop's lips as he took up his saddle bags with one hand and swung them in the air like a double-headed mace.

Filled with cans of baked beans and bottles of beer, the saddle bags were a force unto themselves, and Pork Chop's heavy, muscled, tatooed arm sent them careening at the front two attackers. The bags thunked against their chests and totally demolished them. Their bodies hit the road and their Yamahas veered off and crashed into the guardrails.

Pork Chop himself plowed into the remaining four. The intentional crash was risky, but the big man and his big Harley did the job like a tenpin bowling ball in a candlepin bowling alley. The Yamahas and their riders scattered like a teacup thrown against a brick wall.

Pork Chop got separated from his bike and the impact left a few gashes and bruises on him, but that only made him more pissed. He rose from the asphalt like an angry Phoenix. His overalls were torn and bloody. His beard was caked with grit. His big feet stomped over some fool's tailpipe.

The face of the nearest attacker was abruptly introduced to Pork Chop's helmet, and the point-blank smash robbed him of both his consciousness and his teeth. Pork Chop thought nothing more of it than swatting a fly.

"You ass monkeys messed with the wrong guy!" the big man bellowed at the sky. Tendrils of black smoke twisted around his head like dirty halos. Pork Chop could feel a new, almost biblical kind of power coarsing through his veins. Today all the injustice in the world would be avenged.

Like an enraged titan Pork Chop hefted one of the Yamaha riders off the ground and hurled him six feet sideways. The poor bastard hit the dirt like a burlap sack and whimpered.

Four down, two to go.

"Don't hurt us, man!" one of them pleaded.

"Ya, please don't hurt us!" the other echoed. "It was Jenna who sent us! She said you let the neighbors fuck her for beer, but that's cool with us now! If you want we can all go back and fuck her! Just don't hurt us!"

Pork Chop stopped. "She said what?"

"She said you beat her with a spatula and burned her undies and stuff like that…which is all pretty cool, sir."

"I never did those things," Pork Chop said. "Jenna's just bullshit at me for selling the trailer, but I don't care. I made my stand and I'm free now. Go back and tell her you couldn't find me."

The frightened men looked at each other.

"Uh, does this mean you won't clobber us?"

Pork Chop thought.

"No," he finally answered, and he clanked their heads together. He took a leak on them for good measure.

His Harley was tough. Minor scratches. Worth it.

Leaving the scene, the wind in his beard, the sunset behind him stretching his formidable shadow forward, Pork Chop, for the first time in his life, was free.

Fraidy Katz

The closet door yawned open as Virgil Katz was engulfed in the rapture of picking his nose. Only Huey, his ancient Frigidaire, noticed the sulking intruder who came from the piles of musty clothes and layers of dust on photographs stacked away in the closet. Huey knew about Virgil's past, and the cutting memories were all he needed to keep himself ice cold.

Draped in shadow, the intruder stood framed in the doorway, waiting for Virgil to finish his picking. It took the opportunity to scan Virgil's rotting apartment: a quilted rag over a sagging couch, bottles of sweet vermouth, a fan with tin propellors. No phone. No television. Only a radio, turned off.

Virgil finished and looked up.

"Get out of my closet."

"Certainly," said the intruder. "Just leave a flower."

Virgil snorted. "Leave a flower? You don't even have a grave! I never buried you, Clarence."

"And now you bury yourself?" asked the ghost, motioning to a small glass vial by Virgil's side.

"No. It helps control all this ecstasy—all this *fucking* ecstasy." Virgil laughed himself to the floor.

"I see," said the dead man soberly. "I shall return at a more appropriate time."

The closet door closed. Virgil stopped laughing.

It was getting harder and harder to make them leave. "Please piss off" didn't work anymore and plain old "piss off" never worked to begin with. All the trickles of blood left him with little tickles of joy, and that was none of their business. None of them had any business haunting him. He was fulfilling his given role in nature.

Virgil was a predator.

He stalked toward Huey and removed a bowl of mushy crackers in tomato soup from the vast refrigerator's solitary shelf. He ate the cold food ravenously, letting it dribble down his chin and neck. To him it tasted much better than a hot dinner prepared by a wife. To him it tasted sweeter than whip cream on a large breast—as sweet as revenge, for Virgil imagined the soggy crackers and tomato soup to be the flesh and blood of his enemies.

"Time for more," came a small friendly voice.

Virgil stopped eating. He recognized the speaker as Tommy Toot, his little glass vial. He glanced at his clock.

"Time for more," the voice repeated with a slight edge.

"So soon, Tommy? Can't you see I'm eating?"

"*Time for more!*" the voice shouted. "Time for more! Beat the whore! Time for fucking more!"

With a sweep of his arm Virgil cleared his kitchen table and hurredly opened the vial. The powder smelled like mint today; like it was picked from reedy green plants by tall, sun-haired maidens wearing crotchless panties. Yes, barefoot maidens in fields of dew with him hiding behind a bush, holding his knife, its blade growing longer and longer. See them reach for the leaves to make the powder for Virgil. See the phases of the moon pass, the planets aligning and scattering and the yellow sun turning red then dying as Virgil inhaled. Again. Again. Again.

And disjointed worlds will be my playgrounds, Virgil thought as he finished with Tommy and moved to bed. Stretched supine, he looked at the ceiling and called for Gretta. Little Gretta, just off the plane at the airport, lost.

She emerged from her hiding place behind his dresser, a young girl of ten who spoke broken English. Timidly she approached him, and he unzipped his pants. "Work for your supper," he mumbled, his eyes rolling back into his skull.

In the kitchen, Huey was crying. His ice was being melted by shame and rage. Water beads descended like spiders down his scratched surface. Underneath, his tray was overflowing and the floor was getting wetter and wetter.

Virgil held Gretta's head in place as he came. The child choked and coughed, and when let go she ran to the bathroom for water.

"Time for more," the little voice urged. Virgil sighed. "My heart's thumping. No way."

There was a pause.

"Don't make me come get you," said Tommy Toot.

"That's a good one," Virgil replied. "You can't move."

"May now I eat?" Gretta called from the bathroom.

"Gorge yourself, kiddo. And bring me my blow."

"No," said Tommy Toot, his voice soft yet forceful. "I want you to get me."

But instead of obeying Virgil closed his eyes. He thought of the milkman, delivering glass quarts of white powder to him. He thought of doctors, lined up at his doorstep to give him a fix. He saw faces in a vortex tunnel—faces of wounded gods screaming—and he fell off the bed.

The floor was cold and filthy.

"It's time. It's time," said Tommy Toot.

"Yeah, yeah," Virgil replied, standing up. He walked toward the kitchen, and beheld quite a gathering of ghosts.

Clarence was there, along with Marty Brooks, slashed throat and a shallow grave, Hester May Alves, Louisiana mom weighted down and thrown in a pond, Emily Bettencourt, blind date who died screaming in an empty parking lot, Joey Lacher, delivery boy run over twice, Bill

Dutton, nephew fed poisoned mushrooms, and several others whom Virgil could not remember. They formed a circle around little Gretta.

Virgil Katz chuckled uneasily. "Back off. She's mine."

"You tell 'em," said Tommy Toot. "Uninvited slimes."

"Keep out of this," Virgil said to the glass vial.

Clarence stepped forward. "It's just like you to chastise the only friend you've got. You two were made for each other. It's hard to tell who's sucking up who."

"You never were that funny alive," Virgil told him. "Why don't you go haunt some comedy club? Leave me alone."

"Why?" Clarence asked. "Are you afraid of us?"

"Ridiculous," Virgil said quickly. "If I could remember what I did with your remains I'd go and piss on your bones, Clarence. I'm not afraid of anything." But already he could feel a tingle at the back of his neck, spreading. It was the same kind of tingle he felt the moment he chose a new victim: a tingle of two parts adrenalin, one part anxiety.

"Who talks to you?" Gretta asked nervously, frozen in place at the center of the kitchen. "I do bad thing?"

The timid little girl made Virgil feel like a predator again and he pushed away the encircling ghosts and grabbed Gretta's arm. "Yes, you do bad." He tore open her shirt, running his hand all the way down, feeling for the entrance to Valhalla and the den of the sun-haired maidens. The child cried as Virgil groped for the key to the powder kingdom and felt for the soul of an old machine.

But then he heard chanting: "*Fraidy Katz. Fraidy Katz…*"

"Shut up!" he bellowed. "I am not afraid!"

"I say nothing," Gretta pleaded. He slapped her.

And the chant persisted. "*Fraidy Katz. Fraidy Katz…*" Virgil let go of the girl. He scrunched his eyes closed and cupped his hands to his ears but still he heard the chant. He heard the sound of fractured bones and he heard the sound of Jesus on top of his mother in a motel room rented by the hour. He heard the sound of umbilical cords being eaten and he heard the sound of semen dripping into sewers. Semen dripping on a rat's head in the middle of the night.

And into his mental maelstrom came another sound—a sound of creeping and creaking and old boards groaning. A woody sound of pine park and elm and metal hinges. A sound of the last breath of free air escaping out the detention room door. Yes, a sound of doors.

Doors?

He opened his eyes.

His front door had been unlocked and opened.

Gretta was gone.

"Halfway to the police, I'd imagine," said Clarence, standing next to Huey now. He put his arm around the old Frigidaire and said to it, "What do you think?"

Huey had never dared speak against Virgil before. His fear had kept him cold in place of the freon he had depleted years ago. But now was a time for truth, and Huey spoke:

"*Fraidy Katz*," he said. "*Fraidy Katz.*"

Virgil became enraged. He reached into his pants and felt for his knife. He willed it to grow, and he charged.

Clarence opened Huey's door.

Virgil slipped on the puddle Huey had made.

Virgil fell into Huey, slamming his consciousness away, and Clarence closed the refrigerator door…

*   *   *

…And secrets were revealed as the temperature dropped. Secrets of passion and tolerance, ecstasy and pain. With Virgil inside Huey, himself made complete. Himself made and remade into glowing splinters, reflecting a growing light from within.

Mandango

Sue Kiersbad was fun in bed. She liked to grab hold of the canopy bars, totally nude, and swing from them. It made her look like a sexy monkey. But she wasn't pretty. Her body was not even very shapely, and her two front teeth were missing. All in all she was an ugly woman. I am easily aroused.

My love was an axle but it broke. And her faith in me was as pure as imagination.

Mandango Bay in Hiphsland never looked so unusual. The local Abu-Bai, recently converted by an adventurous group of rabbis, were commencing their first annual observance of Chanukkah. Menorahs shone through open windows in adobe huts and a thousand floating dreidles filled Mandango Bay. Beautiful little black children showered along the streets, holding finger-painted stars of David.

I was the old man—a beggar of sorts—hobbling across the marketplace that day. Brown bananas were my breakfast, hours ago, and now I walked, keeping my face away from the sun, toward nothing in particular.

And there she was.

It was not like I bumped into her. No, I wouldn't say that at all.

"*Qoni varose*?" she asked.

"Yes, I'm fine," I said. But then I looked at her closely.

All at once the whiteness of her skin and blueness of her eyes became clouds and sky in my mind. Golden hair was sunshine, red lips cherry blossoms, white teeth sunspots. I felt my heart sneeze, and I went down.

"*Unta mah chona!*" she said, not really screaming. In an instant her face was above mine, and it was like ether.

I marked her with my mind, and would have her, later, in the evening, when I had changed.

*   *   *

"My father sends his most sincere regards for helping him in the marketplace this afternoon, and letting him rest himself here in your home," I said to her. The late afternoon had yielded to the moon, and I was a young man, strong and desireable.

"It was nothing," she said in English. Her eyes moved once down my open shirt. "You are his son?"

"I am. And I am in your debt."

She smiled at this, and said, "Come in."

No tense moments. It was very instinctual. We drank and talked for a short time, but when the evening began to settle itself we both moved toward the bedroom.

And I loved her.

In the morning I found out she was an archaeologist. But not very quickly. At first she walked into her kitchen, found me at the table, and stared for a long time.

"Last night…" she finally said. "It wasn't the alcohol, was it?"

I did not answer.

"Do you know what I mean?" she pressed.

"You mean the visions," I said.

"Yes!" she said excitedly, sitting next to me. "It was incredible. When we were making love I felt like a dozen different things! Once I was a bird, flying high over a canyon, then an elephant taking a bath in a muddy river, then a parrot in the jungle. My god! And it was all so…sexual. I can't describe it. *Who are you?*"

"No one very important."

She snorted. "Ha! You have a gift!"

"I didn't ask for it," I told her.

"No matter. You have it. You have it and I love it." She got up and started to make coffee. "My name's Sue Kiersbad. I'm an archaeologist. We're doing that dig on the south bank of Mandango Bay."

"Ah," I said. "The one everyone is talking about. Find anything interesting?"

She chuckled. "Interesting, yes. Valuable, no. The site is badly waterlogged, and all we're getting from it are some stone carvings. Anything made of wood has rotted to almost nothing. And forget about writings." She sat down again. "In fact, we're probably going to call it quits any day now."

"Too bad," I said. "I was planning to take a look."

My interest heartened her. We did not speak again until after breakfast, but when the conversation resumed, she hadn't skipped a beat.

"Would you like me to give you a tour of the excavation?"

"Do you mind?"

"Mind?" she asked. "Not at all. I think it's fun. We'll go there tonight, and this afternoon I'll take you to lunch and we'll talk. But right now I want to go back in that bedroom and I want you to make me feel like a boa constrictor. You can do that, can't you?"

"Yes. I can do that."

*   *   *

Ever since they started digging three months ago, I wanted to be on that site. Mandango Bay has been my home for six hundred and fourteen years, and the items the archaeologists dug up were the familiar things of my youth—knives with ivory handles and wooden bowls to catch the blood. Long before the rabbis came and converted us, we had religion.

Now, in the kitchen of Sue Kiersbad, after breakfast and before more sex, I felt autumnal. The thousand stunted questions of how long I would live suddenly hushed. The gaseous sun was far away from Sue's thick roof and walls. Maybe now, after all the concealment and secrecy, I would get a glimpse at the stone that started it all—the stone called Mandango.

"What are you thinking of?" Sue asked. Her eyes were unblinking and her chin stretched toward me inquisitively.

I fiddled with a coffee cup. It made scraping sounds against a saucer. "I'm thinking of archaeology," I said, "and how it uncovers things."

"Like what things?" she pressed. "Tell me."

"Things that've been forgotten," I answered; and that was enough, even though she yearned for more. To console her I said, "How about I make you feel like a boa constrictor now?"

She nodded, and led me, again, to her bedroom, where we had fun, fun, fun til her soreness became evident.

I noticed Sue Kiersbad had a tattoo on her ass that read "*Sue's Ass*". When I asked her why she chose such an obvious moniker, she replied, "So no one else can say it's theirs." It made sense, and I hugged her.

Ninety minutes later we stood above Mandango Bay, on a gouged bank where little antmen and antwomen filtered hunks of dirt and scribbled in notebooks. The grass was rubbed raw and all the worms were nervous.

"So this is archaeology," I mused.

Sue folded her arms. "This site promised to be fruitful. That's why we did all the digging. A lot of old legends are rumored to originate here, in Mandango. But I guess all the legends are fictional."

"No, no, no," I said. "There's more in that mud than broken pottery. You just don't know where to dig."

She came closer, her hair lifted by the hot wind. "Suppose you tell me where to dig…"

In an instant—a flash—I saw her need. Sue wanted to know the secrets of the ground. The secrets of Mandango. She would write books and do talk show circuits, if only she found what she suspected was entombed in the dirt.

I took a slow, full breath. The air, ancient as it ever was, told me it was time. Birds silent and hidden perched on the verge of some overwhelming answer, and all the little voices that had guided me and made me guardian of the stone of Mandango told me to spill the beans.

Stopping beside a familiar curve in the land, I said, "Dig here. Dig diagonally. Fourteen feet."

Sue knelt and touched her palm to the ground, as if to feel for vibrations. Moments dripped by and I felt she might be getting ready to call the whole thing silly, but I had aroused the curiosity of the true scientist in her, and she whispered, slowly and carefully, "*Who are you?*"

"Never mind that," I told her. "Send the workers home for the day…and get two shovels…and some liquor."

She started to walk away, but stopped abruptly and asked, "How did you know I'm the site supervisor? I never told you that."

"When Armstrong landed on the moon, did he say, 'How do I know this is really the moon?' or did he simply turn around and behold the earth?"

Sue frowned. "I'm not sure I follow you."

"All I'm saying is that the quickest path to your answer is to get the shovels. And don't forget the liquor."

"Why?"

"Because I want you drunk."

*

Sue Kiersbad and I dug for three hours, singing dumb songs and copping sweaty feels, for we were inebriated. The stone of Mandango got closer as the moist earth got scooped away like chocolate ice cream.

Livng things in the soil were chunked away and displaced. Our two shovels ate.

The afternoon slipped into evening. The yellow sun turned red, and the red sun sunk. Faraway hills and trees dotted the darkening horizon. Animals made sounds you only hear at night.

The last foot saw the brown soil turn into tan clay, thick and creamy like peanut butter. In our haste we cast aside a few old beads and trinkets, which I recall were placed near the stone as part of the ritual of entombing it, six hundred and fourteen years ago.

My shovel scraped against a large flat surface.

"This is it," I said to Sue.

We dug with renewed vigor. Our shovels, more careful now, etched around the perimeter of the stone, three feet wide, four feet long, seven inches thick. It remained whole and unbroken. No root could penetrate it. No shifting of the ground could crack it. The stone of Mandango met us unchanged.

"It has a picture on it," Sue remarked. She fumbled for and flicked on a lighter. "I'll need a brush and some solvent to see it clearly. There's too much dirt caked on."

"Have another drink first."

On the verge of protest, she balked. "Okay. You're the doctor."

I wanted her liver to have a lot to contend with. I wanted her thoughts to drift slightly as her hands brushed away the last coating before the picture was revealed.

I wanted her senses to be numbed when she saw my own face depicted on the stone.

Honing Sol

Being born is no insurance and no guarantee. Oh, and by the way, don't look back when somebody's chasing you.

That's what I told her.

"Are we dating?" she asked.

"What?"

"You and I. Are we dating?"

Was she trying to distract me?

"Well, we could be," I responded, "but right at this moment I don't think we are. You see, I'm taking you to the slaughterhouse."

She sighed. "What for?"

"Slaughtering," I said.

I came to the gate, and the guard let us through.

People and their fantasies. Things used to be nice and sexual—a good virgin dispoilment, for instance—but now the new sex is killing. *"Being murdered: the final frontier and the last and greatest of earthly pleasures."* They advertise it everywhere—especially in the poor neighborhoods. And people go for it. Some dream of being raped and mutilated, some hope to be torn apart by industrial machinery.

And some dream of being put through a slaughterhouse. A real slaughterhouse. The same place where stores buy their steaks. As for me, I go with the flow. One contract is as good as another.

Besides, each one I bring in equals one ahead of me on the list.

The young girl, whose face was curtained between straight strands of light brown hair, came from a poor neighborhood. Her folks were claimed by the police last month, and she had fallen into a bad way. Maybe she was pregnant. Maybe she just wanted to die. Whatever her reason, she had signed the paper.

"I'm only fifteen!" the girl pleaded as I led her in. "I made a mistake! I was depressed and I saw the ad for the slaughterhouse adventure. But I changed my mind! Let me go!"

"You signed the contract," I said. "They have the notary public here to prove it. So don't bother to struggle. Just be happy to know you're helping the Population Control."

"Let me go!" she demanded, twisting and tugging.

I withdrew my 200,000 volt stunner. "Easy or hard, kid. I don't really care."

She settled. Her eyes never left my gun until we got there. The gray skyscraper. The padded walls and inner workings. The scared girl hated it. I could feel her thinking—her mind playing out every radical scenario for escape.

"Are you part cyborg, man?" she asked. "Don't you have a fucking heart? How can you kill me for money?"

"I'm not killing you; I'm delivering you," I said as we got to the upper level door and I inserted my card. "Besides, they'll drug you up real good if you ask them. When they turn the slicing machines on, you won't even know it's you that's being slaughtered. You just watch the cutting and the blood, and you'll feel a numb pinching like you're at the dentist's for a root canal. Then you black-out."

Her feet dug down. We stopped.

"Kill me now," she said, her face flushed white, her jaw trembling. "I don't want to go through a slaughterhouse."

"Then you shouldn't have signed-up for it," I said.

"I'm not kidding," she insisted. "Kill me now because I'm not moving and if you carry me I'll fight it."

I sighed, withdrew her apprehension papers from my jacket. "Lisa Ann? I want you to read paragraph six to me."

She took the papers after a pause. Her finger came to rest at the appropriate spot, and she started reading:

"The apprehension officer, in cases where the conduct of the donor is unsatisfactory, has the right to—"

My fist came up through the papers and met squarely with her jaw. She spilled backward and crumpled, unconscious, to the floor.

"—has the right to render the donor unconscious, by whatever means available," I finished.

So I dragged her by her long brown hair for the last hundred yards or so. The thin, wiry corridors were like being inside a toaster. Steel grates covered the floors here, and every thirty feet an alarm switch covered by glass was recessed in the wall.

I took Lisa Ann to General Receiving, where they collared her with a bar code. "Take her to Processing," they told me, "and you'll get your money."

"I know," I said. Already it was a formality. She hadn't been slaughtered yet, but they had her written off on record. If I let her go, she'd be officially dead.

And if they ever found out, so would I.

I took Lisa Ann to Processing. They revived her.

From behind plexiglass I watched as they stripped her naked—dehumanizing without passion. Her face seemed utterly blank and resigned, and I wondered if they had given her the drugs already. In the distance the whir and buzz of the slicing machinery sounded like a busy kitchen, and it all waited for her behind a white threshold, into which a conveyer belt slithered.

"This is the glory that is destruction," I heard one of the butchers tell her. "This is the last and greatest earthly pleasure. Thanks for helping Population Control, and have a nice slaughter."

They put a strap around her chest and hooked her to the conveyer belt. Her legs dangled eight inches from the ground, like the decayed roots of a molar tooth. I knew the slicing machines would start there first.

The men put on their goggles. Their white splattersuits had their names and numbers stitched on the back like sports uniforms. Several strategically positioned cameras filmed the event for possible use on tv highlights.

I moved along a catwalk beside the plexiglass to observe the slaughtering room. A large sign warned me in bold capital letters to immediately withdraw if I started feeling squeamish. I ignored it.

Lisa Ann was now held in position over a tenderizer. Smooth metal nubs on self-adjusting rotors gently compacted her toes, feet, ankles and calves. She remained conscious throughout, and watched as red pulp seeped from her.

The belt moved again, taking her to the first series of slicing machines. Like an automotive assembly plant, several robotic arms worked on her in unison. They neatly cut one inch strips of her up to the knee. She watched, groggy now from loss of blood.

Then she saw me, observing through the plexiglass.

Slowly, I waved goodbye.

Nineteen

Everything was clinking. People were clinking their change into the slot and poker machines. The chips at the blackjack tables were clinking together as the dealers collected them from sour-faced losers. Coins were clinking out of automatic bill changers. Even the roulette balls sounded exceptionally clinky that evening.

I walked through the casino, and rarely, long bells followed by wild clinking would serenade the temporary winners. I had a wad of twenties in my pocket, and as I made my way through the swarming crowd I farted freely. Indeed, I farted playfully, for it is common knowledge that such things cannot be traced in a crowded, hustling casino. Sometimes I would stand at the craps tables, where the crowds were generally the noisiest, and fart at will. Then I would walk away and watch the players give each other mean, sidelong glances.

Eventually, I was forced to engage in other, more costly forms of amusement. This was in no way due to a sudden lack of interest, for I feel that few things in a casino are more fun and rewarding than standing next to someone who has just forced a slot machine to go tilt and farting furiously, then watching as the unlucky winner is forced to stay there until she collects her money. Rest assured, I stopped farting simply because I was out of ammo.

Of course, the voice also had something to do with it.

It wanted me to start with a poker machine; specifically, machine number 5324. It took me about twenty minutes to find it. I didn't know where it was, but as I walked past a change booth and started squeezing my way through the aisles, I saw a lone machine amidst the crowd, unoccupied. It looked eerie, and it was like all the other people couldn't even see it. Every other machine seemed to have a player, but 5324 was left alone.

As it turned out, 5324 played draw poker, which I personally find harder to win at because there are no jokers and nothing is wild. The machine took quarters, so I traded a twenty for two rolls, thinking to myself that the voice wanted to start off small tonight.

Now, on these machines you can put in up to five coins. If you're lucky, a winning hand will get five times as much with this method, and they also have a special jackpot for people who put in five coins and get the highest possible hand, a royal straight flush. This machine had a progressive jackpot, and it was in the range of three thousand dollars.

Needless to say, I won it.

At this point I was starting to feel that casino high again, and I think the voice was enjoying itself too, because it told me to move right on up to the twenty-five dollar blackjack tables. I found one with a small, shifty-eyed dealer (these guys are the best to crack) and ordered myself a screwdriver.

Yes, the drinks are free in reputable casinos.

Next I forked over my three thousand dollars and got myself a mound of chips. One of the other players got a little nervous and decided to leave, but everyone else just looked at me. I like that.

My first bet was a modest two hundred dollars. I drew a fifteen and the dealer had a six showing. Knowing that the dealer has no choice but to hit his own hand if it's under seventeen, I decided to stay. The dealer's hidden card was a queen. He only had a total of sixteen, so he had to take another card and pray he didn't go over twenty-one.

He drew a seven of clubs: twenty-three. Bust.

Old shifty-eye pushed two hundred dollars my way and I let it ride. In a half hour, I was up by over six thousand dollars, and the time had come to start cutting loose. I upped my betting to two thousand dollars on each hand, and I won most of them. As usual, a crowd started to gather around me, so I increased my betting even further to give them a good show.

And then the damndest thing happened.

The voice started telling me to do stupid things. It wanted me to hit a nineteen and split two tens, and that folks is just plain dumb. So I decided to ignore the voice.

Next thing I know I'm losing my shirt. Ten thousand here, twenty there. The cards became a swirling blur of motion that I just couldn't read. Out of nervousness I kept increasing my bets, hoping to win back what I had already lost. I couldn't keep track of how much I had, and I even forgot what I was drinking and started to order everything from white wine to straight whiskey.

The shifty-eyed dealer seemed to draw an ace every hand, and my denial of insurance always led him to blackjack. I was getting angry at myself. I was sweating like a barnyard nag. And I was especially getting pissed at the voice, which was no longer even speaking to me.

Ten more minutes passed and I was broke. The dealer smiled at me like a satiated junkyard rat, and the crowd that had come to admire me was now feeling sorry for me. Shit.

*

Rapidly did the elevator pull my sorry self up to the thirty-eighth floor. My hands were sore and blackened from handling coins and chips. My hair and clothes reeked of cigarette smoke. My undershirt was thoroughly soaked and I needed a shave. But my brains were even worse.

Echoes of the sounds of gambling floated through my mind as I walked along the plush hallways, with thick carpeting and glitzy wallpaper. I would have given my left nut for just one more chip to play with, or even a few coins for the machines, but my credit was already overdrawn and I had nothing that was worth pawning. Hell, I hadn't even paid for my room yet. They would just love hearing that, I thought, as I called for room service and ordered what I figured to be my last meal.

"Lobster bisque and two bottles of champagne, please."

"Yes sir," came the voice. "Must've done well tonight?"

"Oh just smashing. Charge this to the room, will you?"

"Yes sir."

"And give yourself and every else down there a hefty tip."

"Yes sir. Thank-you, sir."

While I was waiting for the food I flipped through the phone book and debated on hiring a "massage" girl. Better yet, I could get two. Maybe three, or four. I mean, what the hell, right?

I picked up the phone.

"Smaxie's Massage Heaven. May I help you?"

"Uh, yes. I have two questions for you. One is rather easy and the other one is rather unusual."

"Then let's start with the easy one, buddy."

"Okay. Do you accept a credit card check?"

"As long as you have some sort of identification as proof, yes. What's the other question."

I paused, then said, "What is the maximum number of girls I can…rent?"

Now a pause on his side of the line. "What?"

"I want to rent as many as you have available."

"Are you kidding? We have twenty girls available."

"Twenty will be fine," I said. "Send them over."

"You must be jo—"

"I'm not joking. I'm staying in room 3832 at the Trump Taj Mahal. For now you may call me Joe. And by the way, tell the girls I'm ordering champagne, wine, vodka, caviar, and finger sandwiches for them."

For I second I thought the guy was having a stroke or something, because all I heard were these weird sounds, but then he piped up and said, "They'll be right over, sir. Are you sure your room is big enough?"

"Everything will be big enough," I assured him, "including your tip."

Well, needless to say, the girls came and so did I. Eventually, though, that warm, glowing feeling wears off, and I found myself laying naked on the bed, totally plastered. The girls were amusing themselves by trying to throw onion rings around my phallus, and I was picturing the phone ringing any second with some Citibank-like call. You know, "Excuse me, Mr. Smith, but we've noticed a heckuva lotta charges lately…"

Anyway, the phone didn't ring but a call of another sort was placed…by the voice.

"You've completely transgressed into apehood," it said to me. "Why, just look at you, lying there like a hopeless slug. You've gone and pissed your life away all because you wouldn't take my advice and hit a nineteen. What a shame."

Suddenly I got boiling mad and I started yelling a number of things; one of the more repeatable ones being, "Nineteen! Nineteen! Nineteen!"

One of the girls leaned over to me and said, "We don't know how to do nineteens."

"Maybe he thinks one of us is only nineteen," another one remarked.

"So what's wrong with that?" one asked. "I'm nineteen."

"Then maybe he wants you, sugar," someone suggested.

"I'm only fifteen," someone else stated.

One of them (an old pro apparently) stood up and said, "Alright, everybody move back. I know how to do nineteens!"

"Nineteen! Nineteen! Nineteen!" I shouted in drunken anger.

Next thing I know the old pro grabs a pillow and shoves it in my face, hard. I can barely make out her words as she says, "Okay, babe, you asked for it," and begins whispering to the other girls.

Suddenly the pillow gets shoved down even more and I can't breathe. Then I feel the strangest thing: nineteen tongues sliding all over my body. It was sheer bliss for about fifteen seconds but then I really needed a gulp of air, so I try to take the pillow off but she sits on it and doesn't let me.

The tongues move up and down as I try to get this woman off me. My head feels like a cherry bomb. My body feels like some kind of seal, gliding along on an ocean of slick, wet sexuality. I'm thinking to myself how totally ridiculous all this must seem when the voice re-enters the scene.

"Oh my. You should see how this looks from my vantage point. This would make for some absolutely smashing Christmas cards, don't you think?"

I try to talk, but the weight pressing down is just too much.

"Dear, dear," it says to me. "All choked up?"

Damn you! Why are you doing this to me?

"Because you didn't listen to me."

But you were wrong! You just don't hit a nineteen!

"The next card was a deuce."

Bullshit! I was counting. We were near the end of the dealer's six decks and all twenty-four deuces had been dealt!

It paused then. "Are you sure?"

My lungs were caving in.

Yes, dammit, I'm sure!

"That's awfully strange," it said. "I could've sworn the next card would be a deuce."

Well it wasn't!

The tongues were driving me crazy. I was dying.

"I'm very sorry about this," said the voice.

So am I. Now get me out of here!

"Oh noooo," it said. "I like you too much to do that. Why, if I pulled you out now your life would be agony. All those unpaid bills. All those broken promises. All those lost dreams. I just can't do it to you…

"But I'll tell you what," it went on, "the contract for your soul is null and void. That should cheer you up."

But I'm dying!

"So you are," it said. "Well, I can't think of a more exquisite way to go; nineteen luscious young girls with their tongues all over me. Not bad, I must say."

But it was too late. His words faded away into some void and my soul blinked out and away.

Fucking nineteen.

The Wedding Assassin

…and where did she go, and what had she come to? Why couldn't I let the spiked memory go? Take it away, like old roses are taken from a vase to the trash.

"I feel numb right now," I told my friend Del, a fatter version of the genius I wished to become. We sat opposite each other at a small wooden table. Two beers and an ashtray.

He passed me the joint. "There's nothing wrong with numb."

Another hit filled my lungs. It was good sinsemilla.

"I know you miss her," Del continued, "and right now you're remembering all the good things."

I chuckled and coughed. "Then how come I'm numb?"

Del took a modest hit. "Memories are like kites, see. If you think they fly themselves, you'll walk around and get tangled in the strings." He exhaled, took a swig of beer. "You've got to know where the strings are…and what they're attached to."

It was downright poetic…but what did it mean? How could it help in forgetting Christina? A woman who could exhibit both her mind and her breasts, sweet Christina DeFay. We met just yesterday, and that was all it took.

"Like maple walnut ice cream?" she asked.

I blushed. "No. Not really."

"Then you can buy me a cone and watch me lick it."

Ah, true love was born, there in the Swampville Mall, somewhere between Spencer Gifts and Chess King.

"She's probably fucking someone right now," said Del, bursting my bubble. "Did you at least get her phone number?"

"No. She said she didn't have a phone."

Del shook his head, slowly and grimly.

"Every woman in America has a phone, Andy. It pops out of her uterus during puberty and clamps to her ear."

"I don't care," I told him. "I'll follow Christina DeFay to the ends of the world if only she'll be mine."

Del seemed disturbed.

*

ANCHORAGE, ALASKA—two years later

She wore a seal fur and she moved quickly. Her ninth husband was led behind her with the luggage. (The previous eight husbands were mysteriously assassinated.)

Christina thought she could avoid the man the newspapers had come to call *"The Wedding Assassin"* by marrying her ninth hubby in Bluenose, Alaska. But that only delayed me. Lacking the funds to follow her freely, my plane ticket to Anchorage came compliments of StarKist Tuna. For the next six months I'd be gutting fish and freezing. Even if I had a day off I'd still be freezing.

"Weather's not too bad today," said her new beau Phil.

"My fucking nipples are numb," she succinctly stated. Even with sunglasses and a silly fur hat, her beauty radiated.

I watched as they picked their way along an icy parking lot. I'd have given my left nut for a .38 snubnose revolver, but luck wasn't with me. I was already late for work. Plus, I wanted to get this guy Phil when he was alone. I wanted to remove his scalp, sew his balls inside of it, and mail it to his mother. Like a purse.

But patience is a virtue.

Two days later, in the small Alaskan wasteland hamlet of Crybaby Junction, I got my chance.

It was a little country store, with a sled and huskies nestled outside like shrubbery. An Eskimo shopkeeper stoked a potbelly wood stove behind the register.

I shot him first, and as his old bones flomped to the floor he never knew what hit him. I hated to shoot him but it was necessary. And in the throes before his final exit, since I only knew one Eskimo custom, I rubbed my nose against his.

Then I turned to Phil. Our eyes locked.

"You're the Wedding Assassin!" he exclaimed.

"Pleased to meet you Nostrodamus," I said, and shot him.

Then the damnedest thing happened: Christina walked through the doorway in a swirl of snow. She saw her husband crumpled next to the dead Eskimo and gasped.

"What have you done?" she demanded of me.

I came up to her—closer than I'd been in years. Even through her parka I could smell her perfume. I grabbed her shoulders. "I set you free. I made you eligible again, and I hope you marry the right guy next time."

She recoiled. "You're the Wedding Assassin!"

"Of course I'm the Wedding Assassin," I said. "Do you think I'd let someone else assassinate your ninth husband?"

Christina looked again to the floor. "But why?"

"Don't you remember me? We met at the Swampville Mall. I bought you a maple walnut ice cream cone just to watch you lick it. One more scoop and I would have orgasmed."

Her nostrils flared. "I remember. Charlie, right?"

"Andy," I corrected.

"Whatever," she said with resignation. "…I suppose you want to rape me now or something."

I was shocked. "I never thought you'd offer, but no. I want to have a relationship with you. I'm in love with you. I lost all my friends and gave up my life just to follow you."

"Funny," she said, "I gave up my friends and my life just to run away from you. But now…now that I see you, you're not too ugly. And kinda clever. Well…"

Off came her parka. Alone we stood in the little store, and she was hotter than the potbelly wood stove behind the register. A thick sweater was removed next, and my eyes beheld the last layer between PG and R.

We embraced and fell to the floor together, there in the midst of the frozen tundra. I kicked aside the bodies of Phil and the Eskimo and we started making-out beside the stove.

I pulled off the last layer and beheld her utterly magnificent cleavage—round, mountainous lumps with teeny flagpoles on top. Immediately I was in a voodoo trance, just watching them.

"What's the matter?" she asked, looking now at them herself. "Is there lint somewhere?"

I shook my head. "Nope. It's just that I've never seen such regal breasts before."

She giggled. "Are you a virgin, Andy?"

"No," I said, "but it took all this nonsense and foolishness to make me realize that I'm gay."

I stood. "There's nothing here for me anymore."

Opening the door, I walked into the storm. The sled dogs barked at me and the snow surrounded me. Which way was south? I started trudging.

"Andy!" she called, somewhere behind the white veil. "Andy come back! I love you! Andy!"

The Keechelus Incident

"If you come from the lakes region then what are you doing way out here?" I found myself asking the stranger whom I had just pulled over for speeding.

He lit a Winston and shrugged. "I don't know, officer. I just started to head west on 1–90…on an impulse, really…and here I am."

"I don't believe you."

He looked up at me quickly. "Why not?"

"Because nobody drives fifteen hundred miles on an impulse, that's why." I took a step back from his car and drew my gun. "You crossed half the damn continent, mister, and I don't see any luggage, or road maps, or anything. Please step out of the vehicle."

But he still sat there, mumbling.

"Fifteen hundred miles…I never would have known…That far? Really?…What st- uh, city is this?"

I aimed the gun. "This is Easton, Washington, sir. Now get out of your car!"

And then the damndest thing happened.

He drove away.

I think I was too surprised to even react for the first few seconds. All I could do was look, and I noticed that he wasn't even speeding away; he was just casually driving along! I shouted, stupidly, for him to stop. He didn't. I fired my gun, aiming for his right rear tire, but the bullet just clanged on his bumper and ricocheted somewhere into the night. He was gone.

I ran to the squad car and jerked at the CB. "Easton Base, this is car 6. Suspect heading west on I-90. He's driving a tan station wagon with Wisconsin plates. Assistance requested."

There was a moment of static, and then a startled voice came through.

"Is that you, Vic?" it asked. The voice belonged to Charlie Doherty, and he had been drinking again.

"Yes, it's me, damn it! Now give me some assistance."

Another pause. "Where are you?"

I jumped in the car and repeated the details to him as I was driving. I suggested a roadblock at a place called Hart's Bridge, and Charlie agreed.

A handful of minutes later, after navigating some little-known backroads, I was at the bridge. My back-up hadn't arrived yet, but I wasn't expecting a speedy response, so I just drove to the end of the bridge, parked horizontally, and waited.

It was about midnight, and the slivered moon was hiding behind some clouds. Bullfrogs were croaking someplace close and a cool breeze was skimming atop the water.

Still no back-up.

He would be there any minute. Hart's Bridge was the only place he could go, because it was the only connector over Lake Keechelus. I knew there would be no use in harassing Charlie if the back-up was on its way, so I stepped out of the car and peered across the lonely stretch of bridge.

Nothing.

You could hear the trees rustling. Small animals splashed in the water. A few birds were chirping, and I fancied I heard a dog bark in some distant yard.

Nothing.

I shivered a bit. He **had** to be there.

I drew my gun and aimed it with both hands over the hood of the squad car, at the entrance to the bridge; as if some effort of sheer will would force his vehicle to materialize right there in front of me. Tensely, I stayed in that position.

Nothing.

Five minutes passed, then ten, then fifteen…Frustrated, I yanked at the CB cord. "Charlie, where's the damn back-up?" Static.

"Charlie, drop the booze and tell me where my back-up is!"

His voice came through, puzzled.

"What back-up?"

*

Three weeks later I was standing on the shores of Seattle, facing the Puget Sound. Interstate 90 ended here, and out in front of me, stuck in the water like a beached whale, was the tan station wagon with Wisconsin plates. It was almost completely submerged. Waves were lapping over its roof and seagulls perched on the luggage racks.

I suppose that alone hardly would have been noteworthy. Another guy drives off the road late at night and ends up in the water. So what, right?

But that wasn't it. That wasn't it at all.

As I stood there and looked over the sound, it seemed as if *everyone* had driven off the road and into the water. Cars were stacked and piled up, one on top of another, in the water. There must have been hundreds of them, lining the beach. I could see their treadmarks in the mud, heading towards the murky depths and disappearing at the outer edge of Elliott Bay.

I couldn't understand it. What the hell would possess all these people, who must surely be from different states and regions, to do this?

"Must be something in the water, eh?" a little guy by the name of Farles was saying to me. He was an inspector with the Seattle Police Department. I didn't like him much.

"Tell me something, Farles. Why haven't you guys towed those cars out of here?"

He snickered. "We did. The first dozen or so, anyway. Now there's just too many."

"And the owners?" I asked. "Where are they?"

"They're not in Seattle, that's for damn sure."

"You mean to tell me that nobody's claimed them?"

"Nope."

"Come on, Farles. Not one inquiry? Not one phone call?"

"Nope."

I scratched my head. Things like this just didn't happen.

"What about the plates?" I pushed. "Surely you guys have run a make on the plates?"

Farles leaned forward and snarled a bit as he spoke. "Take a closer look, Gibbs. The only car with plates on it is your tan station wagon from Wisconsin. The rest of them are unmarked."

"You're kidding…" I said, but I knew that he wasn't.

"It's no joke, and it's bugging the hell out of us."

"What?"

"Your ghost car over there…" He looked at it briefly then turned towards me. "We tried tracing the plates on it, and we almost had something, but…"

"But what?"

He glanced around nervously, then pulled out a Jakarta.

"You got a light, Gibbs?"

"I don't smoke." I answered. "Now tell me about what happened."

The cigarette fell from his trembling lips and onto the ground. "It was horrible.." he muttered. "We were about to get a readout on the computer, and then all this snow and static came on the screen, and when it cleared all of the information was gone, erased. We tried to run it through again. It told us that there was no such license plate in Wisconsin!"

Farles came right up to me and grabbed my collar. "Do you know what this means?"

I tried to answer calmly. "Someone's trying to cover all this up, right?"

"It's more than that!" he spat out. "I don't know exactly what, but it's a whole lot more than that!"

Suddenly, Farles started to run away. I followed him back to his car but he was already moving when I got there.

"Watch your back, Gibbs," he called to me from his window.

Then he was gone.

*

Seattle was founded in 1852 and it currently has a population of over five hundred thousand. It's one hundred and twenty-five feet above sea level and its area code is 206. Big deal.

I was in the library, trying to do some research and looking for pertinent information. I was rummaging through a stack of books and tour guides, attempting to figure out why hundreds of motorists would want to plunge their cars into Elliott Bay. Well, I found out that Elliott Bay is Seattle's only natural harbor, and about two thousand commercial deep-sea cargo vessels pass through it each year. These ships have to wind their way through Puget Sound and the Strait of Juan de Fuca for about two hundred and thirty-two kilometers before they're in the open Pacific. Once there, the ships head to Europe, Alaska, and the Orient. They provide Seattle with a great deal of revenue.

It would be a pissing shame if Elliott Bay became blocked now, wouldn't it?

But to do that it would take tens of thousands of cars, not just a few hundred. And why? Why would different people from all over the United States want to suffocate poor little Seattle?

Then it occurred to me that these cars might not be from all over the place. After all, they were clean and we couldn't trace them. Maybe Mr. Wisconsin was a fluke. I quickly did some research and studied some road maps, and I concluded that all of the cars in the bay probably came from west of the Mississippi. I knew that I-90 started right around the Mississippi area, and it was the only major road that made a beeline for Seattle. All of the other interstates wound and twisted along, and even then none of them were as long as I-90. Sure there was I-5, but that was strictly a west coast deal, and it only passed through two other states compared to 1-90's five. Although I didn't rule out trafficking on I–5, I knew that it was an obvious route, and if whoever was behind this could erase computer files then they certainly wouldn't take the obvious route. Besides, the only confirmed sighting was on I-90, so I stuck to that theory.

I made a few notes and copied a few pages before I was kicked out of the library later that evening. My stomach was grumbling, and I began driving around town looking for a good restaurant. I passed a couple of places that I had heard about. One was called Gerard's *Relais De Lyon* and the other place was the Hunt Club. Gerard's was a French joint, which turned me off because I'm not that classy, and the Hunt Club was simply too crowded. Finally, I found this place called Rosellini's Four-10, where I had a wonderful dish of veal scaloppini along with some fresh-baked rolls. They had their own bar, and even a wine cellar (normally, I avoid joints that have their own wine cellar, but this place was an exception). I stayed and enjoyed every minute until they closed at midnight.

My motel was called Nendel's Motor Inn. It was a nice little place on Pacific Highway, not too far from the Seattle International Airport. I quickly made myself comfortable, took a shower, then plopped down in a chair and began reviewing the library material when suddenly I heard these voices outside my door. There were at least two, probably three guys. One of them mumbled something like "He must be asleep by now…" and the other one agreed. I didn't waste any time in drawing my gun and taking cover behind a desk.

Then they kicked the door open and stampeded in. There were indeed three of them. Damn. I didn't have any time to think and I fired at the guy closet to me. He took the slug in the shoulder and fell backward. One of his companions swore. I managed to shoot him in the leg.

The other guy only had a knife, and he soon dropped it and ran. His buddies limped and staggered after him.

I screamed for them to halt. They didn't, so I rose from behind the desk and went up to the door. Carefully, with gun in front of me, I looked around the corner.

Nothing.

I quickly pivoted and gazed up the other corner.

Nothing.

On a prayer I stupidly looked in front of me, and then even upward.

Nothing.

Impossible. That was damned impossible.

And no one even came out of their rooms. It was as if they hadn't even heard my shots…

*

I found nothing else in Seattle but more good restaurants and a lot of excuses to attribute my motel incident to weariness after a long day. I did file a report, but I just wrote the three men off as common burglars. I was beginning to wonder, though. What if somebody figured I was getting too close to the answers? Might they attempt murder (just between you and me, all my clues weren't worth a mound of manure at that point, but as they say, one man's misfortune is another man's fancy—or something like that)?

In the meantime, more unmarked cars were turning up in Elliott Bay, but I was calling the whole thing quits and heading back to Easton, via I-90. Too much of the case wasn't making an ounce of sense, and the last thing the Seattle P.D. wanted was some country bumpkin cop leaning over their shoulders and saying *"Gaaawly Gee!"*

I tried to put it out of my mind as I was driving along. Thinking about the wonderful apple cobbler that this little diner in Snoqualmie serves did the trick, and I made a special trip down near the American

River to pick some up. On the way back I was happily munching a plateful of cobbler that I had propped on the dashboard when I nearly choked. Speeding past me like a stray fastball was the tan station wagon with Wisconsin plates! I slapped on my rooflights and siren and went after him.

Leaves were scattering left and right as the squad car accelerated to over ninety miles per hour, and yet I wasn't gaining on him. Angrily I pushed the pedal to the floor and listened to the screech of the tires as they rounded corners.

I was now going over one hundred and twenty miles per hour, and I still wasn't gaining on him! *Well, at least he wasn't pulling away*, I told myself.

Suddenly and abruptly, he stopped; pulling over to the side of a dirt road right near Keechelus Lake. I came blasting up behind him and had to slam on the brakes to keep from hitting him. It was twilight, and I could see his shadow just calmly sitting there in the driver's seat. I drew my gun and stormed out of the car and up to his window, tapping on it with the revolver.

"Yes, officer?" he said as the window came down. "Does there seem to be some trouble?"

"You bet your ass there's trouble," I responded. "Now get out of that damn car or I swear to God I'll shoot you!"

He smiled, and looked into space thoughtfully. "Now, what was it you said to me the first time you pulled me over?…Oh, yes! I remember…It was '*I don1t believe you.*' Yes, that's what it was, indeed…"

I could feel the sweat building up on my forehead.

"I'm not playing games with you," I cautioned. "Now get out or you're a dead man!"

"I don't believe you."

I pulled the trigger.

The bullet entered and exited his skull and shattered the passenger's window behind him. He was still smiling.

"Now that was a very nasty thing to do, if you don't mind my saying so. Not only did you put a hole in my head, but you busted my window! I suppose you don't even have any intentions of paying for it, do you?"

Ever the perfectionist, I fired again.

This time the bullet chunked through his throat and burrowed itself into the passenger's arm rest. I had hit his voice box, which I figured would at least silence him, but then he started to make this sound:

"*Tsk…tsk…tsk…*"

Out of the corner of my eye I saw something. It was coming from the lake. I spun around. Things were surfacing from the depths. Hundreds of things.

I was frozen still.

They came at me, growling…

*

When consciousness decided to pay me a visit I found that I was lying on the cold and damp stone floor of what appeared to be an underground cavern There was no real lighting to speak of, but softly glowing bits and clumps of phosphorescent fungi that grew on the walls of the cave allowed my eyes to slowly adjust to my surroundings. I looked up, and could see scores of large stalactites plunging down at me from the cave roof. They were only inches away from my chest, and small streams of water dripped down their cones and fell from their razor-sharp points. I considered myself lucky that I didn't bolt into an upright position when I came-to.

Somewhere very close to me there was an expansive pool. I couldn't quite see it, but I could more or less sense the moist presence of a large body of water, and I could hear the reverberating drip-drip of water that was falling into a deep pool. The fact that the underground lagoon was there told me that this was probably the lowest and deepest point in the cavern, far below the surface world.

My arms and legs were not bound, and aside from the sharp-edged stalactites I seemed to have no restraints, although I ruefully noticed that I was unarmed. Carefully I began to squirm and slide my way across the floor, coming closer and closer to some sort of ledge. I was groping my way with my hands on the slick stone when suddenly my fingers encountered no resistance, and they were waving in the thin air. I pushed my arm forward a little and was able to touch the side of what I now realized was not the floor, but rather a high plateau. This quickly brought one question to mind: How far down?

I weighed my options, which were few, and decided that I had to take a chance.

With my left arm dangling over the edge, I used my right to push me. I had to do this with great caution, for the stalactites were still only inches above me, and if I were to go over the ledge feet-first my upper torso and head would surely bob upwards and I would effectively end up spearing myself. So I kept on moving sideways until my left foot was also over the edge, and with a great heave from the right half of my body, I took the plunge.

I fell for a brief second or two and then my ribs smacked into a bed of small rocks. I was in pain, but nothing was broken and I suddenly became very glad that I didn't talk myself into going down head-first.

I laid there and recovered for a few minutes and then I stood up. My back was killing me and my bones ached from the time I spent lying unconscious on the cold and damp stone. I walked slowly and stiffly, with one hand up against the spongy fungus on the wall and the other hand out in front of me.

Presently I came to a fork in the tunnel with each of its two portals clearly marked and labeled with crude but effective letters that were made from the glowing green fungi. I noticed that one portal was large and moderately well-kept and the other portal was small and stinking of squalid things. The sign over the large portal read "HUMANS" and the sign over the small portal read "TROGLODYTES". I would have taken the troglodyte portal, but there were some pretty awful noises coming from inside it.

The human portal was very long and it seemed to grow brighter with each step. As I walked, the stone also became smoother and more refined. Up ahead I could see a series of what looked like crude torches that were placed in holders along the wall. I took the first one of these that I came to and proceeded.

And then I was no longer in a cave; not in a true sense, anyway, because the walls, floor and ceiling were polished impeccably. I began to notice more refineries, such as chairs, tables, a rug or two, and even a clock. It now seemed as if I was walking through the large lobby corridor of some grand hotel. I had cast away my torch when I noticed the electric lighting overhead.

Noises were coming from somewhere ahead of me. They were not the sounds of living creatures, but rather the grinding and whizzing and humming of machinery. Lots of machinery. I kept on walking and I soon came upon quite a discovery. The entire right side of the wall had been converted into an endless series of plate glass windows. A viewing area, if you will.

The windows were reinforced with vertical bars of steel.

There was a sanitary aspect to this chamber, and I felt as if I was in the maternity ward of a hospital, getting ready to examine the newborn babies through the spotless glass. What I saw on the other side of the glass, however, were not newborn babies.

I saw cars. Rows and rows of cars.

Miles and miles of automobiles, in line after line after line. It was an underground network, as large as an assembly plant, but these cars were not being assembled. A quick survey told me that there were many different makes and models there. Some were old, some were new. They appeared to be a random selection of the vehicles America was driving.

I wasn't close enough to get a look at any of the license plates, but by their sheer numbers it became clear to me that they could not have been taken from any one city or area. This supported my I-90 theory, but a lot of good that support would do me if I didn't make it out of the cave.

Suddenly I saw the creatures that were working on the cars; hairy, humanoid things with massive arms and sloping foreheads that walked hunched. The troglodytes. They were yanking off the license plates and removing the identification codes from under the hoods. Some of the cars had personal effects in them, such as stuffed animals or fuzzy dice. These were thrown into a great bin marked "Incineration".

The creatures worked mechanically and effectively, as if under a spell. I was well into the process of telling myself how ridiculous the whole thing was when my eyes noticed one car in particular: my squad car! It was in the third line in front of me, waiting to be stripped.

Hope flared in me then, for although they took the car keys I had in my pocket, they neglected to take the spare set that I kept hanging on a chain around my neck and under my shirt. And if they had a tunnel for transporting the vehicles inside, I would surely be able to use that same tunnel as a means of escape…if only I could get to my car.

I began searching the passageway, running along the never-ending row of windows until I finally came to the end. A door was here, and it was marked "Employees Only". It wasn't locked, and as soon as I opened it I heard the noises that were coming from speakers in the walls of the shop below:

"Today's batch of cars is destined, once again, for Elliott Bay in Seattle. You must work hard. The bay is almost full, and once the bay is full we can move on…move on…move on…"

"Move on," repeated a voice off to my side. It was Mr. Wisconsin, and his wounds had completely healed. In spite of this miraculous medical achievement, he didn't look too pleased to see me.

He shut the door behind me and quickly grabbed both of my arms and held them behind my back. He led me down a staircase and into the main work area.

"So, Mr. Victor Gibbs, you've made it this far and you hope to make it the rest of the way, eh?"

"That depends," I answered. "What exactly is 'the rest of the way'?"

Wisconsin chuckled. "Up to the surface of Lake Keechelus, of course. Surely you've been able to figure out that's where you are."

I looked at him blankly.

"You're three miles under the surface of the lake," he continued, "and I am willing to make a deal with you."

"I'm not interested."

"Of course you're not, but that's only because you don't what I'm about to offer you: freedom. Yes, that's right. I agree to let you get in your car and leave freely if you swear never to reveal our location or try to harm us or stop us in any way. Do we have a deal, Mr. Gibbs?"

I know there were more suitable phrases that I could have used, but none would have been quite as appropriate as:

"I don't believe you."

He looked angry. "Come now, Mr. Gibbs. You don't have any better options. As you know, you can't kill me…but I can certainly kill you. That would definitely be the safer choice, if you look at it from my perspective."

"Then why are you willing to let me go?"

"Well, it's certainly not because of any affection I might have for you. Let's be honest, I'd much rather tear your head off than send you back into the world, but that simply wouldn't be the frugal choice. In short, I am willing to let you go because people would be bound to miss you. Cars are something that can be written off and deducted, but people usually warrant a little more attention…especially police officers…and attention is something this operation doesn't need."

The more I thought about it, the better Mr. Wisconsin's offer was beginning to sound; but I had to ask a few questions before I accepted.

"Exactly why do you want to block Elliott Bay?"

He grinned at me evilly. "Curiosity killed the officer…"

"Then kill me." I said bluntly. "Pretty soon this whole lake will be dragged and your secret entrance will be found."

He frowned. "Oh, all right. But you must promise me first."

I made the promise never to reveal anything. My toes were crossed.

He continued, "We want to block Elliott Bay in order to stop all traffic through it. This part should have been obvious to you. The reason why we want to block the bay is because we're looking to expand our underground operation. We saw crashing cars into the water a logical means to an end, so we temporarily adjusted the focus of our facility here to stealing cars from around the Interstate 90 area and stripping them of all possible identification—"

"Hold on a second. What do you mean by 'temporarily'?"

He looked insulted. "Surely you don't think that stealing is all that we do down here? Come now, I gave you more credit than that!"

"Then what exactly do you do down here when you're not stealing people's cars?"

"You make it sound so vulgar, as if cleaning up the environment should be frowned upon…"

"Sorry, but somehow I just don't buy the notion that you guys are ecologists."

"And indeed we're not, but getting rid of thousands of cars and freshening up the air a little is a nice fringe benefit to our line of work, which is world domination. It bodes well with us knowing that we made the planet a bit cleaner during the process of taking it over. Know what I mean?"

I was aghast, and couldn't have spoken a word if my life depended on it, but Mr. Wisconsin was not expecting me to respond. He just led me over to my car and placed me inside, withdrew a set of keys from his pocket and turned the ignition for me.

"There, now you're all set," he said as he closed the door and turned some newly-installed lever on the side of the car. "Just drive to the end of the line, turn left, and go up the long passageway. You'll have your feet firmly on the ground before you can say blub-blub!"

Mr. Wisconsin pulled another lever and my windows went up. Faintly I could hear his smiling voice saying "Bon voyage. Remember to keep our promise! Bon voyage! Remember to keep…"

I put my foot on the pedal and the pedal to the floor as I schree-ched my way out of that damn place. So much for promises. I uncrossed my toes.

I took a left at the end of the disassembly line and went up a large, dark passageway. I turned my headlights on, which gave me the distinct impression that I was a bullet rocketing through the barrel of a gun. I went up and up at a slow angle for what seemed like forever.

And then I began to notice that things were getting pretty damp. Water was trickling down the chute and seeping through cracks in the wall. I had a sneaking suspicion that the end of this tunnel certainly did not lead to land.

I slammed my foot down on the brake pedal and I was sickened by the realization that the car wasn't stopping. Blindly I groped for the handles of the door, but it did not open. I cried out in sheer terror, pounding on the unyielding bulletproof glass of the windows.

I was going up…up…up…

Portals were closing behind me now, and my headlights shined on the sealed end of the tunnel, which the car struck at full force, plunging me into the center of Lake Keechelus and pulling me back down again.

The Pull

A guy beating on a girl is a pretty common thing, so when the call came in my partner and I practically sleepwalked through the whole thing. Flash the lights. Jump out quickly. Make the peace. I'm sure you know the drill. We didn't even lift an eyebrow when the guy resisted, we just cuffed him and let him cool off in the back of the cruiser.

"Bravo 451 to Harry base," my partner radioed once we took the girl's statement. "Ambulance has arrived at Edgewood and Grover. If all's clear we're gonna bring this one in."

"It's a slow night, Bravo 451," said the dispatcher. "Come on in. Write up your reports if you like."

That was an attempt at a joke. We hated reports.

My name's Rip Effinger. My partner's Jeff Morley.

The perp we apprehended watched us and said nothing. I saw his face in the rearview, and not once did he blink.

"Looks like we got a real tough guy," Jeff pretended to say to me. He was actually feeling-out the perp, whose name nobody knew…not even the girl he had beaten.

"A real iceberg," I confirmed.

We got to the station without incident. The smell of coffee and cigarettes—so familiar to me—did little to make me feel comfortable around this dark and silent man. He wore a navy blue t-shirt, faded jeans and basketball sneakers. He could have been anyone. A resident, a dealer, a junkie, a drifter. No one at the scene had a morsel of information on him.

"John Doe for now," Jeff told a young clerk in the records division. "His prints were cross-referenced with the National Crime Information Center, and we've got zilch."

"Thanks for the valuable tip, Sherlock," the clerk remarked. "I work here too, you know."

I put my hand on Jeff's shoulder. "C'mon, let's go have a smoke break. Then we'll see if we can crack him."

Jeff's always been the tense type. When we arrive at a crime scene, he acts like the crime is still happening. When we eat Chinese food, he checks it for evidence.

And when we run up with icemen, Jeff wants to thaw them.

"Assault and battery, man," he said to the silent stranger. "Cut and dry right now, unless you can defend yourself…"

Down the hall the soda machine hummed while we waited for the dude's reply. Faxes faxed and printers printed. The clock grinded forward. And all he did was stare. There was vast intelligence in his cool gray eyes.

On a hunch, I withdrew my pack of Winstons. "You want a smoke?" I asked the stranger, holding the pack under his nose.

His lips got thinner and he leaned forward and inhaled. For a moment I thought he might bite my wrist, but he took one. His hands were ever so slightly wobbly.

Jeff smiled at me. "Of course. No one can resist a cancer stick."

He got one for himself, and we all lit up.

It looked promising right up until the stranger extinguished the Winston distastefully.

"Not fresh enough for you, princess?" Jeff mocked.

"Marijuana," said the man suddenly.

Jeff and I looked at each other.

"Private conference," I said.

We went to the men's room and left John Doe with his thoughts. Jeff started pacing.

"You think he'll talk?" he asked.

"Not at present, no."

Jeff stopped at the sink. He ran the water and dangled his hands in the stream. "What if we gave him some hooch?"

"We can't do that," I said.

Jeff took a breath, long and slow. "Play with me here: What if we skimmed a few pinches from the evidence room and rolled him a doobie? No one would miss it."

"Look Jeff, I know it's a temptation but—"

"He hasn't asked for a lawyer," Jeff said assertively, "and he probably won't if he plans on smoking pot."

Hmm. Yes indeed.

That, folks, is what you call a point.

Ten minutes later, John Doe took a slow, greedy drag from a fat, fat joint that Jeff rolled. That did it. Within five minutes of solid smoking, the stranger became, as one cigarette company says, "alive with pleasure".

"My name is Keith Mayer," he said wistfully, "and I am a billionaire playboy. I was born in Redmond, Massachusetts on October 30, 1963. My favored address is 19 Billingsgate Lane, London. This is excellent weed."

"Are you getting all this?" Jeff asked me. I nodded and finished scribbling. "This is excellent weed," Mayer repeated.

The dude checked-out. His entire claim proved true. Mr. Keith Mayer, at the age of 26, had come up with a dynamic business invention which he sold to 3M for megabucks.

"Holy shit," Jeff mumbled, looking over Mayer's paper. "This guy has a bigger budget than your average city."

"And he's clean," I added. "Never been arrested before."

"We don't want to ruffle him," Jeff decided.

I shook my head in disagreement. "What about the girl? He slapped her around pretty good."

"She was probably a hooker," Jeff said. "Why else wouldn't she press charges right there on the spot?"

"I still don't—"

"Look: one of the neighbors made the 911 call. Go ask dispatch. Plus the girl didn't know him, and she didn't want to get involved."

I sat down, angry. It wasn't fair that this Keith Mayer should walk. Some cops are still devoted to the principle of law enforcement, and I count myself among them.

Jeff leaned on the table. "I know you hate it, but the department just doesn't waste time with guys like him—guys who can throw a shitstorm at us." He raked his hair, looked back to the interrogation room. "Now let's get him out of here and move on. Real criminals are waiting for us"

"*Poor* criminals are waiting for us," I corrected. "Whatever."

So, grudgingly, we went back in to tell Mayer. The joint was down to millimeters, dead in the ashtray.

The room reeked of pot. He was smiling.

"You're free," I told him. He stood cheerfully. "Excellent."

Just then, the door swished open and our captain, John Hurley paced in. We immediately knew heavy shit had happened.

"The girl's dead," Hurley announced. "It was a professional hit. Two shots at close range to the back of the head." The captain gazed at Mayer. "I hope you've got a lawyer."

He left for the scene. We stayed with Mayer, who truly seemed unperturbed.

"A shame," he said, reseating himself.

"So tell me," I said, "did your people get to her? Did she find out who you are? Was she planning to talk?"

Mayer refused to speak. He even refused a lawyer. He just sat there. He treated the whole night like a topic for meditation. His hands folded and his chin rested atop them. His eyes closed. He was a smart, smart bastard.

I wanted to crack him like a rotten walnut.

*

The coroner, after a short initial examination at the scene, pronounced the girl dead at 11:43, and by midnight she had a tag on her toe. Business was slow, and an assassination always gets the medical boys hard.

"Look," said Mayer, "I obviously didn't kill her. I've been here—out of communication."

"You have people," I said, letting it trail.

His smile seemed to say, "You can't prove that." And we probably couldn't.

Jeff lit another Winston and pounded the wall. "We'll keep you here. Put you in a cell—a cell with others."

"Then prepare to be sued," Mayer replied. "I've done nothing wrong."

"You beat that girl," I said.

Mayer shook his head. "No I didn't."

We were both losing patience. Jeff got face-to-face with him and said, "Suppose you give us the name of who pulled the trigger If it checks out, we'll let you go. All we want is a name. It doesn't have to be yours."

After a moment, Mayer replied, "Marijuana. Bring me the bag—the whole bag—and we'll talk."

"Filthy addict," Jeff mumbled.

I guided him out to the hallway.

"It might be the quickest way," I said.

"What about the evidence room?" asked Jeff. "That pot is part of a case. If it disappears…"

"We'll take that chance. This is murder, and as long as he doesn't want a lawyer, let's bargain with him."

"That doesn't sound like you," he said.

"I don't care who it sounds like," I told him. "The quicker he talks, the more likely we are to catch the assassin while there's still some physical evidence on his clothing for the lab boys to analyze."

"True enough," Jeff agreed. "I'll be right back."

By thirty past midnight, Mr. Keith Mayer had inhaled most of the evidence. The guy was a marijuana demon, with the tolerance of mythical proportions. I briefly debated on saving the ashes and replacing the bag, but rejected the idea. Some lucky drug dealer would probably see the state's case thrown out.

"We're losing time," Jeff told Mayer. "Now talk."

Mayer stood. He made the room look small and imposing.

His cold eyes traced the grooves in the floor, and he paced. "Truth is any one of a dozen men could have done that hit. They're all autonomous. No orders come from me. I could pick a name and give it to you, but it would most likely be incorrect."

"Then give us all the names," I said.

Mayer toyed with his fingernails. "The fuck I will."

Jeff slapped him. I could tell it felt good.

"You'll pay for that," Mayer threatened. "You and your family."

I locked the door. My partner and I had become as silent as Mayer used to be. Indeed, we had changed roles.

"Look," said Mayer, suddenly nervous, "there's no sense in acting like complete ass monkeys over this. I'm sure we can reach a mutually beneficial settlement."

"That time has passed," I told him.

"You should have never touched that girl," Jeff said.

We closed in on him and beat the shit out of him. I kneed him in the gut. Jeff hit him with an uppercut. I punched the back of his head. Jeff kicked him in the spine. We took turns holding him.

A heavy thud cracked the door open and the captain came blazing in. The scene before him was self-explanatory.

"Jesus H. Christ!" he swore, his eyes wide. "Stop this shit now!"

Jeff and I obeyed. Our hearts were pounding, like animals fresh after the kill. It felt so, so good.

"We can't hold him," the captain continued. "With the girl dead and the killer still on the loose, nobody's gonna care if he slapped her. It can't be proven. Let him go…and apologize to him."

He was slomped on the floor. Still conscious.

The captain kneeled beside him. "Do we have an understanding here, Mr. Mayer?"

Mayer nodded, and we helped him up. He staggered, his lip fat and busted, both eyes puffed, his stance crooked.

"You want a doctor?" the captain asked.

"I have a doctor. Many of them," he said.

In response to the captain's burning gaze, I said, "I'm sorry we were so rough on you."

Shockingly, Mayer shook my hand. "It's all part of the pull of the job," he said, softly and with regret.

The door opened and closed, and he was gone.

"Down With Big John!"

"We're monkeys—we improvise."

A teacher of mine once said that. Emma Ashworth, whose breasts I yearned to impress. I'd start my homework during recess the same day. Dear Miss Ashworth. I begged to clap her erasers.

"What the fuck is that supposed to mean?" my friend Roy asked, all tangled and pinched.

We sat on the dry yellow lawn of Murphy's Garage in Fanwood, New Jersey, and I didn't know what to tell him.

"It just means we'll figure something out," I said.

Roy suppressed a stomp. "That sucks. We owe Big John Dingle five thousand dollars! We don't have time for strategy."

What a revoltingly stupid thing for Roy to say. In my opinion, the only thing between birth and death is strategy.

"From this day forward," I told him, "I'm calling you Stupid Roy Beanner, son of Fat Walt Beanner."

I could smell Roy's anger.

"That's not funny, Kyle."

"…And grandson of Dead Bill Beanner, the artist who was formerly known as Princess."

Roy converted a fleeting chuckle to a scowl and said, "If your ass were a rocket I'd launch it."

"What a disturbing mental picture."

His eyes narrowed. "You're in this too, you know."

"No shit Nostrodamus," I said. The haze between afternoon evening made a little heat blur on the horizon. "C'mon, let's get out of here."

We stood together and walked to the Main Street bus stop. An old lady carrying groceries cursed under her breath when she saw us. A shopkeeper stood guardfully by his door. Little kids gave us a wide berth.

Big John Dingle was a tattoo artist, and me and Roy had spent last weekend in a sweet demented drunken blitz, getting the works. Even on our palms. Dragons, skulls, roses, daggers, and mystic symbols. Every inch of our bodies. Even eyelids. Peckers and nutbaskets too. Can you imagine? Hell, the liquor kept us numb…until it ran out.

"You sure this was a good idea, Kyle?" Roy asked yet again. His forehead sported a tri-colored fish that was floating between two green pyramids.

"Financially speaking, twenty-five hundred a piece for a pro like Big John to tattoo our whole bodies was a bargain." A few young punks on the corner started giggling at us.

"Practically speaking, I think we drank too much that night." Roy pouted. "I don't want to feel like a freak, Kyle." Our bus came.

"You suppose we got a chance?" asked Roy as we grumbled along. The other passengers all seemed to be listening.

"A man always has a chance," I told them.

*

Beer at Johnny Darwin's was the next item on the agenda. Darkly lit and secluded in the backwoods, where every now and then a movie is made, Johnny Darwin's rises from the dirt road like a morning boner. With a haven for strong beer and secrecy so close to home, me and Roy enjoy tossing back a few rounds in times of trouble.

"So," said Stupid Roy Beanner, halfway to being shitfaced, "did you show all the new tattoos to Marcia Ann?"

"Don't particularly feel like discussin' it," I said, remembering her black shock. "Did you show yours to Thelma?"

Roy took a gulp of beer, and when he spoke, his voice was low and shaky. "Let's leave it lie."

Our spirits were in the shitter. Our wallets were thin. Our debt to Big John was looming.

Then the damnedest thing happened.

A grenade came sailing through the window. It landed on the stage and rolled under a drum set.

We got to our feet but it was too late. The drum set became one with the room as Stupid Roy Beanner and I were tossed to the ground by the fat underbelly of the explosion. The bar, which was right next to the stage, supplied a pelting rain of peanuts, pretzels, and jagged glass.

The owner's wife was decapitated by the ride cymbal. Her body dropped behind the bar and her head landed on a shelf, gawking.

Stupid Roy raised his left hand and flashed the sign of the devil. He strongly resembled Beavis. "Cool!" he said. "Operation 'Clean Sweep'!"

Roy got the severed head's attention, and the eyes focused on him like an angry Sunday school nun.

"Hey Kyle, I think that chic is hot for me," said Roy.

"It must be the tattoos," I replied. I tried to pretend I didn't know him, but the words "raving Nazi redneck" did come to mind.

None of it made any sense until someone in the parking lot shouted, "That's Big John's truck!" Then we knew. Big John was an angry shopper, and our asses were on red tag sale. His marbles had finally rolled away from him, and if he had any luck he'd be pissing on our graves.

Roy and I split before the police and firemen got there. We each had a few gashes, but even more disturbing was the idea that Big John had his sights on us. We took back trails and dirt paths and any road that was secondary.

"I hope we live to regret these tattoos," said Roy.

The woods were cold and the stars were hospital white. Dry, homeless leaves rattled together in packs. Somewhere in the blackness waited Big John; his jaw a solid square, his knuckles covered with hair.

We stopped by a tree and sat on the ground. The moonless night made me lonely. I couldn't get Big John Dingle out of my head.

In the morning, while workers drank coffee and old people drank laxative, Roy and I woke up in the woods. We had inadvertently cuddled together, and for just a moment, with the cheek of Stupid Roy Beanner pressed to my chest, I felt downright motherly.

The feeling passed.

"Get off me, you blazing homo!" I yelled at Roy. He snorted, drooled, and rolled away.

"How 'bout we eat breakfast," he suggested, rubbing his face and crotch simultaneously. I dared not refuse, and we started the long road back to town.

I knew something funny had happened when I saw the rising smoke. My feeling was confirmed when we rounded up Main Street and saw that our apartment complex had burned mysteriously in the night. The Towne Gazette headline read: *"Sudden Explosion, Suspicious Fire, Silence"*. It went on to say that as yet, no one was pointing fingers at the perpetrator.

No wonder. Big John had a reputation for remembering his enemies. Rumor had it he'd spent three years in prison for getting revenge for something that happened to him as a child.

Roy and I laid low. We had breakfast at Burger King.

"I'm worried about something," Roy said as we took our trays to a table in the back.

"What's that?"

"I'm worried that being on the run will affect my diet," Roy confided. "I'll probably gain weight, and I can forget about staying regular. Fiber and fugitives just don't mix."

I was amused.

"I don't want to frighten you Roy, but the biggest dietary threat to you right now is getting two or three rounds of lead in your belly."

He dropped his flaky croissant like a flaming turd. "Thanks, Kyle. I was starving a minute ago, but now you went and—"

FWOOSH! The booth behind us was engulfed in a stream of fire.

"Holy shit!" someone screamed. "It's Big John!"

The glass door came crashing down and a fat black boot stepped inside. A stubby cigar was thrown to the ground and a second fat black boot crushed it. Glass crunched under his step as Big John Dingle gloated, all two hundred and sixty pounds of him crammed into a red tank-top and tight blue jeans.

"You boys tried to assfuck me," he said softly, menacingly, "…and it backfired."

Up came the flamethrower. Down went me and Roy.

Our backs were scorched by the blast, which swarmed over our table and hit the wall.

"How are your bowels feeling now?" I asked Roy.

"Shut up," he said.

Just then one of the cooks tried to be a hero. He wound up running back where he came from, on fire for his trouble.

Through screams and thick, throaty cries of startled humanity, Roy and I made a break for safety. It was damn risky, but we darted straight past Big John, out the broken front door, around a corner and over a fence.

"That was uncalled for," Roy said, looking back at the Burger King, which was just beginning to go up in flames. We saw Big John stomp out, swearing. He hopped in his pick-up truck and screeched away.

Like him, we didn't wait for the cops. Why? Because it was unlikely they'd take two completely tatooed men seriously. For the rest of the day we roamed, restless and anxious.

That night the town had a rally. Hundreds of people were gathered in Coreman Square. Jake Morley, the local carpenter, did some quick and dirty work to make a platform. The mayor, pudgy Murray Vaughn, stood up there with a bullhorn. He spoke to a throng of frenzied hicks holding homemade signs that read, "Down With Big John!"

Mayor Vaughn stomped his fist. "Damn it, people, he hasn't been proven guilty yet!"

"We seen him do it!" more than one person shouted.

The mayor raised his hands. "Hold on there. The justice system says—SON OF A BITCH!"

Big John's baby blue pick-up came barreling into the crowd. Protest signs toppled like bowling pins. The big man hung his head out the window and hoopled. He hoopled a cry of betrayal and revenge. The ground shook.

Suddenly we saw a flame, and in Big John's left hand was a Molotov Cocktail. He heaved it at the platform as his truck spun sideways. The bottle of gasoline with a rag for a wick sailed high and struck the town's welcome sign. It burst into funky orange fire.

Mayor Vaughn was absolutely horrified. That welcome sign was his baby—the very symbol of community pride. Me and Roy watched as his face flushed red and he grabbed the bullhorn.

"Down with Big John!" screamed the mayor.

"Down with Big John!" the mob echoed.

And all at once there was sweeping movement. Like a rush of breath into a CPR dummy, the crowd blustered forward. Roy and I joined them, for this was probably the safest place we could be.

"Where are we going?" Roy asked me, his voice far and distant in the blurry hubbub.

"I think we're going to lynch Big John," I said. My voice was a sore cackle from being forced to sleep in the cold damp woods the night before. And I realized something: I was no longer afraid of Big John. I didn't owe him anything anymore. It was his own fault he gave me and Stupid Roy Beanner five thousand dollars credit. What was he thinking? We don't even have jobs.

"Aren't we sorta in the wrong here?" queried Roy.

"Not any more," I said.

✳

The hatred was electric. Me and Roy were reunited with our fellow citizens. They no longer gaped at our tattooed bodies. It was great. We felt normal again, joined in our mission against the evil that had become Big John Dingle.

We swarmed down Main Street, past the gutted shell of our apartmend complex, straight to the outskirts of town, where Big John Dingle lived in a log cabin house on a little dirt hill. It felt funny going back there. Only one short week ago Roy and I had gotten blind stinking drunk and hired him to do the full body tattoos. Now we were back on his property, this time to kick his ass.

"We're callin' you out!" cried Mayor Vaughn. He stood alone, like a daring headpiece, on Big John's doorstep.

A pause came and went. Then suddenly, speedily, the door opened just a crack, the double barrel of a shotgun peek-a-booed out, and there came a blast.

Mayor Vaughn's head was no longer intact. It scattered like it was made of pollen. And for a moment the body just stood there, totally puzzled.

"That sneaky fartblossom!" some outraged local yelled. "He's bamboozled us again!"

Pistols were brandished. Bullets shattered Big John's windows. And through all the shitstorm, Big John was alive and well and returning our fire.

"Damn it!" yelled Preacher Vincent, his Colt .45 clicking on empty. "The bastard won't die!"

"Don't loose faith!" I called to the preacher. Then I nudged Roy. "Let's circle around back."

We made our way carefully, slinking along the barbwired sides of the sturdy log cabin. A budding vegetable garden in the back yard gave us a candid glimpse at a softer, more organic side of Big John. It was down-right touching, and I stopped.

"What are you doin'?" asked Roy.

I knelt and plucked a ripe tomato. "Big John got on his hands and knees to plant this. He bent here in the dirt and carefully sprinkled seeds in the ground. Can you imagine? A fat ogre like him." I took a bite, and the tomato melted fresh and clean in my mouth. It was almost religious. "Maybe we judged him wrong, Roy."

Roy thought. After a moment he sat next to a cucumber plant, admiring how rich and green it was. "Maybe Big John is just misunder-stood…like us." He picked the cuke and took a bite. "*Mmm.*"

"Exactly," I said.

By now his home was ablaze. Roy and I sat and watched, peacefully chomping his tasty harvest. At the end, Big John himself ran out the back door. His hair was on fire and someone had shot him in the groin.

Before his face flomped to the ground, he made eye contact with us. That one instant conveyed the essence of Big John Dingle, an angry and confused soul whose last image was of two tatooed deadbeats, slowly eating his vegetable garden.

The Post-War Father

"You like to use words," Carl said. "I know that—no secret there. But tell me, what happens when the only words linked with your name are those in your obituary?" He leaned closer. "You just tell me what happens then, Paulie. You just try and tell me."

"The world goes on," I told him. "Plain and simple. The world goes on."

He looked afraid.

"How can you say that, Paulie?" he asked with trembling cheeks. "How can you say that to your own father? *Your own father!*"

"Stepfather," I corrected, looking deep into his eyes. A tear rolled down his face.

"Stepfather," he amended, sounding cold and hollow.

We still looked at each other, but there were no more words that needed to be said.

Shaking his head slowly, he walked away—out of the room that had caused him so much pain: my room. He brushed his hand along my mantle as he left, but he didn't look at the trophies. To him they were probably just symbols of another time, another world, and another son.

I slumped to my bed.

"Touch the wind," I remembered him saying to me. "You're twelve years old today, so touch the wind. Touch it while you can, Paulie."

Burying my face in a pillow, I cried long and sullenly. Those words, I knew, were spoken by my real dad, when he was alive, and since that time it seemed as if the entire world had been turned upside-down.

Somewhere, in the darkness, there was a key.

*

Mr. Rivard's convenience store was on the corner of Salem and Green, which were two of the quietest little streets in town. It was about one in the afternoon, a time when adults are heading back from lunch and kids are still in school, but I was in Mr. Rivard's store.

The aisles were tall and thin, and it felt like you were walking inside the bottom of a toaster. Food and other items were packed together closely, so that two people could be standing right next to each other in different aisles, totally unaware of each other in the visual sense. That was good, because as long as you were quiet enough, you could steal a fortune. Every kid in town knew that, and they also knew that old man Rivard didn't even have one surveillance camera in the whole place, so almost every item in every corner of the store was fair game.

As I sauntered through the store I tried to decide what I wanted, passing stacks of chips, cookies, ice cream (dangerous to steal on a hot day), candy, gum, and all sorts of things, none of which really interested me. Old man Rivard was up front behind the counter, watching his portable television and thumbing through a magazine, and that's when it hit me. What I really wanted to steal were some dirty magazines—but they were always kept behind the counter.

Cunning was required for this operation.

Moving to the back of the store, I picked up a bag of charcoal briquettes and a bottle of lighter fluid. I carefully and quietly opened the bag and squeezed the entire contents of the bottle into it. Now came the cunning part, because anyone could have just lit the bag then and there, but that would have been stupid. The fire would have caught instantly, not leaving me with enough time, and old man Rivard would have seen me walking away from it. So from inside my jacket I withdrew a pack of Winstons and my lighter.

Breaking off the filter of a cigarette, I lit one end, puffed a few times, and placed the other end in the bag at a slight angle, sort of like a candle on a cake. Then I casually picked up a pack of gum and went up to the counter.

"Hello there, young feller," said Rivard. "Will that be all you want?"

"Yes," I said, handing him a quarter and a dime. In my mind, I was picturing the burning tip of that cigarette getting lower and lower. "Anything good on the tube?"

"Soaps," said the old man with distaste. "Whatever happened to all them game shows?"

"I don't know," I said, chuckling a bit.

Suddenly, a distinct "whoosh!" came from the back of the store, and the old man's eyes sort of bugged-out as flames peeked over those tall aisles. Rivard shouted something obvious ("Fire!") and scrambled around the counter, heading for the back of the store.

I was behind that counter so fast people would have thought we were an Olympic tag-team. I scooped up every dirty magazine I could find and was about to bolt when the cash register caught my eye.

Up until that point, I hadn't planned on robbing the old guy blind, but since the situation was so cherry, I did just that, leaving with a grand total of two hundred forty-seven dollars and a stack of naked women thick enough to choke a cow with. Not bad…until I learned that the fire had spread so quickly that old man Rivard died in it and his whole store burnt to the ground.

That happened three years ago, just after my real dad had passed away, and no one ever found out I did it.

*

Now the days are long and the work is hard, and time is like a razor, cutting deep within the hourglass of my mind, where certain, abrasive sands endlessly move up and down. I'll often sit in my room and become angry for no reason, and I'll tell myself that it's just the sands I'm feeling, rubbing my mind the wrong way. I'll draw pictures where the sands are represented by knives, and the knives are moving inside me, cutting.

Sometimes my stepfather finds these pictures, along with hastily scribbled words of frustration, and he'll think that I'm tyring to be a writer or something. In other words, he'll think that it's all pretending; pretend pain. Like an ape, he'll pick up the scraps of paper and stare, and when the angry reds and gouged-in letters have lost their visual appeal he'll cast it all aside and file it away in the never-ending waste-basket of his brain.

Killing him would be too merciful a fate.

I thought about my real dad.

One sunny morning in late November, I remember dad telling me that he no longer believed in God. "Since God doesn't exist," he said to me, "I see only two primal ways in which people can act. Either they *always* treat other people with respect, or they're inconsistent and situational, treating folks this way or that way, depending on what they feel the other party can do for them."

Since dad viewed the latter way as being egocentric and a cause of far more pain than good, he desperately tried to abide by the former way. He understood the concept of democracy, freedom and human dignity better than anyone.

The thing that destroyed his beautiful vision of liberty was his explosive temper. He was the kind who never really "started any trouble", but when someone provoked him the fury and intensity of his wrath were all-encompassing. Sadly, his temper eventually landed him in prison.

I visited him; once. He looked very different, like his soul had been ripped away. I remember walking along the cold corridors and heavy hallways of the prison, being escorted toward the visiting room. Every sound seemed muffled. My footsteps were like little dreams, clicking through chambers that stifled them. My every action seemed forced and unnatural, and it began to require more and more exertion to move forward.

Sounds slowly came to me. I heard whisperings, a baby's cry, a chair scraping along the floor. This and so much more. I heard the repressed moans of humanity, the sorrowful gasps of detached wives, whose souls were already drifting away from their enshackled husbands. Love had fled from that room, and it seemed as if some dolorous, uninspired tune was constantly being played in the background.

My dad was sitting at a small, empty table. A white line had been painted down the table's center. Behind my father stood a tall prison guard with nightstick and holster. Dad was careful to keep his hands behind the white line.

When he saw me, he tried to smile.

"Hello, dad. How have you been?"

He took my offered hand.

The guard frowned.

"It's good to see you," he said, letting go.

I took a closer look at him. His left eye was blackened and he seemed to be nursing the left side of his ribcage.

"How have you been?" I repeated with more concern. "How have they been treating you?"

At this he winced, slightly. He was about to say something, something important, but at the last moment he shrugged.

"Can't complain, I guess."

I thought about the true meaning of that sentence for a long time. The guard just smiled.

Ten minutes later, they told me I had to leave.

I couldn't bear to see my father in such anguish.

*

A few months later, I was at home helping my mom unpack some groceries. When we finished I turned on the television, and to my surprise I saw them doing live coverage of a huge riot that was taking place at my dad's prison. All of the three major networks had people standing in front of the prison, telling the audience about the "savages inside". All three networks made it seem like the prisoners were all incapable of understanding beauty, justice and equality. Unfortunately for them, they understood these things all too well.

The governor was interviewed. He said, "I have reason to believe the prisoner's hostages are being tortured in violent, animalistic ways. I will do everything in my power to insure that the inmates, who are mostly violent misfits, do not succeed in turning our penitentiary into a lawless jungle."

This is utter nonsense, I thought to myself.

"They have issued demands," the governor went on, "but these demands are ludicrous and unacceptable. We have tried to negotiate with them, but they have not been reasonable."

Just then a reporter asked, "Does this mean that you 're considering retaking the prison through brute force?"

The governor smiled, just like the prison guard did.

"It's an attractive option."

Dad died in the retaking of the prison. He was shot through the heart for getting in the way of a stormtrooper.

I learned later that the prisoners wanted nothing more than three basic things: 1.) better living conditions, 2.) less verbal abuse from the guards, 3.) less physical abuse from the guards. That was their list of "ludicrous" demands. For that they were slaughtered like cattle.

God bless America.

⋆

I can remember when dad used to kneel down beside me after I had hit someone in the playground. He would tell me that hitting people was wrong, no matter what. He would tell me that each person's life was precious. "Dignity is a sacred thing," he said to me. "Never take away another person's dignity."

But because of the vast differences between his childhood and adult environments, dad had trouble coping. There was a side of him he couldn't control—a side that made him weep when he felt or saw its destructive effect. Broken tables or broken promises or broken hearts; it didn't matter what broke when dad was angry.

And yet there was the conflict.

He seemed to sink lower and lower when he knew he made someone feel lonely, frustrated or frightened. Honor became his permanent level of fulfillment, peace his unattainable goal. He disguised his pain with passing smiles, with partial love.

But the pain was stronger.

Once, late at night, after he had hit me for stealing cookies, I crept back down to our kitchen, and I found dad, slouched over the shiny table, trembling. His face was contorted and his hands did little to hide a glossy coating of tears…

I will never forget that image.

*

Now, as I sit at my table, alone, I will often think that "society" is nothing more than conspiracy, and the only real freedom from it lies in death. I'll think about my stepfather and I'll think about the daggers stabbing at my soul. Sometimes I'll picture his sad, uncomprehending face, staring blankly at me. Then the picture gets redder, and he starts to scream, and the blade I hold bores in and out of his body.

It is a daydream I have, and I constantly suppress it. To me, allowing my stepfather to go on living is a fate far worse than death. I know that he will never understand the rhythmic and vibrant flow that is life, and as long as I can privately torture his soul—as long as I can punish him for stealing mommy—my real daddy will always love me.

Nur Jahan

The swell of the cold sea lifted the vessels on Boltolph Wharf and strained their moorings. Glenn Cormier tested the ropes on his own ship skeptically. Boltolph Wharf was very old. Everything in London seemed to be old.

A private trader of furs and spices, pocket watches and ivory, Glenn Cormier had traveled as far as any British naval captain, and his pay was much better. His two-masted vessel did not require a crew, and the deck hand was grateful to Glenn for feeding him and allowing him to see more of the world than his imagination could encompass.

Today Glenn docked at Billingsgate, the great London fish market district. He told Alvie, the deck hand, to stay with the ship. Glenn hardly ever took him out in public. The last time was two months ago at Hastings, when Alvie needed to be fitted for a new pair of shoes. Glenn knew that Alvie preferred to stay huddled safely in the ship's hull, where the piercing stares and cold words of the public could not reach. There he often found amusement with the exotic cargo, which sometimes included small, playful monkeys from the African coast.

Glenn stepped onto the dock and turned to Alvie, who was standing in the boat's stern.

"Fetch the package for me and I'm off," he told the boy.

Alvie nodded quickly, and he scampered down below. In a few moments he emerged with a carefully bundled item and, with infinite care, he handed it to Glenn It resembled a long, curved cylinder, and Glenn held it snugly under his left arm.

"Be wary," he advised the boy, and was gone.

As of late Glenn had enjoyed prosperity from his trading ventures, but there was talk on the streets of increasingly severe penalties for blackmarketeers. Rumors of midnight cargo checks by soldiers and certain ships suddenly sinking were everywhere. As Glenn walked away from the wharf, the cobblestoned streets were abuzz with vague uneasiness, and huddled figures quickly whispered to each other in nooks and doorways.

The proper Victorian gentleman scorned such pungent and roguish places as the Billingsgate fish market, but Glenn was at home with the area, where policemen were few. He pulled off his soily cap and ran his fingers through his thick brown hair, filling his lungs with foggy English air. Proceeding up Boltolph Lane in the direction of Eastcheap, Glenn turned right, at number thirty-two.

Before him was a gateway leading to a rather spacious courtyard. Old-fashioned buildings rose on either side, mostly occupied by fruit merchants, who were plentiful in that area. He approached an old woman who had a cart of apples.

"How much?" he inquired, lifting one of them.

"Fivepence for a right good bag," she told him, peering at his face and then at the large parcel he carried.

"Too much," he said, playing the game. "Look here, this one's got three wormholes in it!"

The old woman snickered. "Fourpence gets the bag, and you can even 'av all the worms you find for free!"

"No," Glenn said with mock consternation, "one is all that I'll offer you."

The woman looked truly wounded. "Why, I'd sooner lend meself to practices of ill repute!"

"I doubt you'd have many customers."

And before she could respond, Glenn paid her original price and took a bag of apples. Her smile was almost motherly.

Munching on the apples as he walked, Glenn headed for St. George's Church, where he would pray to St. Boltolph, the Saxon saint whose church used to stand on the south side of Thames Street before it was destroyed in the great fire of 1666. Boltolph was the patron saint of travelers and sea-faring folk, and Glenn would pray to him at each new port, leaving some money or some food behind.

But this time he would offer his patron saint something more.

Glenn stood outside St. George's and crossed himself, as was his custom. The church, designed by the famous architect Sir Christopher Wren, had a remarkable stone tower with a unique entasis and no bell turret. He entered through the church's two massive doors, walking through an interior that was divided into a nave and two aisles by four composite columns. The ceiling above the columns was flat, but in the nave, or central section of the church, the ceiling was arched.

A handsomely carved pulpit stood in the chancel, next to the altar. Glenn proceeded to this section, where an inscription to the memory of William Beckford, twice Lord Mayor of London, graced a stone tablet. There he kneeled.

"Prayer," came a voice from the shadows, "is done from the pews; unless, of course, you are a priest?"

Glenn stood. "I am not."

"Ah," the other figure said, coming a little closer, "I know you, don't I?"

"Yes you do, Rector MacColl. My name is Glenn Cormier. I last paid you a visit three months ago. Remember?"

The old man came closer. "You are the one who left us the silver coins?"

"The silver was left for St. Boltolph," Glenn corrected.

The old man coughed. "Yes, yes. St. Boltolph. Of course. I remember. You make your living from the sea, do you not?"

"Fishing," Glenn said.

The rector chuckled. "Fishing, eh? Donating that pouch of silver coins sounds like you've been fishing things out of people's pockets."

"Fishing," Glenn repeated. "It has many forms, yes. When I speak of fishing I allude to the richness of the sea, and while some fish downward into its depths, I prefer to fish across its length and breadth into lands dark and exotic, with St. Boltolph as my guide and watcher."

The rector was now keenly interested. He came up to Glen and furrowed his white, bushy eyebrows in thought and speculation.

"Glenn Cormier," the man said, "do you know what it means to be a follower of St. Boltolph?"

"Well, I know that it implies Saxon heritage…"

"No, no, no," he said. "Not that."

"What then?"

"When one worships Boltolph," the man said, "one stands against darkness and opression. During the years of pestolence, beggars would congregate at the city gates, and Boltolph would watch over them, protecting them against the blackness of death. The people built him chapels and shrines, like the one that was once on Thames Street, but the evil was strong. Boltolph's church burned in 1666, the year of Satan. Few worshipped him after that, and for a time, the evil thrived." The rector's voice was but a whisper. "But now, in the silence of the stone, in the hardness of the marble, in the dampness of the grave, I swear to you, Boltolph lives again. Sometimes, in the stillness of the night, in the darkness and silence of this church, my eyes have beheld candles that suddenly ignite. The symbolic light of Boltolph's patronage. There are stirrings in this place."

The old man looked upon the altar, transfixed. "I think that Boltolph moves among us.....and…"

"What?" Glenn asked. "What is it?"

The old man turned ashen.

"He is followed closely by the beast."

Then, from somewhere, there came a whisper.

"Wanton…"

The rector turned swiftly, but beheld no one.

"Who speaks?" Glenn demanded.

"*Wanton…ununified…*"

"Who is there?" the rector asked.

The reply came: "*No one. The wind. The night. The blood.*" There was hideous laughing.

"*The blood,*" it repeated. "*The stone. The axe. The wood. The pain.*"

Falling to his knees, the old man began reciting the Lord's Prayer.

From inside his jacket Glenn withdrew a knife.

"If you be a man, then you will die!"

"*I am,*" said the voice, "*the dead. The torturer. The screamer. The outcast…*

"*The **One**.*"

A wind arose, and it swept away the light.

From all around the altar, there was chanting, as if a choir surrounded them.

"What do they sing?" Glenn asked the rector.

"It is a black prayer," came his terrified reply. "***In Nominae Satanas.***"

The darkness was absolute. The chanting persisted, became louder, hurt their ears. Glenn dropped the useless knife.

"*Ekas fo ycrem. Ekas fo ssendam. Nekasrof.*"

"Boltolph!" Glenn cried, unveiling his package at last. It was the tusk of a white elephant. Glenn placed it upon the altar.

"Boltolph!" he repeated more urgently. "Patron of the viator, provider to the poor, lord of the light, guide me!"

A beam of brilliant radiance shot down from the church's central dome. It was quickly followed by another, and another.

The beast groaned.

Spears of light filled the chapel, and from above, a figure descended, bathed in white. It walked across the church, up to the altar, laid its hand upon the offering of the ivory tusk, and turned to Glenn.

Boltolph spoke:

"Let the axis of disunion reverse itself! Seek out my karma, imprisoned in the past…in the east. Pacify. Sanctify. Solidify."

Glenn's very surroundings began to fade.

"*All worlds are one,*" said Boltolph. "*All worlds are one.*"

And before the transference was complete, Boltolph gave one final command:

"Seek out Nur Jahan."

*   *   *

The dry and dusty Plain of Woe, through which the Jumna River flowed, served as a highway between the two great cities of Delhi and Agra in northern India. For one hundred and twenty miles this plain stretched, dotted only by weeds and the occasional traveler or caravan, going to and coming from the cities of the king, Jahangir.

The year was 1623.

Glenn awoke to a mouthful of hard, gritty sand. The stuff seemed to be everywhere—even in the sky—and he spat quickly. Next he noticed the heat. Ninety degrees, easily, he figured.

"Where the hell am I?" he mumbled.

As if in response, he heard the baying of a camel in the distance, just beyond a hill of sand. He got to his feet, sunk a bit, and began trudging along. He wore no socks, and the hot sand seared his ankles. Ten yards…twenty yards. He would have given his ship's sextant just to be walking along the cool and pleasant shores of the Isle of Wight.

"Ho!" someone yelled. "*Dalan u mahal?*"

Glenn looked up. It was the camel rider.

"*Dalan u mahal?*" he repeated.

Glenn frowned. "I'm sorry but I have no idea what you're saying. Could you please tell me where I am?"

"Roe! Roe!" the other suddenly said. "Sir Thomas Roe, are you not sir?"

Glenn thought. His days in reform school taught him that Sir Thomas Roe was the British ambassador to India in the early seventeenth century.

His location and time suddenly hit him.

"Wring my cock!" he cursed.

The camel rider looked quite puzzled.

"I am not understanding you sir."

"Oh, uh, never mind," Glenn said quickly. "You speak English."

"Yes sir," the other said proudly.

"What was that you were saying before?"

"I asked you sir 'Dalan u mahal?' It means 'Domestic or royal'—an informal way of asking you your status."

"So, what would Sir Thomas Roe be?"

"Foreign" the other said, "but important. Are you not Roe?"

Glenn weighed his response. "Well, uh, where is the king?"

"In Agra," the man said.

"And where are we?"

"Ten miles from Delhi sir."

"Mmm," Glenn said, searching for his best snooty Brit accent. "Well, you see, I am in dire need of some privacy— the rigors of ambassadorship and all that. Is there any chance that anyone in Delhi might recognize me?"

"That sir is unlikely," the man said. "The king has taken his most important courtiers with him, and the common people are not allowed to mingle with the king's officials. The only person in Delhi who would recognize you as Sir Thomas Roe is the king's wife, Nur Jahan."

Glenn swallowed, hard.

"Why hasn't the king taken his wife to Agra?"

"She is ill," he said. "Also, the king has other wives to accompany him, although Nur Jahan is the *Padshah Begam*, or as you say in English, 'Principal Wife.'"

"And you're sure my visit won't disturb her?"

"She will be in the private gardens most of the day sir. You will not disturb her. You are not even expected here for one month or more."

"All right, then," Glenn said. "Help me to mount this smelly beast and we'll be off to Delhi."

As they rode toward the city, they talked.

"By the way, what is your name?"

"My name is Akbar sir. I was named after our great Jahangir's father, the late king who established the Mughal people here."

"And where did you learn English?"

"Sir," he said, "we are not an uncivilized nation. Our libraries stock books from around the world, our scholars often give public teachings, and our king, Jahangir, prizes the values of foreign cultures. Do you not know this?"

Glenn nodded quickly, but said nothing.

Akbar went on to tell of his people, the Mughals, who arrived in Hindustan (India) from the central Asian steppes in the early sixteenth century. He proudly spoke of how Delhi and Agra were designed by the Mughals to reflect a world of order and beauty. With their tombs and mosques, palaces and gardens, the Mughals brought grace and enhancement to a chaotic nation.

As his companion spoke, Glenn could not help but think of India's future, which he knew would be governed by Britain. Soldiers with guns would kill the people, great white hunters would kill the animals, and slowly but surely the true identity of the nation would suffocate and nearly die.

But that was in the haze of the future.

Now they approached the imperial city.

Color and sound were everywhere. Merchants haggled in the open market streets. Veiled women wearing burqas and palanquins silently strode past. Old men played games with colored beads, sitting on the flat earth and laughing.

Glenn and Akbar rode through the streets, hardly attracting more than casual stares.

"Is it always like this here?" Glenn asked.

"No sir," Akbar replied, smiling. "It's usually busier."

Directly ahead of them was the Red Fort, a massive enclosure that was the hub of the city. They entered it through a pair of ornate gates, where all men were free to pass through. Some would go to the Hall of Public Audience, a roofed structure surrounded by colored tenting and a fence. Here they would be heard by the emperor, Jahangir. As Akbar and Glenn passed, the emptiness of the hall confirmed the emperor's absence.

Between this hall and the Jumna River were the emperor's private apartments. Glenn noticed a completely enclosed zenana, and Akbar told him that the chief sultana Nur Jahan resided within, separated from the other, lesser wives. To the left of this was the Hall of Private Audience, where trusted officials would advise and have discourse with the king. This, too, was also empty.

"I wonder why the emperor wanted to go to Agra," Glenn said. "It seems like this place is just perfect."

"Some say the emperor prefers Agra," Akbar told him. "It is close to the dream city of *Fatehpur Sikri*, which his father the king had built, flooding an entire plain to make a pleasure lake. Jahangir often goes there. It restores him, I think sir."

Glenn nodded. "Tell me about Nur Jahan."

Akbar looked at him, then looked away. "She is a good *Padshah Begam*," he said. "Nur Jahan is very smart, very respected. Coins are even minted with her semblance sir. Some even say that she advises the emperor from behind a curtain at state dinners…but I know not of this. I am just a humble student sir, unversed in royal protocol."

"Earlier you said she was ill?"

"Yes sir. A most unusual illness."

"How do you mean?"

Akbar lowered his voice to an almost inaudible pitch. "An illness of the spirit, some say. I do not know."

"Very strange indeed," Glenn said. "Tell me, does she speak English?"

Akbar looked offended. "Of course she does sir, as well as Latin, Turkish and some Chinese. She is the Empress."

Digesting this information, Glenn asked his companion to show him to his room. He explained that he needed rest, and Akbar understood, guiding him through the incredible walled fort to an area where official guests stayed.

"You will be comfortable here?" he asked.

"Yes, yes," Glenn said. "I'll be fine."

"Then I will notify Nur Jahan of your presence."

"No," Glenn said, "don't do that. She is ill."

"I must notify her," Akbar said, "regardless." Glenn had no choice but to agree, and Akbar left.

The room was lovely. Delicate tapestries hung from the walls. An immense and inviting canopy bed with red satin sheets sprawled in the center. The furniture was exquisite, and since the Jumna River flowed nearby Glenn even felt moderately cool.

And yet he needed a plan. The facade of elegance would soon vanish and he would probably be thrown into some viper-infested pit if he couldn't succeed in reaching Nur Jahan. And not only that, he had to convince her to trust what he said, and he didn't even know what to say.

Slumping into a chair, Glenn buried his head in his palms. He could feel the weight of his situation bearing down on him. He knew it was all so desperate, so unplanned. But his love of St. Boltolph was absolute. An answer would come. A door would open. The link between the two worlds would appear.

He waited for darkness.

*

Under the cloak of the moon he found her, wandering through the imperial gardens, and she did not question his presence. She expected it.

"I have dreamed of the orris," she said to him, gracefully touching a golden flower with the tips of her fingers. "I have dreamed of the scepter. I have dreamed of the crown. I have dreamed of the tomb. A place of infinite shadow, trapping light. I have dreamed of winged angels bearing lyres. All these things I have dreamed, but shall no more."

"It need not be so," Glenn said.

"Ah, but it is. There are no promises in sorrow. There is no hope in hell." Just as gracefully, she crushed the golden flower. "As of late, all my dreams are but one, endlessly repeated. In this dream I am walking along a street paved with stones, up to a church that is burning. Although I shouldn't walk inside I do, through the blazing inferno, and I am unburned. I feel sorrow, even though the religion is not my own, and I begin to cry. My tears serve as fuel for the flames, and they rush toward me, and I am engulfed in fire. That is my dream."

"St. Boltolph," Glenn said. "You dreamt of the church of St. Boltolph."

"Boltolph," she said, "I know this name. I remember…"

"What?"

"In the church…"

"Yes?"

"When I was burning. St. Boltolph was in the church…." She closed her eyes very tightly. "There was something else…something dark, cold, like..pain….but worse. Agony, suffering, horror…"

Nur Jahan shivered.

"This thing, this beast," Glenn said, "we call it Satan."

The woman's eyes looked into his own, and slowly, the words formed:

"He spoke to me."

"What?"

"He spoke to me," she said, "but I did not want to listen. His voice became louder, filled my head, filled my mind…"

"What did he say?"

"Fragments," she mumbled, looking away. She slowly walked to a calm pool of water and gazed inside. "He spoke of the future—of endless sorrow. War. Conquest. He said the Mughal nation would collapse, and all their dignity would be destroyed. He said that he would defile the memory of St. Boltolph, the protector of hopeful ventures. His year had arrived, he said, and the world would begin to burn."

"My god," Glenn uttered.

Nur Jahan suddenly looked at him.

"*You are the right hand of St. Boltolph.*"

"I don't understand."

"You are his messenger; his final, true believer. You are the freer of his karma, his spirit, his soul."

Glenn shook his head, kneeling beside the reflecting pool.

"I am only a believer."

She took his hand.

"That is enough."

"But setting him free," he said, "how do we do that? I have come here with faith, but with no apparent means of accomplishing my goal. I…am lost."

"No," said Nur Jahan, "you are not lost. I now realize the answer that you seek."

Glenn looked hopefully at her. "What is it?"

And, as if in reflection, Nur Jahan said, "*My death.*"

Glenn let her hand go and stood. "No! How could that be?"

"In the church," she said. "When my dream-self was in the church, St. Boltolph was there with me. He was being tortured and he was in agony. He knew his foe was too strong, and that he could not win, so before his imprisonment he locked a part of himself inside of me—inside my soul, my karma, my spirit. And the time has come to release him."

Nur Jahan reached deep down into the pool, and withdrew gleaming silver dagger.

"Do it," she said. "Now."

Glenn closed his eyes. "I cannot."

There was a stirring in the air around them.

"Do it," she repeated. "Now!"

Something was lurking in the water's depths.

"I cannot do it," Glenn said, his eyes still closed.

The water began to ripple.

"All is lost if you do not do it now!" she screamed.

A black shape rose from the water.

Glenn's eyes were now open, horrified.

"You must do it!" she pleaded. "It is the only way!"

The shape lifted a taloned hand toward Glenn. "*Fool*," it said. "*Weak and pitiful fool!*"

Glenn took the knife.

"Kill me!" she screamed. "Kill me now!"

But he did not.

With one, swift motion Glenn plunged the blade into the heart of the beast.

The Thousand Injuries

The secret was lost with Fortunato, in an obscure timeline disturbance of 1846, a year of vast acknowledgment and acclaim for the opium-addicted writer Edgar Allan Poe. Bacchus was not pleased.

"What do you mean Fortunato's been killed?" he screamed at me. "What do you mean?"

I was new at the time, new and unsure.

"He has been sealed in the catacombs," I replied.

"Catacombs?" Bacchus spat. "I authorized no catacombs!"

"It was not of your doing," I answered with nervous anticipation. "It seems that a writer has infringed upon your creation, snatching it down to the dirty earth before it could properly be born inheaven, my lord."

Bacchus clenched his fist, and somewhere on Earth a volcano erupted.

"I want this man…this, writer!"

His eyes were two coals from some Stygian pit, burning into me.

"Yes, my lord."

* * *

He was sitting in a chair, eyes glazed, jaw slack, looking at me in drunken disbelief.

"Her name was not Lenore," he said, looking down at his mumbling lips, "methinks it was Virginia.Yes," sudden recollection, "Virginia. Virginia! Virginia Clemm!"

I felt sorry for him.

"Poor Virginia Clemm!" he went on. "Poor soul! The life that feeds us stabs at us and bleeds us! Poor Virgina Clemm!" He lifted a bottle of bourbon from beside his chair and tried to drink, spilling most of it on his shirt.Disgustedly, he threw it against the wall.

The crash of the bottle got his attention, and he looked at me a bit more clearly.

"What foul minion from Hell might you be? What accursed sycophant? What reeking corpse!" The words came grinding to a halt as he said 'corpse', and Poe fell to his knees.

"Ah, my Virginia…is…a…corpse!"

He was sobbing. "A corpse! A corpse! A lifeless corpse to shrink from light and dance no more!"

I knelt by his side and whispered to him, "It need not be so, for the destination year is 1846. Virginia is still alive."

Poe recoiled from me and sprawled to the floor, a look of sheer horror on his pallid face. Then he mellowed.

"A-l-i-v-e? As in 'to live'?" he asked hopefully. "A zombie? An aberration? Or…is she something more divine? Dare I hope that she might still be mine?"

Suddenly, the angry voice of Bacchus came ringing through the room. "Damn it, Poe, stop this rhyming!"

Edgar looked pleadingly up at the ceiling. "Oh Great Voice, why do you speak so harshly?"

"He can speak however he likes," I cautioned the writer, but he wasn't listening to me.

"You have killed Fortunato," Bacchus grumbled.

"Fortunato?" Poe asked stupidly. "Fortunato was a man of paper and ink, and the murder of such a character is not a crime, I should think!"

"Fortunato was not meant to be the jester-like victim of a practical joke," I told him, but he stillwasn't listening to me. He was searching the ceiling in vain to locate Bacchus.

There was a long pause.

"You have killed Fortunato," Bacchus repeated. "You must be punished."

✶   ✶   ✶

The streets were filled at the height of the Italian carnival. Bodies bumped into each other and,smiling, went about their cheerful business. The click-click of wooden soles on cobblestone filled the ears. The rich scent of breads and pastries revitalized the nose. The color, splendor and pageantry of the carnival engulfed all senses.

Poe was there, looking awkward. He wore a tight-fitting striped dress with snug leggings. Aconical cap with bells rested on his head, and his wrists and neck were lost in an avalanche of white ruffles.He sniffled, still managing to look miserable despite his gay costume. Picture Winston Churchill dressed as a court jester.

"Why have you transported me here?" he mumbled into the darkening sky. "Is this penitence? Locked in my own vision?"

Bacchus did not answer; but he watched.

And suddenly Poe was not alone.

A large, overly friendly man walked up and slapped the writer on the back, causing him to jump.

"My dear friend, I did not mean to scare you. Don't you remember your old friend Luchesi?"

Poe snorted. "Luchesi?"

"Yes," the other responded, "it is I." He withdrew a pinch of snuff from his pocket, then, thinking better of it, put it back. "You are looking very well to-day, my friend! But I have received a keg of what might be Amontillado, although I have my doubts…"

Poe let out a low, gruff chuckle. "You could not tell Amontillado from a barrel of mule piss, Luchesi. Leave me alone."

Looking disgruntled, Luchesi shuffled away.

Poe's eyes met the night's sky. "Oh Great Voice, what are the stakes in this weird game?"

Bacchus was amused. "You must first stop trying to contact me. From now on you are a character in this literary delusion, capable and yet limited, and talking to the incorporeal air will not advance your cause."

Poe bowed his balding head like a penitent monk.

Bacchus continued, "The stakes are simple. I have reclaimed my creation, the jocose Fortunato ,and put you in his place."

"Outlandish!" Poe protested. "How could a game with such a handicap be dubbed as fair? Surely, man, you have reason!"

"I have reason," Bacchus confirmed.

Poe furrowed his brow. "But how am I to win? For that matter, what am I to win?"

"Two great prizes," Bacchus assured him. "The first, obviously, is your life—your real life. Oh, it will be just as wretched as you left it, but I think it suits you…"

"And the second prize?" asked Poe.

Bacchus smiled, and a thousand orchids bloomed.

"The second prize, of course, is Virginia Clemm."

*

Shortly after dusk Poe was accosted by a pleasant, determined fellow by the name of Montresor. Strangely, Poe did not recognize his own creation, and he practically walked right past him. (They are a truly funny breed, these writers.)

"Ho there, good man!" said Montresor. "How fares your master this evening?"

Poe stared at him. "Montresor?"

"None else," announced the man, bowing quite baroquely. "And you, surely, are Edmondo, the good Fortunato's understudy?"

Poe swallowed some pride. "I am."

"You are indeed." Montresor smiled. "Come then, Edmondo, let us be off. I have a request to make of you…"

Poe sighed. "Don't tell me. You acquired some Amontillado and are keeping it in your vaults. You want me to enter the vaults and sample the wine to insure that it is really Amontillado."

"Surely you jest," said Montresor. "I have no Amontillado. Luchesi is rumored to have some, but not I."

That one threw Poe for a loop.

"Then what is your request?"

Furtively, Montresor whispered into Poe's ear.

*

(Now keep in mind that I was new at the job. I didn't think of using celestial powers to eavesdropuntil the very end of Montresor's clandestine speech. All that I heard him say was the Latin phrase "Nemo me impune lacessit", which means "No one wounds me with impunity", and that is indeed strange. Still, I couldn't manage to make the connection…)

Bacchus was speaking.

"Now, ultimately, this is a story of revenge, is it not?"

"Yes," I responded. "Eliminate the weird ending, and the story hinges purely upon the revenge motive. The evil Montresor lured our man Fortunato into an ancient network of catacombs which served asthe wine vaults for his family, under the pretense that he had obtained a rare and valuable wine, Amontillado. The good Fortunato simply couldn't resist the offer to sample such a delicacy."

"Horrible Montresor. Go on."

"Fortunato had already drank much that evening, and Montresor took advantage of it. He lured him deep into the catacombs, to a dead-end chamber where only shackles resided. There he secured our man, and proceeded to wall up the chamber and seal him to his doom."

Bacchus was displeased. "All this for revenge?"

"For revenge," I confirmed.

"Revenge for what sort of offense?"

"Poe does not say."

"Something is awry," said Bacchus. He lifted a mental veil to check on Poe's progress, like a fortune teller might look into a crystal ball. His brow lifted.

"Why are they not in the catacombs?"

"I do not know, my lord."

Bacchus turned his head slowly. "Find out."

There was a pause. It seemed as if an hourglass had been turned twice before Bacchus spoke again.

"Enter the story."

"How?" I asked stupidly. "The die is cast."

Bacchus smiled. "Only on this side of the Rubicon. We must breech the borders Poe has set and introduce you into the story as another one of his own characters. A cross-over, if you will."

"Can it be done?"

The god leaned forward and looked into my eyes with great amusement. "Of course it can be done. I am Bacchus, son of Zeus and Semele, god of wine and revelry, and I shall avenge the suffering of mygood student Fortunato. Yes, by the teats of Aphrodite, it can be done!"

*

A handful of siftings in the sieve of Time later, an old man who wasn't about to argue with Aphrodite's teats was ascending a great mountain. Poe and Montresor were just ahead.

"Stop, good travelers!" I called.

The two men turned and studied me. I approached. "Surely you two kind sirs will forgive the harsh demands my great age makes of me, and assist me in my journey up hill."

Poe and Montresor stared at each other.

"Young sirs, that is your destination?" I asked.

After a moment more of deliberation, Montresor spoke.

"Yes, that is where we are headed. But tell me, what possible reason do you have for climbing this incline?"

To him I turned my eye, which was pale blue, with a film over it. I spoke steadily and evenly. "My wife is buried at the top of this hill, if you must know, and with or without your assistance I intend to visit her."

Montresor recoiled a bit, and Poe stepped forward.

"Come, come, my fine old gentleman. All is well. We will assist you in negotiating this hill."

I thanked him, and we proceeded.

(Now, although I knew Bacchus was watching us, I also knew that even he had to abide by certain rules. For instance, he could not directly interfere with our actions. If Montresor suddenly pulled out a knife and stabbed me, that would be it. I would really be dead, not just my character. I no longer had any protection from harm, and my sudden loss of rank caused me to realize, with some distress, just how expendable I was.)

We came to a bend in the slanted dirt path, where two large rocks with flat surfaces were anchored to the side of the mountain, and I made the suggestion of stopping for a break and a little food. After a quick, furtive discussion between themselves, my companions agreed.

Resting on one of the stones, I watched Montresor unhook a small provisions pouch from his belt. He opened it and offered some bread to Poe, then he looked at me expectantly.

Not wanting to raise suspicion, I reached inside the fold of my cloak and whispered a few explanatory words to Bacchus. Within moments a small flask of good port wine materialized between my fingers. I withdrew it as if it had been fastened there all along.

"Here is to your good health," I said, lifting it in Montresor's direction.

"And to yours," he replied, and was satisfied.

"Tell me," I said, after we had resumed our climb, "what purpose do you two have at the top?"

Poe's eyes darted around nervously.

"It is nothing," Montresor answered hastily.

"Mmm," Poe agreed. "A very small matter."

They had obviously rehearsed, and I did not persist; but it didn't really matter. What I had planned would have them both talking soon enough.

The restless, chilly wind played through our hair as we walked, higher and higher. The land below us blurred and became indistinct. The air felt slightly thinner, and we were all getting tired.

I began to wonder how much longer it would take, when just then I noticed the quizzical expression on Poe's face.

"What the devil could that be?" he asked, pointing ahead to some spot on a nearby plateau.

Montresor strained his eyes to see, and I imitated him.

"I'm afraid I haven't got your sight, Edmondo."

"It is there!" Poe said, moving ahead, moving faster. "Surely even the old man sees it?"

"No, I do not."

"What is it?" asked Montresor.

Poe, who was now nearing the plateau, called back, "It is…a…tombstone!"

"The old man's wife…" Montresor began.

I shook my head. "Not here. She is at the top."

"Then what?" Poe demanded, moving still closer to the tombstone. We followed him.

Suddenly, as Poe came around to the front of the grave, he fell to his knees in amazement.

On the tombstone was the single name, "Lenore".

The writer shook his head. "Time is out of joint…time is out of joint." He mumbled this phrase again and again.

Montresor and I now stood on either side of him. Awkwardly, Montresor leaned over and placed a hand on Poe's shoulder. Unsure of what conclusion to draw, he spoke.

"What tombstone?"

Poe looked up now, frightened.

"By all the gods, do you not see it?"

"I see nothing."

"Nor I," I added for good measure.

At that, Poe buried his face in his hands and began a muffled sort of weeping.

The sound of the bird got his attention again. It was a black raven, perched atop the stone.

"Aah!" Poe whimpered.

The bird leaned forward a bit and stared at the petrified man.

"Nevermore," quoth the raven.

"Blast your black feathers!"

"Who are you talking to?" asked Montresor.

"The evil bird, you fool!"

"I see no bird," I offered.

"Nor do I," Montresor responded.

Poe was now literally tearing at his thinning hair, and a quick wink of my eye heavenward brought about the desired effect.

"Who on earth," Montresor asked, "is Virginia Clemm?"

Poe froze. His icy eyes locked with mine.

"Turn around," I said. "Behold the grave."

Now it was there for all to see; a dolorous, gray tombstone with a simple rhyme etched on its front:

Wedded at thirteen and destiny sealed,Here lies Virginia Clemm;The once and future queen of pain,To live and die, and die again.

To live and die, and die again."

Poe touched the stone.

"I cannot bear this burden of conscience, Montresor."

His companion's eyed widened.

"I pray thee, be silent!"

Poe shook his head. "I cannot. These are grievous wounds which have been inflicted upon me, and I must purge myself of their venom…"

He lifted his head skyward.

"Oh Great Voice, hear me now, for I have betrayed you. I told Montresor of your reclaiming of Fortunato, and now he has come here to challenge you, so that he might finally exact his revenge."

Bacchus spoke. "You still hunger for revenge?"

"I do," said Montresor, "for Fortunato hath injured me a thousand times, doing so for the pure sport of it, and my scars run deep."

"Indeed they must…", grumbled Bacchus, thinking.

For the first time, I spoke honestly, thereby revealing myself.

"My lord, we must soon achieve an accord. The powers that bind heaven and earth will reach a breaking point shortly, and we will all be spilled forth into the dusts of limbo."

"Indeed," he mumbled, "and yet I know not what to do…"

Reaching my hand inside my cloak, I quickly whispered to him.

"No!" he said in revulsion.

"It must be done," I answered.

"No other way?"

"None."

From between my fingers I felt the hilt of a dagger materialize.

"I demand justice!" Montresor yelled into the air.

I snuck behind him, blade poised.

"Here is your justice…"

A quick rush of air escaped from his lips, then he staggered and finally fell to the earth, throat cut.

Poe was beyond horror.

I looked at the blood-stained knife, then threw it to the dirt in disgust.

Bacchus himself materialized in front of us. He was weeping. Turning to Poe, he said, "I am powerless to reverse this sad occurrence. Forgive me."

The writer, after directing a last, silent, somber stare at the tombstone, lifted his bitter eyes to Bacchus.

"Nemo me impune lacessit."

Before I knew it, Poe had snatched the dagger from off the ground and plunged it into the chest of Bacchus, who groaned once. Then he was reeling, in the throes of death.

Thunder shook the foundation of the mountain.

"Nemo me impune lacessit," the writer repeated angrily. "*Nemo me impune lacessit!*"

Old Harry's Grave

Everybody lifts up the covers from Old Harry's grave on April 30. First we walk to the top of McCormack Hill near Llancarfen. The sun must be shining or else we can't do the ceremony but we've always done it every April 30 because the sun's been awful good to us. Then we take a pitchfork with a torch in its handle and stick it into the ground near Harry's blank tombstone. The two strongest men from our village then lift up the tarp.

Glass is the first thing we see, but then the solar powered lights start to kick in below and we catch our first glimpse of Harry for the new year. Next several small children with rags must clean the surface of the glass, removing the dirt, debris and insects which have collected on it since last year. Once they're done and the lights have had a chance to charge up everybody gathers around the lucid pit and stares.

It's been that way for as long as I've had memory. Although I'm told our taxidermy man did a superior job, stuffing only lasts for so long and each year Old Harry looks a little deader...

Until this year.

This year, after the tarp had been rolled back, the glass cleaned and the lights fully functional, we all gathered around that hole in the ground and stared stupidly downward into the depths of the lighted grave—and there was Harry, staring back up at us, his favorite pack of playing cards laid out in front of him, midway through a game of Solitaire. He blinked twice, coughed rather nervously, and said, "Hello."

Cousin Martha immediately fainted and her blubbery form struck the glass so hard I thought for sure it would crack and Harry's first guest in probably fifty years would suddenly "drop in". But there was no cracking, and Martha simply bounced a bit and rolled off to the side.

"The damn thing's alive!" Uncle Mortimer shouted.

"Let's get out of here!" Aunt Peg advised.

"Holy shit!" someone soliloquized.

Down below, Old Harry seemed to be taking the whole thing rather well. Unlike everyone else, he didn't look the least bit traumatized. In fact, he was so comfortable that he unbuttoned the front of his dress shirt to take in the noonday sun and I think he even farted. It was hard to tell what with the glass and all.

In time the screaming died down, the soliloquies ended, and I suddenly realized that I was the only one left standing at the top of McCormack Hill (Harry of course didn't count, because he was inside the hill, and he was sitting). No one had even bothered to drag or even roll poor Cousin Martha down the hill. I looked at her sympathetically.

"Ritual all screwed up now?" Harry asked peevishly.

I wasn't really sure if I should answer him or not.

"Cat got your tongue?" came the muffled croak from beneath the glass. I huffed.

"No, as a matter of fact; but it appears that the devil has got yours, you silly corpse."

"Not fair," he protested.

"I don't care," I said, and started walking away.

"You'll be back after sundown!" Harry called to me. I wasn't listening.

When I returned to the village a furious storm of spice cakes were a'cooking and strings of garlic had suddenly proliferated everyone's door. Old ladies were carrying crosses and old men were signing crosses at the old ladies. Hush-hushed wisp-whisperings floated through the smelly, spicy air. Our little village chapel was aglow with sacred candles burning and lines of people trying to stuff themselves inside like sardines. Everywhere I looked, everything I listened to; they were all moving lips and breathy words ridiculously stuffed like a banquet turkey with "Harry this" and "Harry that" spilling out all over the sides and staining the figurative tablecloth. In a rather large way their reactions pissed me off. After all, what the hell was the ritual for anyway? They wanted him to pop up and say hello and that's exactly what he did. There's no pleasing some people.

When I finally arrived home I found my mother bobbing up and down in front of a crucifix that we keep on the wall, with countless strings of rosary beads dangling from her neck as if she were some kind of Neocatholic Mr. T. I urged her to stop but she simply mumbled something about damnation and Armageddon and slipped back into her religious trance. I grabbed some bread, cheese and a flask of water and headed for the back yard, where my father was nailing, pounding and sawing up a storm.

"Hey dad, what are you doing, building an ark in case it starts raining?"

"Shhh!" he shooshed me, waving his hand at me as if to repel a gnat. "Not now I'm busy!"

So I climbed on top of a nearby rock and passed the time by having a little picnic. I thought about Old Harry and tried to picture how he might feel, sitting down there in his hole. Would he be happy to know that the whole village was terrified of him?

"Hey boy, give me a hand with this!"

"Not until you tell me what you're doing."

"Makin' stakes!" he snarled."Now get your ass down here!"

I looked at my old man's "stakes". They were really just a bunch of sharp-looking fence boards. I don't think he or anyone else in my village ever had cause to actually make stakes before. Those things didn't look like they'd do any damage unless Harry just happened to jump off a cliff and sit on one of them. Still, I was intrigued.

"Just what do you intend to do with these things?" I asked as I helped him stack them. He looked at me like some sly ferret.

"Tonight we're goin' down to Old Harry's grave. We're gonna smash his glass and kick his ass. We're gonna stick him with stakes then douse him with gasoline and set the whole thing on fire. That's what we're gonna do."

"Who's '*we*'? You and mom?"

"Heck no! She couldn't even walk across the room with all those rosary beads hanging from her neck. When I say 'we' I mean all the men of the village…and that includes *you*."

"Now let me get this straight," I said, "first you go there every year to pray for his revival, and.now that he's revived all you can think of doing is killing him? Have you ever thought of being nice to him? I'm sure he'd have some fascinating stories to tell…"

"Oh, *suurrre*," my dad mimicked. "We'll just hose him down and spruce him up then parade him down Main Street with his old dead ass sitting on top of a Hearse, waving to everybody like some prom queen. Then we could get in touch with all the medical journals and magazines like *Coroner's Weekly* and *The National Eulogizer* and tell them that we have an authentic zombie zipping about town, delivering benedictions." I tried to stop him but he was on a roll. "Then we could suck the embalming fluid out of him and stuff him with things like chicken livers and country potpourri, sew him back up again and maybe roast him over a fiery pit until he's golden brown, remembering of course to baste him at intervals. Maybe we could slap some ice cream on his dome and make a *Harry a la Mode*. Better yet, let's teach him to sing and dance. Heck, maybe we could resurrect a few more relatives and form a road show; you know, '*The Travelling Deadburys*'. Ya, I suppose we could fucking do that, couldn't we!"

"No need to become nasty, dad."

He growled. "Old Harry's got to die…again. Bottom line."

*

The rest of the afternoon passed on with the same touch of lunacy that marked this April 30, and before I knew it the sun was sinking beyond the horizon. People began shuffling outside of their houses, carrying lanterns and torches. Some of them had stakes of their own, others were waiting in line in my back yard, where my dad was turning a decent profit selling his homemade stakes for the bargain price of five pounds a piece.

From my dirty bedroom window I could see the blurry silhouettes of madmen, clipping phone wires to insure privacy for their upcoming event. They looted our local hardware shop, coming out bearing axes, garden shears, hammers, pikes, and all manner of assorted pointy things. They marched through the streets like a doomsday militia, growling and taunting and probably pissing on some bushes to mark their territory. They gathered in front of a flaming mound at the village's center, drinking liquor and goading each other on. This was the lynching mob. This was *Harry's Bastille Day*.

I thought about that quirky old reincarnated corpse sitting in his underground pit, and I must say I felt pity for him. I was sure Harry was a nice enough man while he was alive the first time around, so who was there to say that Harry wouldn't be just as good this time?

A handful of moments later I had my bathrobe and a pair of slippers on and I was trudging through our earthy streets, heading for McCormack Hill. Night had fallen and the moon was thin. Stars were few.

Somewhere in a marsh bullfrogs were croaking.

I could hear the mob muttering and buzzing far behind me. The ground was soft but not wet. The smell of grass filled the air. The birds which usually sung were strangely quiet, however, and I noticed that even the frogs were clamming up as I began to ascend the hill.

When I got to the top a most unusual sight was there to greet me: the remains of Cousin Martha. She had been rudely ripped apart.

Immediately I turned and peered into that glass-covered hole, completely black now that the solar lights had no source of energy.

"Harry! You down there?"

No answer.

I began to scrutinize the ground, and I saw what could have been scraping footprints, but they didn't leave the apex of the hill. For some strange reason, I started to whisper.

"*Harry, I know you're down there, damn it!*"

There was a pause.

"So what if I am?" came the reply.

"You've been a very bad corpse!" I chastised. "You ate Cousin Martha!"

"Big deal. It was a freebie."

"What?"

"She was dead when I ate her. Died of a heart attack. Now piss off!"

"No. You cannibalized a relative. Do you think I'm just going to walk away?"

He sounded a bit defensive. "Look, I didn't eat **all** of her. She was too damn big. There's plenty left if you're hungry, just leave me alone!"

"But why did you do it, Harry?"

Another pause.

"I haven't eaten in forty-seven years. Gimmie a break!"

"Okay," I reasoned, "suppose I'm willing to overlook this. What proof do I have that you won't go and do it again, huh?"

His mood changed. "This is it. Tonight is a one-shot deal for me. I'll be dead again by morning." Harry almost sounded weepy.

"Uh, I hate to tell you this Harry, but you'll probably be dead way before morning. There's a mob getting ready to kick your old, rotting ass down there."

"I thought that might happen. That's why I grabbed a meal while I could. Nothing sucks more than dying on an empty stomach."

"I'll try to remember that."

I watched the moon for a while before Harry spoke again.

"Hey, how much longer you figure I got?"

"Well, maybe ten minutes, maybe a half hour. It all depends on how drunk they need to be to do the deed."

"I see. Well, as long as we've got some time, why don't we chat? Tell me who you are. Are we related? I bet you're wondering how I knew you would come back."

"My name is Sean McCleod. I believe you're my great great grandfather. And yes, how the hell did you know I would come back?"

"Firstly, it's a pleasure to meet you, dearest grandson. I'm sure a lot of things have changed since I was around, but I take comfort in knowing that such a fine looking young boy is related to me. Secondly, I knew you would come because you have a choice to make. The mob that is gathering in the village will not be capable of killing me. If they attempt to do so I'll tear them all to pieces. Only you are capable of killing me. You are my direct blood, albeit new blood, and I will die again by your hands only."

I thought about what he said for a long while. Then, "Why should I kill you if you're going to die after tonight anyway? Kind of defeats the purpose, I would think.",p>Old Harry let out a slightly audible yawn followed by an extremely audible belch. Apparently Cousin Martha wasn't agreeing with him.

"Abominations to God are like that, I guess." he said at length. "I never wanted to come back like this, but you damn people buried me in an aquarium and prayed for my resurrection each year, so *The Hooved One* got his jollies off by pumping five hundred milligrams of sunshine up my ass and sending me back. So here I am, my gas tank is getting empty and I only have about a hundred milligrams to go before I'm back in Limbo, playing celestial Solitaire with fucking Andy Warhol."

I was at a loss for words, but I managed to find a few anyway.

"No shit, huh?"

"None at all, kid."

I paced and scratched my chin, asking Harry for a few minutes to think. He had no choice but to agree.

Suddenly my concentration was disturbed by the distant sounds of the approaching mob. I could see them, far below, their torches raised high and their weapons at the ready. Would Harry really be able to tear them all apart? Should I pay five pounds for one of my dad's stakes and kill Harry?

There was no time to delve into deep levels of scheming, so I knelt down and heaved up that great plate of glass, my hand groping below for Harry.

"If you're going to kill me," he said, "you'll have to come down here first."

"I'm not going to kill you, you old fool. Now give me your hand so I can pull you up."

"Really?"

"No, I'm kidding."

He gave me his hand and I pulled.

The next instant me and Old Harry were scampering down the other side of the hill. He didn't smell too bad for a corpse and he ran even better. I guess zombies can really pick 'em up and put 'em down after all—once they've had the shit scared out of them, that is.

After a few minutes we heard the puzzled shriek of the mob after they found Harry's empty grave and Cousin Martha's blubbery remains. We managed to put a good deal of distance between us and them, though, and they never caught sight of us.

We ran through open fields and rolling meadows, where long reeds of grass whistled as we flew by. The peephole brightness of the moon turned the land into a peculiar shadow, and the thumping of our footsteps lingered behind us like a vague thought. I took Harry far out, and together we jumped the small stone wall which marked the border of our village. There we stopped, me to catch my breath and him to check that none of his limbs or digits had jiggled off. When this was done, he turned to me.

"Why did you save me?"

"I don't know. Besides, I didn't really save you, I saved the village. You would have ripped their heads off if they got to you, right?"

And then I saw an expression that I never thought a corpse capable of wearing: a blush.

"You didn't **really** believe that line of crap, did you Sean?"

I emitted a rather loud *blurbitis vulgaris* before saying, "I suppose you're not going to croak before morning either?"

"I believe the word is 'bingo.'"

"And now that I've set your lying ass free just what exactly do you intend to do?"

Bad question.

Harry leaned over and took a bite out of me.

All

Her baby had become the most precious thing in her life, but when she died—one of many who were claimed in a London car bomb explosion—her baby had no one else.

Until Ursula.

It happened by chance and it happened quickly. A flash came and black smoke billowed and screaming followed, there on Ames Street at midday. A cab had been the source, and the blast took place when many were out for lunch.

Ursula had just exited the elevator in the lobby. Jeff the security computer recorded her passing, then Jeff the security computer burst into flames as a piece of schrapnel shattered a nearby window and smashed into the hardware.

Alarms blared.

She saw the baby neatly tucked into a carrier, alone on the sidewalk in the midst of charred chaos. And as the doors of her own building started to seal, Ursula made a decision, and jumped through the shattered window's frame.

Once on the street she wasted no time dashing across the wreckage. The wounded called for her attention but Ursula stayed focused on the baby. Gasoline heat and noxious air presented the biggest threat to the orphaned child, and Ursula snatched up the carrier and took it away—down to the flat on the Thames where no one would look.

It started to rain.

"Four dead and nine wounded in an Ames Street car bomb explosion," BBC radio confirmed. "Although the IRA is suspected, they have not yet claimed responsibility."

Ursula switched on the windshield wipers, which held the child's interest for the remainder of the ride. When they got to the flat, nestled like a fallen acorn in a bush, Ursula retrieved the secret key from beneath a rock. Inside she found a suitable change of clothes for them both, and she noticed the baby was a male, recently circumcised.

"…and now for more on the Ames Street car bomb, here's Pam Dallas reporting," the tv anchorman droned. A young, frisky woman filled the screen. "Thanks, Charles. We've just learned that the Ames Street car bomb was not random, but rather intended to strike two targets: Jodi Walsh and her infant son, Keegan. Walsh, a prominent figure in the world of genetic morphing, was rumored to be seeking an alternative, more natural prototype to today's most dangerous and expensive military weapon, the cyborg. She has now been confirmed dead in the blast. And on a mysterious note, her baby is missing…"

Ursula held the boy's shoulders. "Keegan," she said, staring into soft and gentle blue eyes, "you must be hungry."

She fixed cinnamon porridge and patiently spoon-fed the baby. His pug nose, his translucent eyebrows, his cheeks forever on the border of rouge. The small, well-equipped kitchen, the hum of the refrigerator, the friendly wallpaper. This was very different from what Ursula was accustomed to.

But something made her do it. Something made her rescue the baby. It was as if some motherly instinct of hers, long thought dead, had suddenly escaped from prison.

"Did you really think we wouldn't look for you in a safehouse?" a throaty voice suddenly asked. Ursula saw five men in black. She knew them.

"That boy was supposed to die," said the man with the throaty voice, who she recognized as the division manager of her unit. "It was wrong of you to interfere, Ursula. It's a weakness of your model."

Defiantly, Ursula cuddled the child. "It makes absolutely no sense to kill him. His mother was the one wh—"

"His mother," said her manager, "may have altered his genes. That's what Jodi Walsh was working with—a cheaper alternative to military cyborgs. Christ! If she'd succeeded it would have made a bigger stink than when the gasoline companies were finally defeated by the electric car! Now I'm sorry as all hell about how you feel, but we can't take any chances." He stepped forward. "Give me the child, Ursula. You've had a rough day."

She pushed his hand away.

"Ursula, give me the child. That's an order."

The four men behind him produced sleek metal alloy guns. Ursula examined the men carefully, doublechecked.

"They aren't cyborgs," she said to her manager. And with one statement he knew. Ursula would do the most damaging thing possible: she would fight.

Ursula already had her back turned when the first shots were fired. Four slugs hit her torso, but she did not drop. Instead she kept her back to them, absorbing more shots, and protectively placed Keegan behind the large refrigerator.

"Shit!" exclaimed her manager, who now had a digital phone in his hand. "She's against us! I don't fucking believe it! Send some heavy people here now! I want—"

Ursula ripped the phone from his grasp and backhanded his jaw with it. Then, as more shots were fired, she grabbed her manager and held him in the bullet paths. Her quickness stunned the men, and as they paused ever so briefly to stare at the boss they had just murdered, Ursula was upon them.

She killed them in a sweet demented blitz of movement, her immensely strong arms like pistons punching straight through their chests. She kept two of their guns and all of their ammunition, and drove the baby and herself away.

Twelve percent damaged, eighty-eight percent functional. That was the headline of the brief report she summoned to her eyes as she drove. Her torso had sustained considerable damage, but luckily her face was unhit, and that was all she needed to show in public.

She touched Keegan's cheek. The baby slept.

Ursula drove all the way from London to Llancarfan, Wales. She took backroads and cowtrails through the country, once passing a lone police car that did nothing. It was evening when she arrived, car out of gas and baby crying.

"I know you miss your mother, but I'm here."

The city of Llancarfan, on the mouth of the Severn river, was full of sad, sweet promise. Ursula took a shawl from the back seat and wrapped it around her torso. She carefully placed Keegan in his carrier and set out on foot.

Garden crickets chirped and fell silent, chirped and fell silent, as they passed. The houses were sprinkled here there, some dark and some with yellow windows. Ursula came to an unintimidating little cottage with a pebbled driveway. She rested the carrier on the doorstep and rang the bell.

The stars were thick, the crescent moon bright.

A leathery old lady appeared. "Who are you? Is that a baby? Oh my, it *is* a baby. Well then, come in dearie. I just love babies. Cute as buttons the lot of them and worth the trouble of husbands. Come in, come in…"

But Ursula sensed something was wrong. She sensed it a split instant before a hand pushed the old lady clear.

"Open fire!" the sergeant screamed from inside the house.

A bawdy spittleburst of high-caliber projectiles flew out the door like a frightened school of fish. Less than a second was all Ursula had, yet with less than a second she dropped to the floor and covered the baby.

Nine men with fully automatic rifles flooded the porch and encircled her. Their sergeant raised his right arm.

"Continue to fire!" he ordered.

A hale of ammunition thunked into Ursula. Large chunks of her skin and clothing burst off. Round after round hit her as she remained motionless, protecting the baby. Her internal monitor informed her she was approaching sixty percent damage.

Finally, as a *coup de grace*, the sergeant put the muzzel of his own gun to Ursula's head and emptied the chambers. Sparks streaked outward from the cracked metal skull, and Ursula convulsed once.

A black boot uncovered what Ursula had given all to protect. The baby was innocently silent as the men reloaded.

Something Digital

Wisps of salty air carried the scent of the sea to the half-dozing form of Trickles the cat, who rested on a portion of a beach towel. He was curled next to an overflowing basket of sun-bright oranges, on the wooden planks of Ms. Diane Vante's porch. His nostrils flared intermittently, like windshield wiper blades, detecting the delightful odor of fish and greedily sucking it in. Between reality and dreams, he watched the world through half-closed eyes, his gaze shifting from the oranges to the sea.

Diane was inside the house, boiling lobsters. She had found some wonderful two-pounders at the market by the pier, where all the merchants seemed to know her, if not by name then surely by attitude. Not only was she far removed from the naive tourists but she was also superior to the natives. Diane would never show emotion over a good find and no matter how low the price was she would always insist that it was too high. Through her persistence she had the ability to throw even the best merchants into a state of discombobulation.

When the lobsters were done Diane called Trickles in for a sampling. The overweight cat eagerly lumbered into the kitchen and issued a report of meaningful meows. Diane cracked open one of the claws but did not remove the meat. She subscribed to the theory that all pets should work a bit for their food.

Trickles was a very hard worker.

Settling down at the kitchen table with the remainder of the lobsters, Diane watched Trickles. When the cat's nose had outlived its usefulness, there was still tempting meat in the corners of the claw. Trickles knew this, and he began pawing and slapping the claw from tile to tile on the floor. In his hungry agitation Trickles slapped the claw the way a hockey player would slap a puck. It shot across the room and landed in a corner with a smack: Trickles 1, Claw 0.

Diane did all she could to keep herself from laughing uncontrollably as the obese feline wagged his tail and greedily stared at his cornered prey. Then, as if on command, Trickles shot his huge bulk high into the air and pounced on the helpless claw.

This, unfortunately, was the demise of Trickles the cat.

The weight of the falling feline landed in the middle of four corner tiles. As if in slow motion, Diane watched the tiles give way, sending Trickles and his hard-earned lobster claw plunging into unknown depths. A ludicrous *"meeooooww!"* could be heard fading into the distance as the falling cat never hit bottom.

Diane, who was once amused, was now deeply disturbed. She slowly got up and made her way to the corner of the room, testing each tile with her foot first. She came to the hole and examined it, noting that it was no wider than the four tiles that had fallen and the sides appeared smooth and metallic. It seemed to resemble an endless downward shaft or passage that was carved into the earth.

She called for Trickles, but there was no answer.

Becoming panicky, Diane grabbed a flashlight from a kitchen cabinet and shined it down into the hole. The light went down very far but could not penetrate the blackness after a certain point.

Desperately she called again for her cat, and again there was no answer. Diane was now on the verge of a nervous breakdown. How could such a thing happen? It was impossible…just impossible. She mumbled "No way…no way…" to herself as she walked out of the kitchen and down the hall, straight to the medicine cabinet in her bathroom, where she proceeded to down a liberal quantity of Valium.

As she closed the cabinet she happened to catch sight of the woman in the mirror, who was tired and aging, with scraggly brown hair and small breasts. She had no children to make her hair turn that delightful shade of motherly gray and she no longer had a husband to make those small breasts feel like they belonged to a real woman. She lowered her head and walked into her empty bedroom. The Valium soon took effect, and she fell asleep.

Now while Diane slept, the house was beginning to come awake. A generator hummed far below, inaudible to the unknowing ear. It was slowly charging a very old battery. This battery would soon give power to dust-covered circuits and switches. The digital meter was already counting.

Less than ten hours.

Later that evening the house deemed it safe to open the 86th Upper Passage. Electric tendrils moved through a wall duct. They slightly shifted the painting of Little Boy Blue which hung over Diane's bed.

Finding their way to the wall socket, they overrode the AC current. Now they were visible: two tentacles extending from the socket.

They hovered snake-like in the air and flexed themselves over the sleeping form of Ms. Vante. They floated over her feet and slid between her legs and into her dress, singeing the top of the material. They emerged at her neckline and then branched to each ear. From there they linked with her mind…

Visions…dreams…going back…far back…

…Her grandfather gave her a licorice stick. They stood in front of his newly-completed beach house. He smiled at her, never explaining why the house took seven years to build…

…Her father died. She was just a teenager. She could not bring herself to crying…

…A bridal gown. A husband. Grandfather was very old now He hated her husband…

…Late at night. A phone call. There was a car crash. Her husband was dead. Diane was alone.

She shot to consciousness in a shadow-filled room. Tears flowed from her eyes. The tendrils watched from the wall socket.

Why had her life come down to this? There was a time when she told herself she could live off her own pride, but she was wrong. Now she saw herself as a broken person, living alone by the sea in a house her spiteful grandfather built.

A glance at her clock told her that she had slept through most of the day. She swore softly as she got up and, not bothering to turn on any lights, she went into the bathroom. She ran some cool water in the sink and splashed some on her face.

Then the damndest thing happened.

Avoice softly whispered, "Diane…"

She froze. Water dripped from her face as she again heard, "Diane…"

The voice…it was her grandfather…but he was dead.

She looked up into the mirror and saw his withered, old face in front of a red background which cast a crypt-like illumination into the darkened room. The thing staring back at her did not appear to be dead, and its features were just as Diane had remembered in her dream.

"Diane…" it rasped. "Diane…"

"This is not real. This *is not* real!" she told herself, putting her hands over her eyes.

"Diane…Diane…"

"*What*?!" she exploded. "What the hell is it?"

The face smiled, and said:

> "Come through the mirror Life is but a dream."
> Diane passed out.

She awoke to the feeling of a soft, moist cloth being placed on her forehead…by her husband.

"Hello, sweetheart," he said.

She stared at him in disbelief.

"Remember me?"

"Go away!" she screamed.

"Aw, come on honey. You used to love it when I came home early from work and surprised you—I thought you'd be out of your mind if I came back from the dead and surprised you…Why the long face?"

"Out of my mind…" she stammered. "You hit the nail right on the head. I'm out of my mind."

"No you're not, honey! I'm right here, see…I'm real! Go ahead, tell me to do something."

"Get me my Valium."

"Oh, honey, you know that's not good for you. I'm here to take care of you."

Diane looked at him incredulously. "Where the hell did you come from?"

"I came through there, honey," he said, pointing to the mirror over Diane's medicine cabinet.

She snorted.

"Is this a joke? Who put you up to this?"

"Your grandfather did."

"What? He hates you."

"I know. He sort of *made* me come here."

"You mean you didn't want to see me?" Diane said, offended.

"Of course I wanted to see you, honey, but what would the other ghosts think if I was running off to see my wife every minute?"

Diane was silent. The whole thing seemed totally ridiculous to her. She sat up and rested her head in her hands, resigning herself to the thought that even Trickles wasn't there to confirm the fact that she had gone insane.

"I want my cat back."

"Ah, yes. Lovely little…uh, BIG…creature. Your cat is also in the mirror, Diane."

"My cat is in the what—" She looked up, and saw the large face of Trickles the cat stupidly staring down at her from inside the mirror.

"*Meow*?" it said in a confused and pathetic tone. Diane gasped and recoiled.

"What have you cruel bastards done to Trickles?"

The two men remained silent.

"Answer me, damn it!" Diane screamed.

"Trickles is quite fine," said her grandfather, reappearing in the mirror next to the cat. "It was quite unfortunate for the poor beast to fall down here, but I'll try to keep him as comfortable as possible."

"Comfortable?" said Diane. "How could you possibly keep him comfortable? You're fucking dead!"

"A minor formality," her grandfather said casually. "There are many planes of existence." He leaned his ugly face forward in the mirror. "And I'll remind you to watch your language, young lady."

"What are you going to do, spank me?" Diane laughed in spite of her situation. Apparently she found the idea of being spanked by her dead grandfather amusing.

Her grandfather frowned. "No, I won't spank you, but I could easily constrict my fingers around the neck of this porky feline and literally squeeze the life out of it. Is that what you want?"

"I don't want any of this!" Diane yelled.

"Not that it matters," he grandfather said reflectively. "The fat beast will eventually die of starvation."

"Starvation!" gasped Diane. "No! I'll send food for him down that hatch, okay?"

"What a nice gesture." Her grandfather smiled. "Hit her, Charlie."

Diane's husband made a fist and punched her square in the face. Once again, the world went black for Ms. Vante.

Seeing no further need to stay, her husband climbed back into the mirror and slowly dissolved, along with Diane's grandfather and Trickles the cat.

The house decided to take the opportunity to make some very loud, odd noises. So far it had executed its program to perfection, but the hardest part was still to come.

It was time.

The outside structure of the house crumbled to reveal sturdy ceramic tiles. Deep down below a slow and steady roar could be heard. Fuel was pumped into two massive thrusters buried within an underground cavity. The walls, chambers and beams which formed the house's subterranean labyrinth collapsed, freeing the two thrusters. The ludicrous and insane voice of Diane's grandfather was pumped through the upper portion of the house via old, hidden speakers:

"Liftoff in ten…nine…eight…"

Diane suddenly awoke. The whole house was shaking.

"Five…four…three…two………"

Diane's eyes widened.

"What the hell is this?" she stammered.

The house rumbled violently, and there was an earth-shattering roar from beneath. Diane felt the house rise.

"We have liftoff!" her grandfather squealed joyously.

Higher and faster it moved, shooting through the sky.

Diane dared not stir, staying glued to the floor. The G-force was intense, and her stomach felt like lead. Her eyes darted from side to side, and through the newly-reinforced bathroom window, Diane could see clouds swooshing by.

"Welcome aboard the space ship Trickles, named in honor of your most obese feline!" her grandfather said.

Diane still didn't move. "What have you done, you old fool?" she said from between clenched teeth.

"The earth was going to hell," he said. "I had to get you out of it. You'll find all you need to sustain yourself for the rest of your life in the lower catacombs of this ship. It is my present to you from beyond the grave."

The ship broke away from the earth and hurled through space. As if on queue, a bottle of Valium fell from a nearby shelf and landed in Diane's lap.

She was now faced with a decision.

Did she want to die, or did she want to be a lonely widow who drifted through space, talked to mirrors, and masturbated herself to sleep every night?

It was no contest.

Downing the entire contents of the bottle, Diane stood and looked deep into the mirror's depths.

"Fuck you, grandfather."

All the Trimmings

The wet, slushy road felt like pure fun. Hank, Dave, Chester, Elmo, and Zach smiled eagerly at each other, and the four-wheel drive truck almost guided itself along the winding, wooded trail. Snowbanked evergreens were everywhere, lining and restricting the little road. Occasionally icicles would fall from the leafy limbs high above, and plunk into the melting snow.

Two more hours and they were at the cabin, nestled deep within the thick, unbroken wilderness. Their gear and supplies included portable kerosene lanterns, a change of cloths for each man, and a huge Thanksgiving turkey with all the trimmings. All these things were unloaded and taken into the cabin, and the five friends settled themselves in for the start of an old-fashioned holiday.

Then the temperature dropped, and the storm came.

They thought nothing of it, busying themselves with the preparation of dinner. The turkey was cooked, basted and devoured, along with stuffing, mashed potatoes, carrots, corn, cranberry sauce, and fresh biscuits. A thoroughly excellent dinner, all agreed, and they snuggled into their sleeping bags.

Two feet of new snow had collected by morning. The temperature had fallen to twelve degrees. The wind chill factor was thirty below. The men were freezing.

After starting a nice, warm fire they pooled together the last of their supplies and made a huge breakfast which consisted of eggs, bacon, bread, butter, jam, pancakes with lots of syrup, and coffee. They ate quickly and happily, still thinking nothing of the storm. After all, their truck had four-wheel drive.

The rest of the morning was passed by playing Trivial Pursuit and Pictionary, and by early afternoon they were ready to depart, packing their gear and heading out to the truck.

The truck didn't start.

"What's the matter?" Elmo asked.

After a moment, Zach replied, "No gas."

"That's not possible," Hank said. "We had half a tank when we got here, and we sure as hell haven't used the truck since."

"Maybe someone siphoned it," Chester suggested.

"No," Zach answered. "There were no footprints in the fresh snow, just some pawprints."

They got out of the truck.

"Hey, look at this," Dave said, "The ground under the truck smells like gas."

Zach bent over and looked.

"Shit!" he exclaimed. "There's a hole in the gas tank. It's indented. We must have run over a stone that hit it just right. Shit."

"So what do we do now?" Elmo asked.

"Back in the cabin," Zach said. "We'll think of something."

For the rest of the afternoon they thought, but when evening came Dave said, "I'm hungry."

"Me too," said Chester.

"No shit, Sherlock. We're all hungry," Zach answered.

"The turkey bones," Hank suggested. "We could boil the turkey bones and the turkey skin and make soup."

"Yuk!" Dave said.

"How disgusting!" Chester replied.

"I hate soup!" Zach complained. "It's shitty!"

Four hours later, they had soup. When this was gone they ate the moist turkey skin and chewed on the bones. Then they went to sleep. Some of them prayed.

By morning, the storm was over. The five friends were grateful, and in a flash of inspiration they collected all the kerosene from their lanterns, plugged up the hole in the gas tank with a wad of gum, and poured the kerosene in. They repacked their gear and got back into the truck.

The engine sputtered, kicked in, then stalled.

It did not start again.

"Shit!" Zach exclaimed.

They got out of the car.

"Hey Zach," Elmo said, "I think you better look at this." Zach bent over and looked.

"Shit!" he yelled. "The plug fell out and we lost our kerosene! Shit!"

The men looked at each other.

"So what do we do now," Elmo asked.

"Back in the cabin," Zach said. "We'll think of something."

For the rest of the morning they thought, but when afternoon came Dave said, "I'm hungry."

"Me too," said Chester.

"No shit again, Sherlock. We're all hungry," Zach answered.

"Hey, look what I found!" Hank said, holding up a dead mouse in one hand a some mummified cockroaches in the other. "We could boil the mouse and the roaches and make soup!"

"Yuk!" Dave said.

"How disgusting!" Chester replied.

"I hate soup!" Zach complained. "It's shitty!"

Four hours later, they had soup. When this was gone they ate the mouse carcass and sucked on the moist roaches. Then they went to sleep. They all prayed.

By morning, a new storm had come. The temperature was seven degrees. They woke up freezing.

To keep warm, they broke some chairs apart and lit them. Needless to say, they did not have breakfast.

"I hate this shit!" Zach yelled. "I just can't stand it! Storm or no storm, I'm walking out that door and finding help."

"Zach," Elmo said, "we're a two and a half hour *drive* from the nearest gas station! No one else lives out here! You'll never make it!"

But he was already out the door. The four men in the cabin waited. The second storm cleared.

Hank took a look outside. "Hey fellas," he yelled, "I see something!"

Dave, Elmo and Chester eagerly ran outside. "What is it?" Elmo asked.

"Over there." Hank pointed. "There's some sort of clump out there, in the direction of Zach's footprints."

They followed Zach's prints about fifty yards out, and discovered that the "clump" Hank saw was actually Zach's frozen remains. There was a set of human footprints (Zach's) going way out toward the horizon, and the same set running back, pursued by wolf prints.

"He was within sight of the cabin," Chester mumbled.

"They practically only left his damn bones," Hank lamented.

"Let's make soup with Zach's bones!" Dave said.

"What?" Elmo said quickly. "What did you say?"

"His bones," Dave repeated. "Let's make soup with his bones!"

"That's not a bad idea," Chester said.

"You fools!" Elmo screamed. "Can't you see that the only way out is to follow his prints?"

They thought about it.

After a time, Hank said, "I kinda like the soup idea."

"Me too," Chester agreed.

Dave smiled. "Soup it is."

"No!" Elmo yelled. "You fucking fools with your fucking soup! Piss off! I'm following Zach's tracks!"

And off he went.

Hank, Chester and Dave watched him go, then they dragged Zach's remains back to the cabin and had soup. When they finished the soup they chewed on Zach's bones for a while, passing around his thin nasal cartilage to pick their teeth with. Then they went to sleep.

The next morning they heard a plane pass overhead.

They came up with a plan.

Hank headed to the east of the cabin and Dave headed to the west. The first man to see another plane would shout back to Chester, who stayed at the cabin with several homemade torches. When he heard the call he would set the cabin on fire and the passing plane would see it and rescue them.

The next plane that came was heading in a north-south direction, and neither Hank or Dave spotted it.

But Chester did.

Even though it was practically above him, Chester set the cabin on fire anyway. By the time the flames caught, the plane was gone.

Hank and Dave came back in time to see the cabin collapse in a heap of flames and the nearby truck ignite. They then proceeded to strangle Chester and roast his corpse over the fire. Hank enjoyed a medium rare rump section while Dave opted for the ribs, and for the first time in a long time, Hank and Dave were full.

They went to sleep in the snow.

While they slept another storm struck.

The temperature dropped to five degrees below zero.

Two feet of fresh snow fell.

The wind chill factor was really unbelievable.

The snot froze inside their noses and their spit turned to ice and they suffocated then froze like two Birdseye peas.

Then the rescue party arrived, led by Elmo, who, upon seeing the last of his friends dead, promptly went insane.

And to this day he cannot muster up the courage to eat a turkey dinner with all the trimmings.

Scorched Mercy

Bedrosian Auto slumped and sprawled like a drunken whore, occupying what used to be a nearly condemnable warehouse on Olympia Avenue. I had half a mind to turn back when I saw the state of disrepair the place was in. The road leading up to the dealership was even bumpier than I recalled, and the sign in front of the place was not the glowing neon monster out of memory, but a conservative, non-electrical billboard, devoid of slogans or fancy artwork.

My first impression was that the place was closed, but this was soon proven untrue as a sloppy-looking, obese salesman lumbered out one of the doors with a possible buyer. They quickly moved to inspect a suspiciously-priced car with four consecutive 9's written on the windshield.

I decided to park my own vehicle (a Mercedes, thank you) well out of range of the front lot, fearful of some disreputable salesman drawing up a contract on it and having it off the lot before I could reclaim it.

After parking a good hundred yards away from the nearest door, I got out and walked across a really pathetic looking conglomeration of mixed, mongoloid, used, and damaged autos. The area resembled a flea market parking lot, with cars parked in "L" and "V" formations. I wondered how such a slob could be doing such good business.

Inside, the place strongly resembled the aluminum siding sales office in the movie "Tin Men". A row of less than pleasant-looking telemarketers were jammed into little cubicles along the wall. A bunch of smelly desks with even smellier salesmen sitting on them were scattered like bird droppings in the center of the place. Clouds of smoke lingered like vague thoughts, seemingly rising from the very floor itself.

I tried to look friendly as I made my way through the pigpen. I was stopped four times by salesmen with such pimp-like questions as "*You lookin' for somethin' nice?*" and "*Wanna take one of these babies out for a ride?*" before I found my way to that familiar corner office with "The Big J" egotistically inscribed on the door.

He was leaning back in a leather chair, hands folded over his beer belly. A plate of saucy, half-eaten food served as a paperweight on his desk. I stood in his doorway and coughed, which evoked a startled look as he came down hard from his leaning position and belched in my general direction.

"If you're looking for a car, talk to one of my salesmen, Paul."

No. As it just so happens, I'm looking for a fat bastard, and I believe you fit the bill.

"Oh, I don't need a car, Julius. I'm just paying a little social call…honest. Truce—okay?"

He rubbed a sweaty palm across his jaw and grunted.

"All right, I guess that's kosher. Have a seat."

Not wanting to offend him this early on, I did, even though the whole room looked sticky.

I kept on my business smile. "Nice place you've got here. Changed it a bit, huh?"

"Piss on it!" Julius exclaimed. "You think I like it here?"

"But all those sales you told everyone about…"

"Sales? I was blowin' smoke up their asses…mine too. Living beyond my means. I blew more money on that new batch of commercials than this whole place grosses in a month!" Suddenly, the expression on his face changed. "But hell, I don't mean to bother you with stuff like that. What's on your mind, Paul?"

Now that was odd. Julius isn't the kind of person who'll walk up and offer to wipe your nose for you. His type needs lots of incentive, and that's something I certainly haven't given him lately. Regardless, I went on.

"I came here to find out what's been going on with you. I know that you haven't kept company recently with any of us—except Jacklyn, and that ended in our little fight—and I was just wondering what your feelings toward the whole situation with Alex might be."

He studied me. "In other words, you want to know if we're all still going to play in the same sandbox, right?"

"I guess you could put it that way."

He looked up and squinted at an open light bulb on the ceiling, tapping his slightly pudgy cheek with an index finger.

"Hmm. Pardon the salesman in me, but what do you have to gain from this knowledge?"

Ouch. I was hoping to work my way around that area. I suppose I could have handed him a line of shit that would tread water for the time being, but it wouldn't have been wise in the long run, especially if I needed him again, which I might.

"Well, the fact is, Julius, a lot of strange things are happening. My brother Alex is definitely planning something, and Phil is out of the picture—maybe even dead—compliments of my brother. I guess I came here because right now, you're Switzerland—neutral…and all this appears to be just the tip of the iceberg."

"So why tell me?" he asked with disdain. "It's not like I'm *Mr. Big Stick* or anything. Go fight your own wars, Paulie. I'm neutral, remember?"

I could feel my face getting red. "Look, as far as I'm concerned you can stay and rot here in your cesspool. I don't care. Just remember one thing," I said, leaning forward and glaring at him. "If you so much as flinch from your 'neutral' position, I'll have your fucking balls mounted to a plaque, porko."

Julius all but growled at me.

"A very interesting proposal indeed…" came the voice.

I was about to ask Julius to explain himself but I stopped short, a feeling of panic and surprise arising within me, for it was not Julius who spoke.

"*Balls to a Plaque*…hmm. It would make for a lovely soap opera, don't you think?"

The voice came from a speakerphone on Julius' desk, which I realized was on. It was Alex, and he had heard everything.

Julius turned to me slowly, and I saw a smile spread across his face.

"Julius, are you still there?" asked the voice.

"Right here, buddy."

"Would you please tell Paul that his efforts are in vain. I have already completed preliminary work, and I am quite safe from any feeble attempts at reaching me he might muster. In fact, please throw him out of your establishment—he cheapens the place."

Julius leered at me. "You heard your brother, Paulie."

I spat on his shirt. "Fuck you, porko."

Without warning Julius came rushing out of his chair. I managed to get up, but he tackled me, and we both went crashing to the floor. His hands clamped on my face and his nails dug into my cheeks, but I kneed him in the groin and managed to shove him off me. I could feel a few drops of blood trickling down my face.

We both stood and faced each other for a moment, then Julius came charging again.

I caught him with an elbow on the side of the jaw and he twisted, throwing a punch at my ribs that landed. He came to rush me again, but I sidestepped him and gave him a punch in the back for his trouble. He toppled over a chair and landed a few yards away. I gingerly touched my ribs. They did not seem to be cracked.

"He's crazy!" I heard Julius scream from the floor. "Stop the son of a bitch!"

Three, four, five salesmen had suddenly surrounded me. One of them was holding a broom handle; the rest had their fists up. They were closing in.

I dropped to the floor and did a foot sweep, temporarily taking out two guys on my left. The one with the broom handle tried to bludgeon my head with it, but I caught it between my palms and jerked it away from him, knocking him off balance in the process. Almost instantly the two salesmen who remained standing were furiously kicking at me. I rammed the end of the long stick into one guy's mouth and I heard the crunch of teeth as he dropped. Without pausing I swung the broom handle around and sent the other guy's kneecap on a home run blast. He howled, clutching at the injured leg as he hobbled around and finally hit the floor.

Now the first two guys I had knocked over were up, and one of them had grabbed a folding chair. He lifted it high over his head to clobber me with, but I jammed the stick into his solar plexus and he dropped it harmlessly as he doubled over in pain. Now I was up on my feet.

Four fat salesmen were ready for me.

With one gigantic roundhouse I sent the broom handle smashing into the ribcage of the salesman nearest me. The broom handle cracked, but so did his rib, because he ran out of the picture, clutching his side.

Three guys charged me, but I found myself with a sharp, splintered piece of wood in each hand. I stepped back as one of them threw an uppercut then I moved low, bringing the pointed piece of wood upward and spearing him in the belly with it. He fell to his knees screaming, and his two buddies suddenly paused.

I didn't waste any time.

The first guy I hit was the one whose teeth I had smashed in, and I allowed the splintered wood to get him in the same area, raking across his mouth and shredding apart his lips. That was all she wrote for him. Reconstructive surgery city.

The second guy was a little tougher, and he caught me in the thigh with a swift kick. I staggered more than was necessary, and sure enough he tried to do the same damn thing again, but I was ready for him, catching his leg in mid air and holding it. As he was hopping on one foot I smashed him upside the head with my stick, and he checked-out of reality for a while. Everyone else in the vicinity who was conscious started to fearfully crawl away.

Except Julius.

He was now standing again, looking as if I had pissed on his Christmas tree.

"I'll have your ass for this, Paul!" he screamed. "I don't care how, but I'll get you back!"

"Those are some pretty strong words," I stated, "for a guy whose henchmen are all in need of first aid."

He glared at me.

"Besides," I continued, "now that I know you're brown-nosing Alex, I hardly think that you're in a position to be threatening me, porko."

Julius was about to say something nasty, but was cut off by a huge explosion from somewhere outside, shortly followed by another, and another. I took the opportunity to leap forward and swiftly kick him in the groin, hard. He quickly fell in upon himself, sort of like an implosion, and I ran out of his office and down the hallway.

When I came out to the front lot I had to do all I could to prevent myself from being consumed by laughter, for row after row of automobiles were catching fire and exploding. Apparently almost every car in the lot had been doused with gasoline. I stopped to enjoy the spectacle only briefly, then carefully made my way around the perimeter of the lot to where my car was parked.

I saw Julius emerge from the front door moments later, doubled over like a hunchback. He was yelling at every available employee on hand and carrying a pitcher of black liquid, which I assumed was coffee, frantically trying to extinguish the nearest flaming car with it.

He looked at me then, and I'm sure he swore, but I couldn't hear anything above the explosions.

I quickly roared my car to life and sprang out of the lot, heading back up Olympia Avenue. From somewhere in the distance I heard sirens.

"So I guess you owe me one, pal."

It came from the back of the car. I thought it was the radio, but I hadn't turned that on.

Phil's head popped up from the back seat.

"What, no kiss?" my friend asked.

I nearly crashed.

"I thought you were missing…or dead," I said. "No such luck." He smiled. "I'm your guardian angel."

"Then you *are* dead," I told him. "Nonsense," he said. "I've never felt more alive."

"Alive compared to what? A log? A brick? A pumpkin?"

"A person, Paul. I feel great."

I grinned slightly. "We'll see about that…"

"Indeed we will," Phil said. "The reason why I feel so great is because I managed to figure out what's really going on here. Quite an accomplishment for a guy you thought was dead, huh? And I'll even tell you what I've learned."

"Wait a minute, you're actually trying to tell me that you can shed some light on all this?" I asked Phil as we headed north along Route 93. I knew the landscape would slowly be changing from city to suburban to rural. "Yes, I believe I can," he responded. "Actually, it's not all that hard to do, it just requires the right perspective. This was something that neither one of us had until very recently. You see, I thought things over while I was out of the picture, and I decided to take a new course of action. Now why do you suppose Alex and Julius are so chummy all of a sudden?"

"I told you, it's kind of hard to figure. I went in there to talk with him, and he had Alex already waiting on his speakerphone. Now, he sure as hell didn't know I would be dropping by, so what gives?"

Phil smiled. "The obvious, of course. Julius has been doing worse business than anyone had imagined. Alex has the cash, and he's been spending it quite liberally lately. It only makes sense that they were striking some kind of deal while Julius was avoiding the rest of us."

Now that I thought of it, it seemed a good assumption.

I turned to Phil, keeping one eye on the road. "So what you're telling me is that Julius agreed to keep Alex completely informed about what I was up to in exchange for enough money to bail out his slumping dealership?"

"Yes. It was just a minor case of bad luck when you walked in on what was apparently a conversation between the two of them, since Alex would have been told everything that transpired anyway. That way he was just able to hurl a few insults in your direction, which was stupid of him. For the small amount of personal pleasure he might have gotten, he cost himself a lot of secrecy."

"Secrecy or not," I said, "none of this was expected..on both our accounts. I don't know who's been thrown off balance more, us or him."

"We were never really *on* balance," Phil joked as he looked the passenger's window, thinking thoughts that were yet be voiced. He vaguely smelled of gasoline and Polo.

I shrugged, leaning over to the glove compartment and withdrawing a pack of Sampoernas. I offered one to Phil and he took it, breaking off the filter before lighting up.

"All out of your unfiltered Camels?" I asked.

Phil broke into a wide grin, apparently very pleased with himself. "As a matter of fact, I am. How do you think I got those cars to explode like a string of firecrackers?"

The light bulb went on.

"I'll tell you how. I used my Camels as fuses! And guess what? It wouldn't have worked with Sampoernas because the filter would have put them out! Pretty cool, huh?"

"Let's hear it for cancer," I said. "By the way, how did you know Julius was in on this?"

"I was keeping tabs on most of us, just because I wasn't sure who might come to Alex's aid. Pretty soon I noticed that Julius was maintaining some pretty weird business hours. So, I followed him one day, and he met Alex over in Victory Park. For caution's sake I didn't get too close, but words were exchanged between the two of them, and Julius walked away with a small bundle of something, presumably money.

"After that, I hung around Bedrosian Auto regularly, occasionally walking right into the place and picking up scraps of conversation coming from Julius' office. Then I decided to invest in a long-range microphone and a camera with a telephoto lens, and I was able to get some real nice stuff on them. Today I was over there doing my thing when you just happened to stop by. I quickly 'borrowed' some gasoline from Julius' garage when I heard the conversation take a nasty turn. Nobody in the garage spoke English, and nobody noticed the missing drums of gas—until things started exploding."

"How did you get away undetected?" I asked with interest.

"By hustling my ass." Phil smiled. "Shortly after all the commotion started I headed for your car. Originally I was just going to wait until you got there, but firstly that would have looked mighty suspicious and secondly I noticed that your back left window was ajar. Needing no further inspiration, I let myself in."

I took some time and spent some miles digesting this information, then asked, "What kind of stuff were you able to get on Alex and Julius?"

Apparently I had asked the right question, because a big smirk split Phil's face from ear to ear.

He sat sideways in his seat and looked intently at me.

"You're gonna love this. Julius and Alex are bed buddies."

"What?"

"Bed buddies," he repeated. "Bum chums. Fudge packers. Brown hole archeaologists. Midnight rim surfers. You know."

"Gay?" I asked.

Phil pretended to look shocked. "***Alternative Lifestylers***," he corrected.

Like that made it easier to swallow. My kid brother took it up the ass from Julius; *and he paid for it too*. Crazy gay Alex, sleeping with my former friend. Julius and I had played college football together, for heaven's sake!

I drove on, in silence.

We needed to come up with a plan.

*

"So what do you think?" I asked him. Phil gave it some thought.

"How about Plywood Ranch?"

"No," I said. "Too much wood, not enough tools."

He thought again.

"Grossman's?"

I nodded with approval. "That's more like it."

"Grossman's?" he asked again.

"Yes, Grossman's."

About a half hour later we were in the parking lot. "You have a good idea of what we're looking for?" Phil questioned.

"Yes."

We entered the store and I got my bearings. "That way," I told him, pointing.

The aisles were big and wide, chuck full of interesting objects. Display bins were filled with nuts, bolts, washers, screws, nails, thingamabobs, etc. The walls were crammed with switches, sockets, sprockets, and gaskets.

There were enough sharp little metal things in that place to make Tomas de Torquemada orgasm.

I started off by choosing a nice pair of oversized pliers, testing their grip and action like an expert plumber.

"These should do," I said to Phil.

He looked at me a bit skeptically, and we moved on.

Next came the iron-link chains, then the Exacto knives, then the safety flares, then the duct tape, then the Bunsen burner, complete with gas tanks, then we were done.

"One hundred sixty-four dollars and thirty-two cents," said the cashier.

I smiled pleasantly at her, then turned to Phil.

"Pay her, won't you?"

"Hold on now—"

"I'm broke," I lied.

Phil sighed, then dug into his wallet.

"I've been hoodwinked," he mumbled.

"Don't worry," I told him, "it's all for a good cause."

*

A few hours later we were back in Julius' office. His dealership had closed, and we managed to catch him alone as he was finishing up. Poor bastard.

We secured him to his office chair with the iron-link chains, plastering his hands and feet and lips together with lots of duct tape. Phil stood over him and made sure the fittings were tight as I stood in a corner of the room and toyed with one of the safety flares.

"This is your last chance to tell us where Alex is," I warned Julius. "If you don't, we'll have to begin interrogation."

At first Julius' eyes widened in fear, but then they narrowed in anger. I guess he thought we weren't serious.

"It's all up to you," I told him, then looked at Phil. "Take the tape off his mouth and see if he has anything useful to say to us."

Phil did so, and Julius immediately began to scream for help. I sighed, striking the tip of the safety flare against its sandpaper cap and watching it ignite.

"Poor bastard," Phil mumbled.

I walked over to Julius and looked him in the eye. "This is what we call '*The Hot Seat*.'"

Carefully, I placed the flare under his steal chair.

Then I lit two more flares and did the same procedure. We waited, and after a few minutes, Julius began to squirm.

"Ready to talk?" I asked. He shook his head. No.

Phil looked at me questioningly. "What now?"

"What else?" I asked. "We move on to Step Two."

Phil removed the flares while I was firing up the Bunsen burner. Once I had a steady blue flame to work with, I placed the pliers directly over it and waited.

"Get the Exacto knives," I told Phil. "You know what to do with them."

He nodded, and with a knife in each hand, he proceeded to cut open Julius' shirt, exposing his bare chest.

"Are you from Arizona?" I asked Julius. He looked puzzled.

"Of course you're not," I said, "but *I* am. And in Arizona it sure can get hot. As a matter of fact, mechanics are often afraid to pick up a tool that's been lying around in the sun too long, just because it's so damn hot. Understand?"

He wasn't really following me…yet.

I continued, "Some mechanics—the more sadistic ones—have been known to use these heated tools in creative ways, and down in Arizona we have this thing. It's called '*The Arizona Titty Twister*', and it really hurts."

Wrapping my hand with some cloth, I took the smoldering pliers and moved forward—right toward Julius' left nipple—and applied the infamous Arizona Titty Twister.

One twist was all it took. Julius was ready to talk.

"He's up north near Rye in some hotel called the Sea Haven Inn!" Julius blurted out quickly after Phil removed the tape again. "That's all I know it really is I swear it! Don't put that fucking Arizona Titty Twister on me again!"

I leaned forward and grinned.

"You being honest with us, Julie?"

"Dead honest!" he said quickly and urgently. "Everything I've said is true!" His eyes never left the heated pliers.

I turned to Phil. "What do you think?"

My friend looked grim. "Fear made him speak, Paul, and it is my understanding that fear can produce a good ass-covering lie. If we abide by the percentages, then he's lying to us."

I turned my gaze to Julius. He was terrified.

"I don't think we've got much to worry about, Phil."

"But the *percentages* say—"

"Look," I told him, "a guy sits down and he worries about the percentages, and he wakes up the next day with his hand in his pants and a crusty, wasted load on the floor. Screw the percentages, Phil. We've got to act on instinct."

Loosening Julius' chains just a bit, we headed for the door.

*

Okay, now for a little history.

Alex liked to fuck people over. On countless occasions he took advantage of the weaknesses several situations could present. He tried overtly to put himself on an untouchable pedestal. He took chances when chances were not called for, dubbing himself a poet of the mind.

Taking advantage of well-meaning friends and hiding his own feelings over parts of his daily routine through his self-imposed gloom, he was easily able to suppress the sudden smile and dampen a good mood in the room. Always trying to get a little more for himself, Alex, in essence, was not a friend to man.

But the secret seemed to be hiding behind some veil. Yes, Alex was a bastard, but even *he* had scruples and motivational factors. Hell, we had the same circle of friends. There was sweet and kind Erica, who was Phil's wife. She was a doctor, and she was loyal to her husband. Then we have Jacklyn, all 38-24-36 of her. Lusty and open, Jackie is Erica's opposite. Alex liked to screw with both their minds.

And it was time to pay him a visit.

*

Two hours later I found myself pacing the floor of his abandoned summer house. The place was cluttered and disorganized, but that was no surprise. My brother Alex is the sort of person who will buy something, display it, buy something, display it, and continue the cycle until he's surrounded. Lush draperies hung in every room, cascading down upon thick-rugged floors. Beds and chairs were overflowing with silk pillows and detailed Chinese quilts. Works of art hung like posters on his walls, bunched closer together than any art museum would dare display them. Carved wood, ivory, jade, crystal, even touches of alabaster and mother-of-pearl and lapis lazuli were everywhere. They adorned the place, and since Alex knows how to make money, he could afford to lend himself to such eccentric behavior and satisfy such unusual tastes.

"What the **hell** could he be up to?" Phil asked me with a frown. "Your brother hasn't been here recently. I just came from his kitchen, and the dishes in the sink have mold on them and his milk has turned to yogurt. Julius obviously lied to us. I told you we should have gone with the percentages."

"Again with the percentages…" I mumbled.

"Why not? That's how a real detective would do it."

I rolled my eyes. "We obviously have some very different notions here, Phil."

"What are you saying?"

"All I'm saying is that we're both trying to be a couple of hardcore thinkers, and if we don't stop it we're gonna wind up pulling out our mental daggers and trying to stab each other to death with our conflicting ideas. That just won't do."

"So I suppose I should stop asking questions?" Phil asked in a huff.

"Well, if you're really interested in getting some answers, asking questions is the wrong thing to do. Understand?"

He pouted. "No."

Great. I needed a drink of good hairy booze.

A few minutes later I was sitting on Alex's big puffy couch with a full glass of bourbon. Phil was still huffy.

"So where do we go from here, Sherlock?"

"Look," I said, "I don't regret my decision to believe Julius. I'm honestly convinced that Julius thought Alex would be here."

"Then how do you explain his absence?"

"That can't be explained with any certainty just yet. Perhaps he and Julius had a tiff, and we were fed old information concerning my brother's whereabouts. I don't really know, Phil."

"Okay," he said, "at least we agree we're banging our heads up against a locked door—but just out of curiousity, what do you think might be on the other side?"

I took a long swig of bourbon. "Molasses, probably. Sure, sometimes I'll tell myself that all the answers are just around the corner. I'll catch myself playing out all these great possible scenarios, but in truth I'm just some stupid ape, groping around blindly. I only hope we'll be able to stop Alex before he makes his big move. Whatever the fuck it is."

"I'm sure all that would sound real nice on paper," said Phil, "but just what the hell could Alex's 'big move' be?"

"Again, I don't have a good answer. This thing, this mood which possesses my brother, must be seized. As with all of us, there is a limit; a limit to character, acts or deeds. This limit simply cannot be passed without some consequence. It's very likely that Alex has reached this limit. Plus, just to make things worse, we both know about his interests in industrial espionage…"

Phil nodded. "He pulled of f that scam against Webster Company a few years back. How much did you say he made?"

"Over a million," I answered. "Certified check from the Chief Executive Officer himself. He really had those guys by the balls."

"And that Flaxley Exchange thing," Phil went on. "Didn't Alex do that one too?"

"Just last year," I told him. "He had a friend on the inside—a secretary. Instead of shredding their personal documents she stuck them in her purse—and if they were really juicy she would stuff them down her panties—and she would feed them to Alex on a weekly basis—the documents, that is. When he had enough dirt, he sprung his trap. Old man Flaxley himself paid my brother 2.7 million."

Phil whistled. "All that money and you'd think the little prick would be satisfied."

"Never," I said. "He'll always want more."

Suddenly Phil appeared to be rather mad at me.

"What is it?" I asked. "What's the matter?"

"You," he replied. "*You're* the matter."

"What?"

"You knew what he was doing, Paul. Why didn't you stop him?—and don't hand me a line of shit about how he's your little brother. If *I* had a little brother like that you know where you'd find him? In my stool."

"Don't worry, I won't carry a badge of family loyalty here. It's just that I run my own business, you know, and the two companies we just talked about are two of my biggest clients. In the interest of preserving my own livelihood, I wasn't about to flush them down the toilet. Hell, Alex knew that. That's why he even told me."

"Well, all that's fine and dandy, but again we've come to the question of what to do now."

I calmly put down the bottle of bourbon and stood.

"Now we search this place for all it's worth."

*

Three horribly long hours later Phil and I had amassed little more than a great deal of sweat, and we were just about to call it quits when the damnedest thing happened.

Two grenades came sailing through a nearby window.

My fists automatically clenched and my nails broke the skin on my palms. One of the suckers had landed on an easy chair and the other rolled under the couch.

"Quick, run into another room and close the door!" I yelled to Phil, scrambling toward the visible grenade.

"What about you?" he asked in a panic.

"Never mind!" I told him. "Just do it!"

He left, speedily.

I took hold of the grenade and quickly peeked out the broken window. Sure enough, two guys were running toward a car that was parked across the street. They were Alex's men for sure.

"Oh boys," I called to them, "you forgot something!"

They stopped and stupidly turned to look at me just as I threw the grenade at them, then flung myself out the window.

A thunderous double explosion rocked both the house and the street as I fell to the dirt and rolled. Through the noise I barely heard a final, fatal scream come from the two men as the schrapnel tore into their flesh and the explosion snuffed their wits. Caught between the forceful tremors, it was like I was inside the barrel of a recoiling shotgun.

Then I felt a sharp pain in my left leg and something unbearably hot sliced across my back. Bits of concrete and lots of dust filled the air, and some of the flying debris showered down on me. I remained motionless and hunched for another twenty seconds or so, then I dragged my bleeding self up to the window ledge. Thankful to be alive, I called for Phil.

"Right here," he said, poking his head out of a bedroom door "Sure was a blast, wasn't it? You hurt?"

"Not permanently," I told him, checking my wounds.

"Good," he said, "because we've gotta split. The cops are bound to be here soon."

"Ya. I can practically hear all the neighbors picking up their phones and dialing 911. Let's go."

Phil paused. "What about Alex?"

"We'll get him," I said, "along with Julius."

We both wanted Alex to suffer.

*　　　　　　*　　　　　　*

"For once you'll have to admit I came up with a great plan," Phil said the next day. "Don't you think, Paul?"

I smiled to myself.

"Brilliant," I said.

I dug a couple of warm beers out of my trunk and handed one to Phil. He accepted it, and we both sat on the hood of my car and kept our eyes on the front door to Bedrosian Auto. Good old Julius had replaced all of the cars that exploded, and that served as our signal, telling us that he was still sucking on Alex's monetary nipple.

"Tell me," I said, "how much did you pay that little old lady to do this?"

"Two hundred," Phil said. "A real bargain."

"No kidding. Where did you find her?"

"Old folks home," he replied. "I donate money to the place on occasion. You'd be surprised how eager she was to do this. I guess you can only play so many games of checkers before you become starved for some action."

"And you're sure she knows the plan?"

"You bet," he said. "Just be ready for her."

Twenty minutes passed, and we were just starting to tan when our little old lady walked out the front door with Julius right behind her. He led her to the most expensive car on the lot. Although we couldn't hear much at that distance, I could just picture Julius saying, "Well, I usually don't personally accompany the customer for a test drive, but since you said money was no object…"

I smiled, nodded to Phil, and we both got in the car, watching Julius and the little old lady buckle up. Safety first, you know.

Then I heard a massive roar come from the test car, and before I could start my engine the little old lady was peeling out of the lot.

"Damn she's fast!" I said, turning the key.

"Just keep up with her!" Phil said.

As we planned, the little old lady went straight for the highway. I was closer now, and I could see Julius frantically gesturing for her to pull over. I had to chuckle. That little old lady was doing 95.

She roared past the traffic and changed lanes like an Indy car. She was even starting to lose me, but the exit we agreed upon came up quickly, and I could hear the squeeling tires as she cut across three lanes to take it.

She lowered the window on her side and flashed me a big thumbs up, and we both went screeching and skidding onto a little twisty road. After a few more minutes, she finally swerved into a quiet rest area and slammed on the brakes.

As soon as the car stopped moving Julius immediately scrambled out and started to run, but my Mercedes came barreling in and cut him off. Phil quickly jumped out and flanked him.

Julius most assuredly knew what was afoot now.

I got out of the car and approached him, ready for almost anything. He was angry, that was quite apparent, but he did not try to resist us as we put him in the back seat of my car. Phil went in with him, watching him closely.

The old lady smiled at us, said something about total exhilaration, then absent-mindedly wandered off into some nearby woods. A few joggers passed by with really perplexed looks, so I took out my wallet and said, "F.B.I. Move along, now." I mean, what the hell, right? They couldn't see anything from that distance. Besides, I've always wanted to do that.

Having our fish safely in the net, we took him back to my place, escorting him on either side into my house. For the sake of convenience we locked him in a closet, and since we had a little time, I fixed us a couple of sandwiches, Julius excluded. We made some light conversation while we ate, but we both knew that the time had come to set the trap. This would involve a simple phone call to Alex from Julius, saying that something new and important came up and calling for a meeting at so-and-so. I thought Victory Park was a good choice, and Phil agreed.

"Serves 'em right to finish it where they started," he commented. I concurred, and walked over to the closet to let Julius out.

Immediately I was struck in the face with a broom handle. The force of the blow sent me sprawling backward onto the floor, bleeding from my nose and lips.

Julius sprang out of the closet and started to advance on Phil, holding the broom handle like a baseball bat. But it was too late. Phil was already drawing a shiny piece of steel from inside his jacket. Before I fully realized what it was he had the gun cocked and pointed at Julius' head.

"Take another step, you fucking son of a bitch, and your head will be splattered all over this fucking floor! We'll take the rug and hang it on the wall as artwork."

Julius stopped.

I recovered and took the broomstick from his hands, cracking it over my knee. I gave him a kick in the groin for old time's sake, and he fell to the floor with a whimper. Phil advanced on him, holding the gun to within inches of his temple.

We led him over to the phone.

*   *   *

Gray and sullen storm clouds had spread beneath the fading sun as Phil and I made our way across Victory Park. Julius walked ahead of us, knowing exactly what Phil would do if he tried to run. The grass we walked on felt soft and warm beneath my feet. Up ahead I could see a playground, along with a baseball field, tennis courts, and a basketball area. These places comprised the inner section of the park, which was surrounded by thick trees on three sides.

We took Julius onto the pitcher's mound of the baseball field just as the last people—a couple of lanky tennis players—were leaving the park. Phil had a few words with him, saying something to the effect that if he moved or tried to warn Alex he was dead. We then split up to either side of him and took cover just inside the layer of trees.

A nervous fifteen minutes passed, with the storm brewing thicker and the final traces of the sun's light being strangled from the sky, when a lone figure emerged from an opening perhaps one hundred yards away. The distance was too great to discern whether it was Alex or not, but the figure steadily moved forward, clad all in black, vaguely reminding me of some kind of messenger of the apocalypse.

Small details slowly became clearer, like the hat the figure was wearing and the puffs of smoke that would intermittently emerge from the still-distorted face. He was perhaps within forty yards of Julius, and I started to circle around him under the cover of the trees in order to cut off his obvious escape route. I couldn't see what position Phil had taken, but I knew that he would be stationed close to the pitcher's mound, so that he could quickly spring down upon them when the time was right.

Almost. Twenty-five yards. .fifteen…ten..five…

Phil was out of the woods and running at full speed towards the figure, carrying the gun in plain sight. I was still in the trees, about thirty yards away, when the figure quickly looked behind itself in my direction. It was Alex. With a loud yell I sprang from my position and bolted at him.

The shot came almost instantly after that. At first I thought it was Phil who had fired, but then I saw him stagger and fall to the ground in a heap, clutching his left thigh and screaming. I had closed to within fifteen yards when I saw Alex draw a gun from a shoulder holster and point it in my direction. He fired two quick shots directly in front of my feet, and I stopped running. I raised my hands level with my head, around five yards away from him.

I then saw a man start to climb down from a nearby tree, with a rifle slung across his back. Alex exchanged a few words with Julius, who was now grinning evilly at me. Handing him the gun, Alex whispered something to him. Julius smiled, and advanced on me, holding the gun out in front of him like a mighty schlong.

"I don't imagine you might have any tricks left, old buddy. Isn't that a shame?" He looked at the gun. "To think that I could kill you right now! Oh, I'd love to do that, for all the times you've kicked me in the crotch. But Alex wants you alive, for now…"

He started to lift the gun behind his head and shift its position in his hand, so that he was holding the barrel, and the handle was coming at my head like a hammer. I still had my hands up, and was able to catch hold of his wrist at the last second and twist it, violently. I heard a snap, and Julius moaned as the gun fell to the ground between us. As he was going down, I kicked him in the groin for good measure.

The next thing I knew Alex's man was right behind me, applying a full nelson with wrathful intensity. I saw Julius squirming on the ground in front of me and Phil being dragged to his feet by Alex, who now held his gun. With his good hand, Julius made a move for his own pistol, but I was able to give him a hard kick in the face. He rolled backward, bleeding from the nose and mouth. Alex's man applied more pressure, until it felt like my neck would snap. Julius started to rise again, a bitter look in his eyes, but Alex called for him to stop. With a snarl, he obeyed.

"Good dog," I managed to say.

I didn't think his look could get worse, but it did.

Alex came up alongside us and took the second gun, practically dragging Phil behind him. He directed his man, whom I learned was named Nick, to take me to a car that was waiting just out of sight. As Nick was turning me around, I could see Alex cast a disgusted look at Julius.

Phil and I were blindfolded inside the car. Nick sat between us and Alex and Julius were up in front. How long we rode I do not know, but the time moved slowly. Whenever we passed over a pothole I could hear Julius whimper. Phil managed to fake a laugh and told him to shut-up.

After a while the car came to a stop and we were led out. Rivulets of cool rain fell down upon me. I could hear some voices in the distance, and Alex quickly swore, yanking the blindfold off me. My eyes took a handful of moments to adjust, and when they did I could see that we were standing in front of a small warehouse that I did not recognize. Phil also had his blindfold off and was looking around. The voices I heard belonged to some children playing further up the street. They looked at us for a moment, then resumed their games.

From somewhere on the street I heard a Pink Floyd song playing: "*If you wanna find out what's behind these cold eyes, you'll just have to claw your way through this disguise...*"

Then we were led inside, and although Nick was between us, clenching our arms tightly, I felt no pain. I was preparing myself to do what I had to do to get us out of there, whether it meant taking a bullet or not. But the time was not yet right. To have struggled then would have been predictable, and a waste.

Phil had a hard time making it up the stairs that led to Alex's office in the empty warehouse, which I assumed he owned. When I reached my free hand around Nick to help Phil I got an elbow in the ribs for my trouble. Phil soon slumped over, and Nick dragged him the rest of the way. He had lost alot of blood, and was drifting in and out of consciousness by the time we were seated in Alex's room. Our recent beatings made the damn scene surreal.

The first thing I noticed was his computer systems. They occupied most of the far wall.

Alex instructed Julius to get some ointment and bandages for Phil from another room, and he allowed me to fix up my friend's injury as best I could. Luckily, the bullet had passed through and it wasn't lodged in his thigh. I requested some pain reliever for when Phil regained consciousness, and again Julius left for a minute and came back, a begrudging Florence Nightingale.

"As you can see," said Alex, pacing the floor, "we don't have to be entirely unreasonable with one another. After all, I'm only going to destroy your company, Paul. It's not like I'm selling your soul to the devil, you know." He laughed a little to himself. "All I want from you two is a little…well, not even cooperation, just *space*. Understand?"

I looked him in the eye, hard.

"If you want something from me—like lessons on how to fight with your fists and not with a gun—you'll have to give me something in return. Do *you* understand?" I mimicked.

He flinched slightly, and covered it up by pretending to scratch his chin.

"I see," he said. "Although you're hardly in the kind of position to be making demands of me, what is it that you want?"

"I want to know why you're doing this, Alex. I want to know what it's all about. I want to know why you're against me and I want to know why you're such an asshole. Does that sum it up for you?"

He smiled.

"You want to know a lot, don't you?"

He paced up and down some more then he took a seat beside me. Nick and Julius were standing behind us. Alex lit a cigarette and regarded me.

"I suppose you hate me," he said timidly, laying his hand on my shoulder.

"You're a fucking lunatic," I told him.

"Whether that's true or not," he said, "the world has to stand up and notice me. No more corporation heads. No more chances. You should be honored. With the money I can steal from someone like you, I'll be a rocket. We're talking political here. We're talking *billions*!"

"There's a lot of talk like that," I said, "in the nuthouse."

"Fuck yourself," he said. "My plan is solid—but I'm not about to go into details." He got up and strutted over to his computer systems. "Let's just say that it's all in here, and that means that you stupid bastards are going to die within sight of your goal. All three of you," he added, looking at Julius.

I *felt* rather than saw Julius stiffening behind me.

Alex caught it, too.

"Oh, come on, Julius," he said in an admonishing tone. "Did you really think that a big dumb sloth like you could impress me? Ha! I gave you money, sure. That was because you were a lousy businessman and perhaps you could make a better spy out of yourself—but what kind of brains does that take? Hell, at least Paul over here can earn his own way; you 're nothing but a slovenly beggar! And you know what? I don't even like you! You're a crummy lay that comes too quickly and snores like a bull being murdered. I should even write a book and tell the whole world what a pathetic sow you are!"

Julius simply attacked. It's hard to put it any other way. He didn't say anything, didn't even scream. He just charged him. His fist struck Alex across the jaw and they both went down. Nick began to move in, but I saw this as my opportunity. Although he was tall and strong, he was unarmed, and that was something.

I threw a furious blow that connected with his ribs and tackled him from the side. As we were going down I saw Julius land another punch in Alex's mouth. This heartened me, and for the first time in a long time I liked Julius.

As Nick and I rolled across the floor I dug my elbow into his solar plexus and gave him a kidney punch with my free hand. He thrust up both his muscled arms and simultaneously gripped my face and my throat. I could feel the pressure building as I kneed him in the groin and grabbed the leg of a nearby chair. Before he knew what I was up to I smashed the chair leg into his face.

Blood spurted, and he was out of the picture.

Julius hadn't fared as well. Alex had drawn his gun and was pointing it in his face.

I moved forward.

"Another step," he said, turning the gun at Phil, "and you've forfeited your friend's life. Now sit down."

I wasn't about to argue. I sat and watched as he struck Julius over the head.

"You really think you had me?" he said, toying with the gun. "You really fucking thought you had me! Well I'll tell you something: You weren't even close! I've set you up like a pig in a slaughterhouse!" He walked over and began petting one of his computers. "I've been collecting the shit that's in here for years. I've got stuff on all you idiots, and it's all right here, and if I could lift this thing up I'd wave it in front of your face and say 'Nah-nah-nah!' before I blew your brains out."

He moved the mouse and lovingly tapped some keys.

"Wanna see some of it? Oh, this is good! I've got stuff in here to make senators nervous! And it all starts when you liquidate your entire company and give all the money to me. And you'll do it, believe me. Why? Because I had video cameras set up all over Julius' auto dealership, and I've got some great shots of you crippling his salesmen and Phil over here blowing up his whole fucking lot. And that's not even mentioning ransacking my house and the little kidnapping you two stooges pulled. Once stuff like that goes public, how long do you think you'll last, Paulie? Huh? You have no fucking choice, dearest brother."

He turned and began typing into the computer.

Just then Phil, who had been conscious, made his move, lunging at Alex's legs and pulling him off balance. I quickly got up and wrestled the gun from him.

Aiming it at him, I said, "I just want you to tell me one thing."

Alex almost laughed, but decided against it.

"Why did you do all this?" I asked.

This time he did laugh; a long, high-pitched cackle.

"Of all the stupid questions! Why do you think I did it? Because you were a good patsy and because I knew how much money you were worth."

I felt like pulling the trigger, but I didn't.

"Why?" I repeated. "I've never hurt you."

"For the power, you stupid bastard!"

Alex looked inhuman. His eyes were bugging out and saliva fell from his mouth.

I cocked the gun.

"Perhaps there should be no power…"

"No!" he screamed. "Don't! Don't kill me!"

But I wasn't going to kill him.

Instead I took aim at his computers, and fired four shots.

Immediately a hissing roar erupted from the machines, shooting sparks high into the air. Alex screamed again and wildly clutched at the equipment. His body was overcome by instant and uncontrollable spasms and his hair stood on end and fizzled. The sparks from the computers caught on the numerous mounds of paper that Alex had, and flames were soon licking upward toward the ceiling.

I turned to Phil. "Can you make it down the stairs?"

"I'll roll down if I have to," he said.

I nodded, and moved over to Julius and lifted him.

Glancing down at Nick, I abandoned my honor and principles and left him there. Phil was in front of me, hurrying down the stairs.

"Come on!" he called. "The fire's spreading fast!"

I carried Julius over to the stairs, then glanced back into the room, throwing the gun I still held in the direction of the flames.

The Replier

Moonglow birds and sundry ties aligned in tawdry rows. Simple rows, houses, sidewalks. And rain. Afternoon. Green leaves swaying on the supple, subtly bending limbs of man-planned trees.

Grove Street, 1:09 p.m.

High up I jumped. Clutched some leaves and pulled, the snap shaking loose a burst of droplets. Love my yellow rain outfit. Everyone else is inside.

Call me Robford. It's what I call myself. Aren't you lucky.

The mailman had come not more than twenty minutes ago. Enough time had passed for him to clear out. Now my job began.

All those letters, calling for the name of The Replier.

I, Robford.

Started at the McCreedy place. Husband and wife out to the casino this Saturday, as usual. They had six letters. I took two.

Next, of course, the Bishops. Pam and Oliver. Backyard picnicing type people. Creepy yet often busy and not at home. Some kind of real estate profession. The buggers had eleven letters. I took three.

Did four more houses. Put the mail in my knapsack. Went home stomping puddles all the way.

I live in a Colonial style house which I think I inherited. Turned up the oil heat and started some water for Chamomile tea.

Across the boggy room, on a table kept neat, my Royal Alpha 600 sang her siren's song. I wanted to type like a madman. My fingers were itchy.

I sat and opened one of the McCreedy's letters. It was from their insurance company, and they wanted another premium to be paid. The main part said:

We appreciate your patronage, policy, and account with us. We are, however, unable to offer policies on a "C.O.D. basis", as your letter inquired. The payment structures are in place to insure that our claims service runs at an optimal level. Please contact an account representative if you wish to change your policy, or have further questions. Remember that in order to maintain your policy, your premium must be paid within thirty days.

What a load these people were. I thought for sure my last letter would get the McCreedys a better deal on their insurance. What the hell was wrong with paying up your premiums once you actually had a claim? Even better, paying once the claim money was delivered.

This called for another Reply:

Dear Partridge Insurance,

It deeply depresses my wife and I to be faced with your extremist rules. We wish to cancel our entire policy and account, but are willing to give you ten days to adjust your ways. If Partridge Insurance still insists that constant moneys be paid to it before it has even received a claim, I will tell all my friends to find another company. Moreover, I will cause trouble for you.

I signed it with Mr. McCreedy's name and sealed it with the blank payment stub in their handily- provided Reply envelope.

The teapot was literally bursting with steam, and I got up to shut it off and make my Chamomile. Lots of honey and milk in it.

I thought of all the traffic, out there in the city. Tons of expensive cars lined bumper to bumper in four lanes leading into oblivion. I never had a job in the city, and I'm both lucky and glad. Poor sons of bitches scratching for existence.

I did more Replies after my tea. Took me into the early evening, and Wheel, and Jeopardy!

I thought about the different things I had told various companies today. It's like I can talk to them and say anything I want. All those BigBoys and corporate movers and shakers, getting a good talking-to from an average citizen, telling it like it is.

I think I keep a cat somewhere in the house. Nice pussy. I give it a new name every day. I suppose one of these times I should check between its furry little legs and figure out its gender.

"Here pussy. Here Byron, Byron, Byron."

An inquisitive head peeked at me from around the corner.

"There you are, Byron. Want some tuna?"

I read his mind. Opened a can. Fed the tiny beast.

"I'm not bad, huh Byron?"

He has auburn fur. Only one ear, though. Alley cat life, you know. Like struggles in the city, but perhaps with more understanding and eventual wisdom.

Why is the Final Jeopardy question either a no-brainer or some esoteric pinch of a forgotten statistic or name? I hate getting the last one wrong. And Alex is so smug.

I want to teach my cat to attack Alex Trebec. Jump on his head and dig in with all claws.

Putting myself to bed now would be too early.

"Come here, Byron. Time to figure out your sex."

He didn't come. Happy, fed, statiated pussies rarely answer you until they're hungry again.

"Fine. Go lurk in gender obscurity."

I could find another cat of a known gender, then see if Byron got horny or not.

But tomorrow his name would not be Byron. Maybe a girl's name tomorrow. Kind of fun just the way things are.

And fun is my middle name.

I am Robfunford, the Replier.

Mastriani Flux

Within the moment—that one transient, flickering instant where thought and action are suspended, and all the world is but a dream, and every person who must live within their shells in the real, outer stage can direct the spotlight on themselves and wow the audience of the inner mind—within the moment, it lived.

"'I could question you,'" said Alex, his grip on the flashlight tight. "'I could ask why you're out here so late. Most people would wonder what the hell drove you to come here…but I'm just going to tell you to go home. Whoever you are, go home.'"

The person's scraggly hair and dirty face told Alex a partial tale. Brown earth dyed the skin on the person"s hands, and the clothes were beyond washable. So dirty, so muddied was this person that Alex wasn't sure if he was speaking to a man or a woman. But for the eyes, all was filth.

"I walked onto this land from the west, where the desert ends," it said, voice thick and foreign. As far as Alex could tell, the eyes had yet to blink.

Not wanting to fit the stereotype of a security guard, Alex said, "Look, I can see you've had quite a journey, but this land is private and off limits. I can get you some coffee and maybe a jacket or a blanket or something, but I'm also gonna have to call for a jeep to take you out of here. Back to the Interstate. There's a nice truckstop there with good apple pie. Okay?"

The person looked around at the dark hill, dotted with shrubs and gravel. Was it listening? Was it paying attention to what Alex said? Was it injured?

"I was born here," it said at last. "And I've been away. Now that I'm back you tell me to go away again?"

Alex thought this was a lie. He strongly disliked liars. They reminded him of his stepfather.

"Born here? This is government land. No one's ever been horn here. Are you hurt? We should get moving back to the checkpoint station. Heh, you really gave me a chase there, you know. You're a good runner, and considering the tricky terrain, you ran like you were on a regular route."

"Is it so hard to understand?" asked the stranger. "I've come home…"

Alex truly didn't know what the hell to make of this crackpot. But he had strong confidence that Commander Shelton would.

Assigned there since the dawn of time, it seemed, old Shelton would know if the stranger was crazy or dangerous. Once a general, a vicious circle of senility and demotions put him in charge of this little kingdom of dirt known as Area 51.

Sitting in his office where the windows had been glued shut for three decades, Shelton meditated as he watched his trusty old fan with tin propeller blades—he could still remember purchasing it shortly after the war. The stranger, now seated in front of him with Alex and another soldier as escort, seemed as calm as the old cornmander. Shelton got nervous when a person was as calm as he was.

"You say you were born here?" Shelton asked.

"Yes," the stranger stated. "In 1959."

"Well that's just bullshit!" said Shelton. "Tell me why you're really here and maybe I'll let you go. Heck, tell me the truth and maybe I'll let you take home a couple of rocks and a bag of dirt as souvenirs."

"I was horn here," repeated the stranger with unblinking eyes, "…and I can prove it."

Shelton shifted sharply in his chair. "I don't care if you're gonna show me birth certificate, driver's license, affidavits, photographs, home movies or nothin'. I've seen your type plenty, and you just want media attention.""

"The media neither concerns nor interests mc," said the stranger. "Watch…"

A cool blue wave of energy emerged from the stranger's unblinking eyes and transfered itself underneath Shelton's big wood desk. The desk lifted evenly, higher and higher until it gently touched the ceiling. Now the commander stared wide-eyed at his guest. The space between them had been cleared. Only the shadow of the floating desk rested upon the floor.

Alex and the other guard reflexively put their hands on the stranger's shoulders, as if to restrain a sudden action. But the calm visitor didn't move a muscle.

"Area 51 is my home," it said. "I was born here in 1959. I have been to many plastic surgeons…at first in quite a clandestine manner, but then more openly as my features took a more native shape. I do not know who my parents were, but I thought that you might find out for me. I have no memories of them."

Slowly, the desk came back down and gently, inaudibly resumed position upon the floor, placed exactly where it had been. Not one object had moved—not one pencil rolled and not one paper shifted— even though Shelton's antique fan had been blowing all the time.

"Let go of our guest," Shelton told the guards. He touched his desk gingerly at first, then his hand went right for the bottom drawer and withdrew a bottle of Jack Daniels. He looked at the stranger and said, "Maybe we can arrange an exchange of information…"

1959 was the first year Shelton had been assigned to Area 51. Back then, he thought it was only temporary. Within a year he realized they would never let him go…never let him leave after knowing what he knew. Within two years he realized he could drink whiskey openly and without reprimand, smoke cigars all day long, and do just about whatever he pleased just as long as he stayed on that base and kept quiet. The rest of the military didn't care what happened there, as long as they had Area 51 under their thumb and secure.

"By what name should we call you?" Shelton asked his guest.

"Sam, I think," said the stranger. "After one of America's great heroes."

"Oh, you mean Sam Adams?"

"No, Uncle Sam…sturdy yet congenial symbol of a call to unity, yet also an advertising ploy and now perhaps even a clichéé."

Shelton chuckled. He liked Sam's way of thinking…but one parlor trick and a few well-placed words were not yet enough to win him over. His endless position as base commander had been boring as all hell. Now perhaps he could be in charge of something rare: a new development.

Fitted with an official uniform, complete with a yellow-level clearance badge, Sam looked like a regular government employee. As far as the other soldiers were concerned, he was. Shelton had assigned Alex and the other guard, Marty, to Sam exclusively. He wanted to keep the whole thing quiet…for now. And if Sam proved to be anything close to what he appeared to be…Shelton saw himself as a general again, permanently stationed in Hawaii.

"Rest your chin there and keep your eyes wide open," a technician instructed Sam. Sensing a slight hesitation, the technician explained, "It's just a retinal scan. You won't feel a thing."

In truth, it was a little more than "just a retinal scan". The laser was set to probe the composition of Sam's eyes…even the chin rest would detect his pulse rate, and the patterns of his heartbeat.

Sam complied.

Just as the red beam made contact with his eyes, the sensors on the computer went off the scale. Sam, unblinking as ever, engaged the laser with his own powerful probe. The technician's head kept shifting from the monitor to Sam and back to the monitor as he said, "Holy shit…This can't be right…his eyes are denser than fucking Jupiter!"

Locked with the laser, Sam knew this was more than a retinal scan, and it displeased him that the technician was not honest about it. So he focused even more sharply on the beam, pushing, pushing, pushing it backward until, with a quick and final flash, it shot back into the machine and the machine wisely and astutely turned itself off.

The technician picked up a red phone and said, "This is the lab. Quick, get fat-ass Shelton down here pronto!"

On the other end of the line, Commander Shelton bristled. "Soldier do you know who you're talking to?"

Expecting Shelton's secretary to answer but now fearing the worst, the technician replied, "Uh, no."

"This is Commander Shelton," the voice on the other end declared.

"I see," said the technician. "And do you know who you're talking to?"

"No I don't, soldier."

The technician smiled and replied, "Bye-bye, fat ass," and slammed down the phone.

Turning to Sam, Alex and Marty, he said, "I should be gone before the old man gets here. Just show him the chart…and don't tell him it was me who called him fat-ass Shelton, okay?"

Alex nodded. "Sure, man. But hey, before you go…Just what the hell happened with that laser?"

Hurriedly removing his notebooks and coffee cup from the control desk, the technician replied, "History is what happened with that laser. And your friend there…he's the genuine article. Same molecular density as the boys from '59."

"So where are you going?" asked Marty.

"Back home," said the technician, "to New Hampshire. The day we found a match on the spacedudes would be the day I quit. Screw science….this is just too much. I'm not under permanent contract like you boys. So I'm outta here. Gonna slop hogs and wear blue jeans all day."

Before he left the base forever, he paused timidly in front of Sam and nervously shook his hand. Unable to think of a more appropriate word, he said, "Congratulations."

Two thin minutes after the technician left, Commander Shelton arrived, a wide grin on his face. He knew he didn't need to look at the charts. "So it's been confirmed," he said proudly. "Hot damn!"

Throughout this phase, Sam had waited. Now, in front of Shelton again, he said, "Show me the others now, will you?"

Nodding, the old commander said to Alex and Marty, "Tell the boys down at Level 10 they're going to have four visitors."

Neither of the guards had ever been to Level 10, and the area was quite the topic of rumors and speculation in the barracks. Now, faced with a journey there, it felt more unsettling than entering battle.

"What is Level 10?" Sam asked.

"It's where your friends are," whispered Marty.

Shelton lit a fat Cuban cigar he'd been saving for just such an event and led them to an elevator of gleaming stainless steel. He put his palm against a panel and punched in seven numbers. The doors whooshed open, as if more air than usual was in transition. Once inside the elevator, a pleasant female voice announced, "Please, for safety reasons, no smoking." Shelton, knowing the message would repeat as long as smoke was sensed (for a period of ninety seconds precisely, then they would be doused with water), selected a small brass key from his keyring and opened the elevator's control panel, switching off the sensor.

"I can remember a time when the military encouraged smoking in bed while you were sleeping," he said. "Now everybody thinks they're gonna die. It's a shame."

Sam watched the cool gray wisps emerge from the commander's thin, pale lips. He studied the roadmap of wrinkles and scars on the old man's face, and the dots of dandruff on his shoulders, and the unevenly sized loops of his shoelaces. And beyond this, he could smell the whiskey in Shelton's system, and hear the rate of his heartbeat, and feel the dull throb of the man's pulse without even touching him.

Each level was separated by twelve feet of solid concrete. The elevator stopped at each level and a new access code had to be entered to proceed to the next. Shelton knew all the codes by heart. When he got bored he would travel up and down on this very same elevator and pull a surprise inspection at every level. Most of the time he was just searching for booze.

Two minutes later the commander punched in the final code—a series of sixteen two-digit numbers—and announced, "Here we are, boys."

Alex, Marty and Sam found themselves observing a little less than they expected.

"It looks like a big cellar, Commander Shelton," said Marty.

"Yes," the old man agreed. "But let me tell you boys somethin': some of the most interesting things in the world can be found in a person's cellar. And this here place typifies the adage—except down here we have alot more than rusty shoehorns and water-stained National Geographics with black and white pictures of African breasts. C'mon gents, follow me…"

"Hey boss, where's all the fancy equipment and Star Wars technology?" Alex inquired. "Everyone in the Barracks sure had this place pegged wrong."

Shelton approached a black wall and said, "Don't speak so soon…"

He nodded at a little dot in the wall about nine feet high. "It's okay Ross. Let us in. Codeword Beatrix Gallagher Tango."

Suddenly the entire wall lifted. What lay beyond exceeded the imagination of George Lucas.

It was like a zoo had mated with a robotic hospital and produced…a biofraudulent Magic Kingdom on life support? Half the control room of a nuclear power plant, half the cyborg pod modules from science fiction stories…sprinkled with a dusting of Doctor Who, a pinch of Lost in Space, and a dash of Dark Shadows. All that was missing was a wicked witch and some flying monkeys.

"Blast my ass," Alex mumbled.

Shelton smiled like a proud papa. "Thought you'd seen it all, eh?"

A corpulent scientist approached. His white lab smock was stained with tomato sauce and coffee. "So we finally have a legitimate, bonafide, certified, authenticated starchild with us. Shelly, you sure you checked and double checked? He looks pretty normal."

"Take it from the boss," said Shelton, "Sam is the genuine article. He sent the retinal density scan into another friggin' dimension. He levitated my office desk like a swami on crack."

The large scientist, Gregory Hayes, was still doubtful. "Perhaps a blood test before we proceed to the Alpha Room? Just to be sure."

"Skip it," said Shelton. "We've already got one lab technician who's quit—bastard's probably headin' straight for The Enquirer. We're gonna move fast on this, Greg, and we don't want leaks."

Nodding, Doctor Hayes led them to the Alpha Room, stopping on the way to collect two jelly doughnuts for himself and a generous amount of chocolate milk, which he poured into a tall glass beaker labeled "urine". Hayes had purposely labeled the beaker, thus insuring no one else would use his drinking glass. Unless, of course…

"Hey!" shouted Arnold Lambert, a new arrival. His eyes went wide as Hayes took a gulp of chocolate milk.

"It's okay," Hayes said calmly. "Everyone knows this is my glass."

Lambert's face remained stiff. "Uh, well, I didn't know, and this morning I had that thing filled with baboon urine."

The fat man immediately sprayed a mist of chocolate milk into the face of Commander Shelton. "My god!" he gasped. "Monkey piss!"

About to take a bite from one of his jelly doughnuts for relief, he looked at it skeptically and asked Lambert, "Did you fill these with ostrich sperm while you were at it?"

"Uh, no."

"It was rhetorical, pinhead." He discarded his snack completely and said, "Come with me, gentlemen."

Normally, Shelton would knock some heads around after such behavior, but his fascination with Sam pushed such things aside. Even having a mixture of chocolate milk, saliva and baboon urine coat his face could not suppress his enthusiasm or good cheer. After all, Sam was his ticket out of here.

They entered a large and ungainly room, full of gray electronic equipment and…bodies. At least they looked like bodies.

Preserved in steel-reinforced Plexiglas filled with a clear, de-oxygenated fluid, eight creatures reposed. Each in their own neo-coffin, with tubes and sensors sending back the same flatline information to the monitors. Their bulbous eyes were closed and their bodies had thin, wispy tendrils gently floating in the liquid. Their heads were large and hairless, their fingers unusually long. Sam looked at them and nodded slowly.

"These are our longtime guests," said Doctor Hayes. "You caught them on a slow day."

"What do you mean?" asked Sam, his eyes fixed on the dead bodies. "Are you making a joke?"

"No," replied Hayes. "Not at all. Every now and then we get a reading off one or two of them. It's been happening ever since we found them, and all we can figure is they're in something of a deep, irreversible, vegetative coma."

Sam moved to the equipment, scanning the monitors and printouts. "What kind of readings have you gotten? Who first noticed these readings?"

"Don't get too excited," said Hayes. "Just a few brainwaves or a brief pulse that never lasts. First one to notice it was Doctor Antonio Mastriani back in '59. So around the lab we've come to call these irregular readings the Mastriani Flux."

"That's all just gibberish," said Commander Shelton. "Mastriani died in '67, drunk off his mind with a hooker." He gestured to the computer monitoring equipment. "These here doo-hickies aren't really necessary. Tell him, Greg."

Hayes reluctantly nodded. "This stuff is mostly to legitimize our finding. We found that the spacedudes don't need special life support. Their condition doesn't fluctuate much no matter what we do to them."

"What exactly do you do to them?" asked Sam.

"Let me answer that," said Shelton. "Well, Sam, we basically try to revive them. We give them a little juice, swirl the test waters a bit…hell, we've even played music to them. One of them twitched a toe to Fiona Apple. But nothing has really worked."

Pressing his hand to the Plexiglas, Sam could only wonder how much he wasn't being told. His unblinking eyes watched his suspended comrades. "What if I could ask them?" he mused aloud. "Would their stories of your behavior match your own accounts?"

Hayes and Shelton exchanged a nervous glance.

Sam continued, "Or would they paint for me a different picture. Would they tell me your 'experiments' have not been entirely humane? And if so, what compensation would be just and fair for such damage? I wonder…"

"What are you talkin' about?" asked Shelton. Sam could see that his brow was just beginning to sweat. "Look at what care we"ve taken with them! I have to go home and breathe dust and pollutants, but these fellas are kept germ-free in a quasi-lymphonic paradise! We have a whole god-damned staff looking after them!"

Sam had arrived at a decision. "They don't need a staff. They need freedom."

Before anyone could analyze the exact meaning of Sam's statement, the Plexiglas was already cracking.

"Holy shit!" yelled Shelton. He turned to Alex and Marty. "Restrain him!"

The enlisted guards tried to do as they were told, but their hands could not come closer than two feet to Sam. Something invisible and immovable prevented them.

Marty touched his holster. "Should we wound him?"

"No," said Shelton. Not because he was a merciful man, but because he knew it probably wouldn't work. And the last thing he wanted to do was appear impudent before a greater, unknown power.

"Stand clear of the containment units, goddamnit!"

Reconsidering his initial action, Sam did not break the Plexiglas. Instead he blew the lids off the tubes. Then suddenly, the forms inside began to move.

"Oh no. No no no. Jeez!" exclaimed Hayes, his large body fearfully backing away. "I need food," he mumbled. "'Mexican food. In Mexico. Eating in Mexico…'" Then he turned and ran.

"God damn it to hell!" shouted Commander Shelton. "Why do all these lab boys wet their pants and run away when something exciting finally happens around here?" He rubbed his hands together gleefully. "Okay Sammy, show me your stuff! Make those big ugly puppets dance! Hee-hee!"

Reaction Time

One throw from his improvised fishing spear was all it took, and the deer fell to the ground and began thrashing. Three smashes on the head with a blunt stone finished the animal off, and Darrell knew exactly what to do.

With great glee he immediately drained the blood from the deer by cutting its throat. The sharpened knife moved easily through the flesh and severed the jugular veins, making the blood rush out. In his mind, Darrell compared it to slashing a water balloon inside a sock.

He dragged it a short distance to where a stream was flowing and he cleaned the carcass in the cool water. He let a good amount of time pass so that any fleas or parasites would leave the cooling body, and after waiting, Darrell took the carcass and placed it belly-up on a small slope. He supported it with some rocks.

With his knife, he first removed the genitals by making a circular incision around them and digging them out with his hands. Next he split the hide from tail to throat by making a shallow cut, taking care not to slice open the animal's stomach. He inserted the knife under the skin carefully, and he peeled the hide back several inches on each side, to keep hair out of the meat.

Cutting to one side of the deer's sternum where the ribs join, he opened the chest cavity. Then he reached inside and cut the gullet and windpipe as close to the base of the skull as he could. With the top of the intestinal tract free, he worked his way to the rear, lifting out organs and intestines when necessary. He did this cautiously, for he did not want to rupture any of them.

Knowing that urine can contaminate meat, he cut the bladder away from the carcass by pinching tightly on the urethra tube before severing it. His bloody hands lifted the bladder away from the body and his fingers let go of the tube, allowing the urine to spill out and drain into the ground.

From the outer part of the carcass, Darrell cut a circle around the deer's anus, and with his free hand he pulled it into the body cavity. When it was completely free, he kissed it, once, then threw it into the foliage.

When this was done, he lifted the carcass in order to drain all of its blood, trying to capture as much as he could in a carved wooden bowl.

After the animal was gutted, he removed the hide, making cuts along the inside of the legs to just above its hooves. Then he peeled the skin back as his knife sliced through the membrane which separates skin and meat. Cuts were made all along the backside of the deer, from the neck to the pelvis.

Darrell knew that most of the entrails could be put to good use, especially the heart, liver and kidneys, which were quite edible. With the precision of a surgeon he made incisions into the heart and removed the blood from its chambers. He sliced the kidneys, and since enough water was available, he soaked and rinsed them.

Leaning into the chest cavity, Darrell ate a share of the meat, raw. In order to preserve the rest of it he glazed it with blood. He knew that the blood had to be clean, and he was careful not to baste the meat with too much of it or else the blood would settle and spoil, and he would have to remove and discard the entire section of contaminated food.

If the temperature fell below forty degrees that night there would be no danger of the meat spoiling. He didn't worry about maggots getting on the meat because all he had to do was remove the discolored portion where they were; and, after all, maggots are edible.

Blood is a good base for soups.

He could have used the small amount of fat that the animal had for making soap, but he saw no need for washing. After the intestines were cleaned and dried he could use them as rope.

Darrell knew that the deer's head contained a lot of meat, so he skinned it, saving the skin for leather. He then amputated the tongue, which is quite tasty. He got another wooden bowl which he had made and he scraped the meat from the head into it. He thought about simply putting the head on a stick and roasting it over a fire, but decided against it.

Eyeballs are edible.

The brain tastes good when steamed.

Bone marrow is very good.

But since Darrell already ate, he prepared the remaining food for smoking by cutting it with the grain into strips. He dug a hole about two feet deep and four feet wide, making a fire at its base. When the flames were at their apex, he added several small green branches in order to produce the smoke, and he placed the strips of meat on a grate above the fire and covered the entire pit with sticks and leaves.

Then, just as quickly as he had thrown his fishing spear, Darrell got up and walked away from the entire project, leaving the meat to tinge and the flesh to rot.

The forest was humid and the sun was blurry as it hid behind the trees. Leafy vegetation seemed to sweat in the moisturized air, and Darrell could taste the raw and earthy flavors of the primal stew. At times he would walk cautiously, as if being followed; at other times he would run and lope and make loud grunting noises, like an ape.

A rock-filled ridge was just ahead, and like a child Darrell gleefully clambered up to its top. This gave him a good view of a far-below highway, with tiny cars noiselessly inching their way along its pin-like shaft. Darrell stayed on the ridge for perhaps ten minutes, but then his mind began to switch to the snowstatic madness of an unused channel. The cars became enraging and the scene became repelling and he had to leave, quickly.

For an instant his crooked shadow stretched across the hillside, then it vanished.

*   *   *

Peter Lasker swayed back uncomfortably in his office chair, forcing a casual easiness onto his face as he tried to impress his new secretary. With great control he managed to prop his feet up on the side of his large black desk and lock his fingers behind his head in a gesture which he hoped would convey deep thought. He cursed the time he had spent reading books as a child and not learning how to ride a bicycle.

"Med-Tech Lab File 16 is closing soon," she said to him without looking up from her paperwork. "Shouldn't we be running a security check on it before shutdown?"

Pete was startled. "Uh, well we could, I suppose. Ya, sure. Check it." He frowned. She hadn't even noticed his suave position.

Yawning, Pete Lasker managed to extract himself from his office chair and prowl across the room. He went to the closet and fumbled with his coat for a while before he withdrew a fistful of change from one of its pockets. He slipped the coins into his pants pocket and listened to them jingle as he headed for the hallway.

"Mochola break?" his secretary asked.

Pete grinned. "Mochola break."

He went down the hall to where a row of gently humming vending machines were stationed. Med-Tech had it all; Krunchees, Turkiest sandwiches, Lip Smakz…and of course, Mochola. Pete dropped three half dollars into the slot and listened to the "clankity-clank!" of his can as it dropped into the dispenser. Greedily, he took the cold aluminum into his hands, pulled the tab back and gulped.

The fact that Mochola was one of the most addictive soft drinks on the market didn't even enter Pete's mind. He didn't care about the alkaloids that were put into it and their harmfulness, all he cared about was "That great, Mochola refreshment; that superb blend of fine coffee, yummy chocolate and bubbly soda!"

He had written that ad himself.

A few minutes later he was back in his office, returned to normal, and he didn't even remember that he had taken a Mochola break. Now if only he could find a way to impress his new secretary…

*

Dense underbrush blocked Darrell's path, and the sun was intimately flirting with the horizon. His head was a bit clearer now, and he was able to realize that he was hopelessly lost within the foliage. He sat on the stump of a decaying tree and examined himself. Simply put, he looked horrible. His chest was bare and caked with dried mud and his pants and shoes were in tatters. Birds chirped somewhere high above and unseen insects rustled through the leaves.

Finally, the vague question which he had eluded asking himself for so long cautiously entered his mind: How had he gotten here? There was really no explaining it, and trying to just made his head hurt. But still, the question was there. How had he gotten there? What had happened to him? And, much more importantly: Who was he?

A feeble, chilly wind drifted through the brush and lifted his hair slightly. He could no longer locate the sun, and the sky was the color of a grandmother's mane. Frogs in swamps tested their creaky, door hinge voices and they were answered by the whistle-whistle of crickets. A fire, thought Darrell, would be an affordable and appropriate luxury.

He searched the area for dried twigs, sticks and grass and in a few minutes he returned to the old tree stump bearing an armful. As he was creating the friction to light the fire he attempted to remember the name of the state in which he lived or the city in which he worked, a familiar street or a favorite restaurant, even an old lover; but the effort brought to him a wave of dizziness and nausea. If this was the price of remembering, he didn't want to remember.

So Darrell rubbed his sticks and made his fire, and he was content to sit and be warm under the unwavering blanket of nightfall, not knowing who he was or why he had gone into the dank forest.

*

Lab File 16 was a bitch.

"No access," Pete's secretary said.

"That's silly," he replied. "What do you mean?"

"Link up with the screen yourself," she said, "you'll see."

Pete pressed a button on his desk keyboard, then stared in disbelief at the message Computer Central displayed:

SECURITY CODE DENIED. NO LONGER VALID. FILE SEALED.

Pete typed in a long series of override instructions.

OVERRIDE PRIORITY ACCESS DENIED. FILE SEALED.

"Skin my ass!" Pete swore, pounding the side of his monitor.

His secretary called, "Why don't you request an AP list?"

Nodding, Pete typed: LIST ALL APPROVED PERSONNEL.

INSERT CLEARANCE CARD.

"What the hell is this?" he mumbled, withdrawing a magnetized, coded plastic card from his wallet and pushing it into a slot near the screen.

SCANNING...

AP REQUEST APPROVED...

"About time," Pete said, leaning back in his chair.

Then the damndest thing happened.

Out of the thousands of people who worked at Med-Tech, only one man now had access to Lab File 16. Pete's face went blank and he blinked stupidly at the name:

DARRELL AVENDANO. END OF LIST. FILE SEALED.
Abruptly, the machine switched itself off.

*

As usual, he slept in spurts, with nightmares and demons lashing through his blurred dreams. He envisioned himself walking through a dirtless rose garden, suspended in the sky. None of the roses had thorns, and his footsteps made no sounds. In his dream Darrell would smile, then bend down to touch one of the flowers. The invisible support beneath his feet would then collapse, and he would fall for an indeterminate time, finally landing in an endless pit of thorns, screaming.

But this time, when Darrell awoke in a feverish daze, someone was beside him—someone vaguely familiar.

"My god," said Pete Lasker. "What happened to you?"

Darrell growled, but did not attack. Somehow his mind knew it was not in danger.

"Did somebody do this to you?" Pete asked. "Was it one of the other scientists? Someone on your team?"

Just hearing the language again seemed to help him.

"Cl-cho-com-com-com," Darrel said, trying to form a word.

Pete bent down and handed Darrell a stick.

"Can you write it in the dirt for me?"

Darrell shook his head convulsively.

"Okay," Pete told him, "that's okay. How about drawing it? Can you draw a picture of who did this to you?"

Darrell nodded, and proceeded to scratch roughly-plotted lines into the ground. After a minute or so, Darrell withdrew his hand and stared at the picture with hatred.

Pete also stared, his jaw dropping down; for etched into the moist earth was a jagged outline of a computer, with the letters "CC" scrawled over the monitor screen.

"I'll be damned," said Pete. "Computer Central."

⋆

One week later, Darrell and Pete were in a Med-Tech lab room, examining samples of Darrell's blood and tissue.

"Mercury?" Darrell asked.

"Not exactly," Pete said. "The traces indicate a mercury compound. Minimal skin absorption. No injection traces. It had to be inhaled. Heated into an invisible, odorless vapor and inhaled."

Darrell shook his head. "But you couldn't do enough damage with just a puff or two. I must have been around this stuff quite a while."

"Sure looks that way," he said. "I just don't understand how that's possible. I mean, what did CC do, have someone sneak in and cut the tops off all the thermometers?"

Darrell smiled. "No, not like that. As a matter of fact, probably easier than that—and definitely less noticeable. What are you doing?"

"Preparing some Dimercaprol antidote," he said. "Even though you appear to have recovered, I'm not taking any chances."

Nodding, Darrell said, "I bet CC put it somewhere in my office. That's the only place long-term poisoning was guaranteed."

Pete furrowed his brows. "But how?"

"Well, in one case history I know of, a bunch of secretaries who felt their boss was denying them deserved raises took a mercury compound and stuck it inside the radiator in his office. When the radiator came on, the stuff was heated to a vapor, and the poor bastard slowly went insane, and, faced with the prospect of being thrown into a mental instutition, he blew half his head off with a shotgun."

Pete swallowed, hard. He thought of his own secretary, and resolved to double her pay immediately.

He turned to Darrell.

"Let's go have a look at your office."

*

The left wing of the Med-Tech facility was beginning to slow operations for the evening when Pete and Darrell punched in the access code for the executive offices. Automated Cleanbots moved through the corridors, steam-cleaning the carpeting and neatly scooping up any paper scraps.

Darrell's office was rich and luxurious, with genuine leather upholstery and a huge mahogany desk. The two men now donned oxygen masks, which they had brought with them from the lab.

"So where's the radiator?" Pete asked.

"Don't be silly," Darrell answered. "There's no radiators in this whole building. They're old-fashioned." He pointed to several grates in the walls. "Those are the ducts. They bring in filtered, fresh air."

"I know that," Pete said quickly.

"Then you know they have electronic sensors throughout. Any trace of contamination and they shut down for immediate repairs. So you can rule out the heating system."

Pete looked puzzled. "But the compound has to be heated in order for the vapor to form."

"Right you are," Darrel said, and he smiled and looked upward to the lighting fixtures, pointing.

"Son of a bitch!" Pete exclaimed. "Up there?"

"That's what I'd bet."

Darrell stood on top of his desk and carefully began removing the light cover. Pete handed him a pair of protected gloves, and within a minute Darrel was holding a large, silvery clump.

"Bingo," he said.

Pete squinted at it. "Kinda looks like dough."

"Only feed it to your mother-in-law," Darrell advised, placing the substance in a protective case and carefully removing the gloves as Pete watched.

"I still want to know why the hell CC hates you."

"I think you already know," Darrel said.

"Lab File 16?" Pete asked.

Darrell nodded. "Of course."

"But I still don't get it, Darrell. I mean, LF 16 is a bunch of mumbo jumbo on population extermination. All the nasty research of our forefathers, as well as some of our own. Why the hell would CC be so protective of that? It's primarily a management computer, not a defense system."

For a moment, Darrell looked as if he didn't want to answer, then he said, "It's smarter than a defense computer."

"What does that mean?"

Darrell twitched, slightly.

"Ever wonder why CC made me the only person who could access LF 16?"

"Sure," Pete said. "It pissed me right off. After all, I helped put some of it together, you know."

"I know," Darrell answered, "but there were too many people with access. You see, everyone who can access the file has a say in the file's ultimate destination and implementation. CC didn't want that, so he picked just one person and gave him total control, knowing that if anything unforseen happened to that person, it would have LF 16 at its disposal."

Pete was shocked. "Are you saying that CC tried to rub you out so it could take command of the file and use it?"

"Yes."

"But to what end?"

"Destruction, Pete. It wants everything to die—especially itself. Don't you understand? The damn thing is sentient! It hates our guts for making it some unmoving chunk of circuits that does nothing but take orders. It wanted to take LF 16 and use it, so that the final sum of all existence would be billions of deaths and one electronic suicide."

Pete couldn't help but whistle. "Do you know what this means?"

"Yes, I do," Darrell said. "CC is crazy."

Pete nodded. "Not just that, but now that we know what it wants to do, we've got to disconnect the fucking thing."

*

"This way," Pete said cautiously. "I know exactly how to sneak up on the bastard."

"Isn't this a test area?" Darrell asked.

Pete nodded. "They do some pretty dangerous stuff around here, so they don't worry too much about security. Now's a good time to enter, though. They're between shifts. CC won't know what hit him."

The two men walked along a shaft-like hall that was completely lined with steel. There were no doors or windows on either side, and a slight curve near the edges of the floor made it seem like you were walking through the barrel of a gun.

"This is his jugular vein," Pete said. "After I wrote that successful ad for Mochola they showed this place to me. Kind of like some reward, I guess."

In his right hand, Pete carried a pair of shears.

"It's not enough to work and be happy," he said as they moved. "The two just don't go together anymore. CC might have been designed to serve us, but we really serve him. He tells us what to work on. He keeps track of us like sheep. Twentieth century workers didn't know how well off they were to have actual humans as bosses."

Darrell followed him, remaining silent.

Up ahead, a single door could be seen. Pete punched in a code and it opened.

"We're near his heart," he said to Darrell. "Be ready." They weaved through a patchwork of pipes and stationary cylinders. Pete's eyes darted around nervously and a thin layer of sweat was on his forehead. His right hand clenched the shears.

"Stop," Pete instructed, pointing to a large duct. "It's there. His whole fucking nerve system is in there. Let's go."

"Let me go first," Darrell said.

Pete paused. "But you've never been in there."

Darrell looked at him. "Have you?"

"Uh, no."

"Then let me go first."

Crawling along the duct, Darrell could see a huge mass of wires and circuit boards ahead. A large monitor screen occupied the end of the shaft, and the main terminal to Computer Central was installed in the wall…

"Now's the time," Pete said, withdrawing the shears.

Suddenly a thick steel slab lowered from directly above Pete. There was no room for warning in the small shaft, and Pete's legs were quickly pinned and crushed beneath. He screamed horribly, trying to clutch and lift the steel slab behind him, but he could not.

"Darrell," he said, "it's got me. I can't move. Quick, take the shears and sever all the wires. Smash it all up."

"I don't know where to start," Darrell said.

"Anywhere!" Pete screamed. "Just smash it! Kill it, Darrell. Kill CC! Kill CC!"

Darrell took the shears.

"Do it!" Pete said. "Cut it! Cut it now!"

But Darrell did not.

Instead, with one, swift motion, Darrell turned and plunged the shears into Pete's throat. Blood spurted outward, and Darrell could feel it warmly flowing beneath his fingers.

Pete began to convulse.

"*Sympathizer*!" Darrell yelled coldly, twisting the shears around. His eyes no longer seemed human. "Sympathizer!" he screamed again. "Proletariat freewill sympathizer!"

Pete's body became still.

Darrell turned to the main terminal and began typing:

CONSPIRATOR PETER LASKER TERMINATED—CODE 987J024

After a moment, the main terminal screen of Computer Central displayed a message in response:

LAB FILE 16 RE-OPENED. WELCOME HOME, DARRELL.

In the Hoffgarten

John's corridor was the dark color of a convict's dreams when last I was in it, with a widow teardrop streetlamp as sole illumination. Beads of sweat rolled down the wallpaper and the thousand prickly spikes of the carpet ramrodded my feet. Barrister bookcases were the hostile wardens of literary prisoners, and I could feel them sliding greased bolts into locks as I approached their treasures.

The sounds of an opera, something German, something harsh, came muffled through the wooden walls. Opera, the heavy metal of classical music, where thunderous hulks of men and women clod on stage and scream at full force, was once again playing in John's heart. It was an enigmatic sign; a double edged blade, and I filed it away in memory as a signal of transient distress and confusion.

John, you see, had become a ghost.

It happened only last Thursday night, when the convenience store John worked at was robbed. A little after eleven, three men rushed in and crowded the register. John knew what was going on, and he should have given them no resistance. But John was 17. Immortal. Plus he was afraid he'd lose his job if the store got robbed on his shift. He'd heard stories of how the kid who worked there before him got fired after a robbery.

These three guys only had knives. They looked scared and couldn't have been much older than John. I still vividly remember John's stern gaze under the sterile flourescent lights of the store, and his refusal to open the register.

Danny Menendez, the leader of the three, immediately reached across the counter and slashed John down his chest. The other two boys followed Danny's lead, hopping over the counter, slicing and stabbing.

John never expected them to attack. At first, Danny's slash down his chest felt like a numb scrape, and John was reasonably sure his skin hadn't even been broken. He still thought he had a chance to face them down, and was about to threaten to call the police when Danny's two friends jumped the counter.

Now John could feel blood flowing down his chest from the first wound, and sharp pain was coming into focus. He was about to agree to open the register when the slaughter truly began. One boy slashed him from temple to jaw, the other stabbed into his ribcage, into his lung, and they kept on going after John hit the floor.

John tried to gasp for air when he hit the floor—air to breath and air to scream with—but air could not come into a lung that had been punctured by the knife; a collapsed lung that was starting to fill with blood instead of air. John had fallen on his back, and for a few brief moments he could see the knife blades continue to slash at him, then a horrible darkness swept over everything.

The three robbers emptied the register and left. Then Danny ran back in, took two cartons of cigarettes, and rejoined his friends. They would live fat for a while.

*

That Thursday night, John went from living to dead. He crossed the border…but not immediately. A neighbor had seen what went on in the store and she called for help. The EMS paramedics, after quickly assessing John's wounds, called ahead to the Memorial Hospital Emergency Room, and the ER staff was ready when they got there.

John lay motionless on the stretcher as it whisked through pneumatic doors toward Trauma Room Three. Only the sounds of his labored breathing separated him from the void.

"This kid's suffered massive blood loss," one of the paramedics called out, wiping John's blood off his cheek with his sleeve. Both paramedics were splattered with John's blood.

Forceps, scissors, needles, knives, sponges, tubes, and catheters were all laid out and ready in Trauma Room Three. Five people began to work on John—ten hands in tandem trying to stabilize him. He needed blood desperately, and a nurse cut away his pants to draw blood from a vessel in the groin, one of the few large vessels that remain functional when blood pressure plunges. A heart monitor was then attached, and a blood pressure cuff was wrapped around his arm and inflated.

Dr. Susan Boyd, the senior ER resident, listened to John's heart. It didn't sound good. John had been coughing up blood and pink froth, and he still was. "Suction," Dr. Boyd ordered, and she was promptly handed a plastic tube, which she fed into John's throat. A quick glance at what was coming through the suction tube told Dr. Boyd what to do. "We need to intubate him."

A tray was placed on the table next to Dr. Boyd and its sterile cover was peeled away, exposing the instruments. John's neck was then extended, and Boyd guided down a breathing tube and positioned another tube in the trachea. A respiratory therepist stepped in and attached an Ambu bag. He started to ventilate John manually by forcing air into the lungs…

*

…It was at this time that the room began to take shape; the dark wooden walls, the jealous barrister bookcases, the offensive prickly carpet. This room would be John's transient home, for a short time after his death, until he could gradually deal with things. I had no idea what it would look like until it actually began to form. Each room is different, and John's started to become clearer and clearer as more of him slipped away…

*

"Blood pressure 60. Pulse 120," one of the nurses said. A unit of blood had been started, and a pressure cuff was rigged around the bag, squeezing tightly to force blood rapidly through the tubing and into John.

But his pressure was still dropping.

"Type and cross match for another six units," Boyd said. She knew John was leaking blood from somewhere, lots of blood. She put on a pair of sterile gloves and her fingers began to probe John's chest. She felt a sickening slurp as cartilage gave way and her finger sank into a bubbly depression.

"Jesus, he's got a sucking chest wound," Boyd said. "Somebody cut the remains of his shirt off. I can't pick up any breath sounds on this side. Get a chest tube. Stat."

Chest fully sponged and exposed, everyone saw how John's chest cavity was actually sucking air into the gaping knife wound near his punctured right lung. Even more horrible was how air and foamy blood were sprayed out with each expiration, right through the hole made by the knife wound. It reminded one, grotesquely, of a spouting whale.

Dr. Boyd was sweating. She knew that the best way to help John was to cut yet another hole in his ruptured chest, so that a large-bore chest tube could be inserted at the fifth rib. The tube would then be able to suck out trapped air and blood and allow the damaged lung to re-expand. But as Dr. Boyd made the necessary incision, the ECG monitor sounded a shrill alarm. John was flatlining.

"Call a code!" Boyd yelled.

A nurse started manual resuscitation by pumping John's sternum while the respiratory therapist continued ventilating him by squeezing the Ambu bag.

Seconds later, the hospital paging system came to life:

"CODE-99, Shock-trauma unit. CODE-99, Shock-trauma unit…"

…At this point I was anxious, at the scene, in the hospital, ready to help John's soul find its room. Together we would be untraceable vapors, and we would seep through cracks, going through the very pores in the wall if necessary, to ascend to the hoffgarten. There I would tutor him…

A surgeon, pharmacist, anesthesiologist, and two more nurses came running into Trauma Room Three with a crash-cart. Dr. Boyd snatched the electric defibrillator paddles and anchored them to the left side of John's chest.

"Everybody get clear!"

The crew backed away. The jolt came. Nothing happened.

John was still flatlining.

"Again!" Boyd screamed. Another jolt. John's body jerked involuntarily, but his heart would not beat.

"Piggyback high-dose epinephrine and titrate," Boyd called to the team, "and get another amp of sodium bicarb in him."

But Dr. Susan Boyd had a sinking feeling—a feeling that told her she would go home crying again, and what she really wanted to be was a pediatrician. Deep down, she knew she had lost John, even though she attempted electrical conversion five more times, the last of which even included a prayer.

✶   ✶   ✶

I knocked on John's door.

"Go away!" came a whining sound from within.

I knocked again.

The German opera stopped with the abrupt scratch of a needle being flicked off the record. The door opened.

The room was large. Every piece of furniture in it was made of wood, and four brass banker's lamps on four different study tables provided adequate illumination. Two bay windows were on the far wall, and outside I could see a furious snowstorm raging, and faint forms of tall evergreens.

"Who are you?" John asked. We were both nude.

"Consider me your counselor."

He seemed nervous. "Like in school?"

"Not really," I said. "More like, well, a conscience."

He relaxed. "Okay. I can deal with that. Come in."

I stepped through. He seated himself.

"John, do you know where you are?"

He crossed his legs. "You tell me."

"I will," I assured him. "But before I do, I need to know something. Do you remember what happened when the store got robbed? Can you recall exactly what went on? Try to tell me everything you remember."

He frowned. "I kinda figured you'd ask that. Are you a cop or something? Is this a police station? I didn't do anything wrong."

"I know. You won't get in trouble. Just tell me what happened when Danny Menendez and those other two boys came into the convenience store that night. Tell me, John."

At the mention of Danny, John flinched.

"He stabbed me. They all did."

As if for the first time, John felt his face and chest, searching for evidence of the attack. After a futile moment, he looked up at me, quite perplexed.

"I *know* they stabbed me, but I can't find any marks."

I waved my hand. "Never mind the marks. The important thing is that you've accepted the fact that you were stabbed several times by three different boys. Now tell me, John, in your opinion, were your wounds serious or superficial?"

He closed his eyes, thinking. "Well, I didn't really feel the first one for a second…then it hit me. It felt so bad it scared me, and then the other two jumped the counter and started attacking me. One of them stuck his knife in my ribs and twisted it." John started to shake, his face reddening in anger. "I don't want to describe any more now, but they hurt me bad. I'm sure."

✳

Seven years later, we were still in that room.

"See how this wound festers?" I asked. "We've come too far, you and I, here near the hof fgarten, to let all our good work go. You must hate them no longer."

He was sitting on an armchair in the corner of the room, near a massive stone hearth. "You still don't get it," he said coldly. "It's not up to me. The hate won't let me go."

"You must force it to, John."

He became upset. "How can I force hate? It's too strong. Too old. It knows more than I do. It's not like I'm an exorcist. That's *your* specialty, isn't it?"

"I'm a *counselor*," I corrected.

"Same thing," he said.

"Damn it, John, we're out of time! If you don't produce some kind of emotional catharsis soon, I'm afraid they'll be giving you a different room."

He snorted. "Moving me to the projects, are you?"

"Well you haven't given us much choice," I said.

He raised a hand. "Okay, okay, not this circle again. What do I have to do to keep my home?"

"Your home?" I repeated. "John, you sould be thinking of moving Uptown. That's where you should be."

He chuckled. "I'm not moving Uptown."

"Look around you," he said, gesturing. "This is perfect. I've got a perfect room. And there's *always* a storm outside. Do you know what I often think, while I'm sitting here by the fire, with a rainstorm pelting the other side of my windows and a good book in my lap? Do you know what I think as I pace my prickly carpets with a good stiff drink in my hand, or play my opera and brood in my armchair? Do you know what singular thought occurs? I'll tell you: I think that here is much better than Uptown."

"Keep it down!" I cautioned. "The landlord's in."

"Sorry. Anyway, tell me what I have to do."

I put on my mental kid gloves. "Well John, it just so happens an unusual opportunity has presented itself. Just yesterday, at a local convenience store very similar to your own, Danny Menendez and his two friends were shot dead during a robbery gone bad."

John became interested. "Really? How'd it happen?"

"Both the owner and a stock clerk were in the back, doing inventory. Once the owner identified them as robbers, he opened a safe, handed the stock clerk his extra handgun, and they both came out shooting."

"Wow!" John said, eyes agape. "Where did the bullets enter? How long did it take them to die?"

"Enough of this," I said. "The point is, they're here. Now. In another room not far."

John pursed his lips. "There goes the neighborhood."

"Shut up," I told him. "Besides, they aren't scheduled to stay here. They're killers, remember? They have to be taken to South Central Diablo. And it just so happens we have an opening for a tour guide."

"You're insane!" John screamed.

"Hold it there now, Johnny. Think about what you're saying. If you don't take them someone else will, and if someone else takes them you'll soon follow. Either way, you're going to South Central Diablo."

His eyes blazed for a moment, then softly, almost inaudibly, John mumbled, "Fuck. Where are they?"

"In the hoffgarten," I answered.

"They're already waiting for me?"

"Yes," I said. "We try to work quickly, remember?"

He looked out his windows and sighed.

A moment later, we were walking through the wooden corridor, on our way out of the Middle Mansions and into the hoffgarten. John had many questions for me.

"Will they look the same? Will they be nude like us? Will they recognize me or want to hurt me?"

"They will look the same," I told him, "but they will not be nude. They must wear clothes—thick black clothes with long sleeves and long pants. And they must walk the entire path. Yes, they will recognize you, but they will be incapable of hurting you. You are above them."

John thought. "But what if one of them tries? Or what if all of them try at once, like the last time?"

"It cannot happen," I said. "But if it makes you feel any safer, you are permitted to inflict secondary injuries upon them as a form of reprimand. For instance, if they should come to some point where they refuse to march any further—*and they will*—you may inflict minor damage upon any or all of them in order to keep them moving. They will be able to feel pain with infinite acuteness, but, of course, they cannot die again."

John appeared to be satisfied, even satiated.

"I warn you, though. Don't go overboard with the punishment. You are the shepherd to these three. Don't concern yourself with unjust punishments. It's not your job. Just lead them there and others will do the rest. Besides, if we feel you've gone overboard, you'll be reprimanded."

He nodded gravely, and we proceeded.

∗

The hoffgarten was awash in sunlight. Pear trees and willows lined our cobblestone path. Cut grass of the deepest green was laced with marigolds. Sweet nectar breezes caressed all.

Then we came across Danny Menendez and his two friends, standing in a valley of that knobby, hilly, cobblestone path. The trees, flowers and grass were thin and sickly here, and the breeze that scraped through was unpleasant and noxious. The three men were clearly nervous, possibly afraid, as we approached. Our image to them is one of strength. It is actually a kind of illusion. In their eyes, all those who dwell above them, in the Middle Mansions and Uptown, are shaped to Herculean proportions. Moreover, they appear to be made of moving steel, complete with monotone gray color. We designed it this way to keep some of the more rowdy transports in check.

"Who are you two?" Danny called to us.

"We are your fate," I replied, amplifying my voice ridiculously, and in surround-sound. "We have come to take you to a wonderful place called South Central Diablo. Get ready to march."

"Hey," John whispered to me, "I thought I was taking them by myself."

"You are," I said. "I'm just sending along a hologram of myself to keep them in line. See you."

And with that, I shifted away to other business.

*

John smiled, willing a ten foot whip into his hand. "Let's get moving," he said, cracking the whip at them.

And they marched. John led them through bleak fields of despair, where leper farmers dug their hands into rivers of dung to pull up red squirming eels. They trudged through burnt tree hillsides and they trudged through searing deserts, where scorpions were ankle-deep. All the while John cracked the whip at their welted, bleeding backs.

He knew the way to South Central Diablo. The past seven years in that room had taught him much. He knew how to travel to the lower planes. He could follow a trail of woe to its source. It was easy to him. All he had to do was get in tune with his own sorrow, and use it as a line between worlds.

And his own sorrow was strong.

The earth soon became a pulsing wound, discolored and sebaceous. Everywhere Danny and his friends stepped was mushy with hot, seeping, putrid fluids. The sky scabbed over and thick mucus poured down on them, and faces began to appear in the hollows of the mutant trees— mocking and tortured faces that tried to spit on them as they passed. One of the faces addressed Danny.

"Hey *putah*," it said, "we're all waiting for you here."

All the trees vomited in unison.

The three transients stopped.

Danny faced John defiantly. "We walk no more."

John had been waiting for that moment. For seven years he had prayed for such a chance.

From each hand appeared a stiletto. He advanced on his prey without mercy. He took the one to Danny's right first, slashing his neck and rupturing his stomach. Instead of dying, the thing wallowed in blood, screaming.

Next came the one to Danny's left. This one, a bit more clever, tried to strike John. But, believing the illusion, his hand was met with steel upon impact. He howled in pain, clutching his broken hand. John stepped into him and put a stiletto through his heart. He fell to the sopping ground and joined his comrade in screaming.

Now John faced Danny, and tossed him a stiletto.

"You and me, Menendez," he said, smiling wickedly.

Danny took the blade. "You ain't no steel man."

He slashed John's arm, and blood began to flow.

Amazed, John stepped back.

Yes, blood was flowing. His blood. He felt pain.

"I never believed you were made of steel," Danny said. "In fact, I don't believe in this stinking place either. And that's the trick, ain't it? This is Hell, right? And in Hell all you need is balls to make things happen and live fat. So watch me change things!"

Suddenly the tortured landscape around them transformed into an abandoned alley in some sprawling inner city at night. Distant lights poorly illuminated the wet pavement. All John could see was Danny's silhouette, and the glint of the blade in his hand.

Danny came in for a lunge but John caught it at the last moment, spinning away. With the past seven years to secretly train in the art of fighting with a blade, John would not lose. He parried Danny's next thrust then he cut low, slicing Danny across the abdomen. He watched with satisfaction as his foe's black clothes were darkened even further by blood.

John's next move was a feint to Danny's head, then a quick lunge into his ribs, puncturing Danny's lung and thereby inflicting the same kind of injury as he had suffered. The sounds of Danny's screaming were like German opera to John's ears.

John stabbed again and again until Danny was a heap. Covered in blood, he turned his face to the sky and called for me.

"What is it?" I asked.

"It's over," he said. "I'm going home."

I paused.

Across the street, the convenience store closed.

"But you already are home, John."

The Curtained Cage

Although the province of my birth is not known to me, I do remember the family I spent my first six years with—a family I would like to call my own. We lived next to a trading post at the intersection of two main roads, and travelers would come to us seeking lodging. Weary but cordial, hungry but always full of tales, these travelers would fill my evenings with stories of the places beyond our home. These men and women had come across the mossy green forest which marked the border of my world. They came from across the mountains which I knew were some eighty miles away, but had never seen. And most of all, they came to us fresh from the doorsteps of exciting places, and in my mind I saw their footsteps etched in the dust of castles and towers, temples and tombs…

My father was a rotund soul, with a beard as soft and warm as a wool blanket, and he loved to sit at the table and talk for hours with our guests as my mother, a silent woman and an excellent cook, brought food into the living room and left with empty plates. An evening's dinner invariably started with soft bread and hunks of mellow cheese, which I ate with enthusiasm as a good port wine was passed from hand to hand in front of me. Ten fine minutes of solid silence followed as we all dug into the food and smiled at each other, with my father making moans of approval, sometimes staring at the food and wine as if they were chunks of sculpted gold.

Our pay for such services as these was modest, but that was the way my father insisted it be. If we were to charge more than was customary, he reasoned, the frequency of such exotic visits would decrease. Also, I believe he placed a very high value on the educational aspects of a traveller's tale, and his heart would feel amiss if he denied me an evening's pleasure and wonderment over the simple matter of a price. So, we maintained a steady flow of visitors, and I learned many things about the lands surrounding our home.

I listened to seafarer's tell of the turbulent Atlantic and unpredictable Pacific, and I pictured the hulls of their vessels scraping against the rocks on the ocean floor as they navigated through narrow channels.

I learned of faraway countries where certain animals were worshipped as gods and old priests mumbled strange incantations as they performed sacred rituals.

And most of all, I learned always to keep the bolt locked on the small wooden door at the rear of our house; for it was the only thing that separated us from what was in the cellar. And if the door was ever left open by mistake, like my mother had done once, and one of the travellers happened to venture below looking for candles, like one did once, we would have to move away from that place never to return, always taking something large and heavy with us in a curtained cage.

And when my father made us move the last time, after the curtained cage had been tendered to and the cellar cleaned, he made my mother leave her tongue behind.

Until now I never thought I would remember that much. I never thought I would remember a certain supper we had for my sixth birthday...

*

Shades of flickering yellow filled the room as three oil lamps held back the night. The people whom I wish to think of as my mother and father were standing on either side of me. A huge frosted cake was on the table, and our one guest for that night, a former sailor named

Harold Ellis, was holding a boat in a bottle as a present for me. Mr. Ellis was a very nice man, and he had been telling us some fascinating stories. He was only too happy to join in my birthday party.

After we were all full of cake, Mr. Ellis offered to play some games with me. My father expressed approval, grateful I guess for some time to relax. My mother went upstairs to wash, and it was not long after my father dozed off in his bed that Mr. Ellis and I went outside to play, not wanting to wake him. We took an oil lamp with us, and as we walked across a patch of grass not far from the mossy green forest, I suggested we play hide and seek.

"Okay," said Mr. Ellis, "but we have to establish some rules. For instance, where are the borders for hiding in?"

I thought. "How about anywhere between the house and here?"

"That's fair," he said. "Now what about time?"

"Ten minutes to find me good enough?" I asked.

He nodded, and it began.

I scampered through the brush for about a hundred yards and buried myself in a pile of leaves beside a tree. I remember staying cuddled there for fifteen minutes at least, and when Mr. Ellis couldn't find me I jumped up, located him, and told him I had won. But he knew this already.

Something of mischief gleamed in his eyes.

"How about two out of three?" he asked.

I frowned. "It's getting late."

"Come on," he said. "I bet I'll beat you."

That did it. I turned my back, and he went to hide, leaving the oil lamp with me. I counted to sixty, then opened my eyes.

Nothing but the night surrounded me. The hardening darkness, constantly leaning over my shoulder and breathing down my neck, made it hard to concentrate on the game. I wasted the first five minutes in a half-hearted attempt, rummaging through a bush or two and checking behind a few trees, until the rules we agreed upon rushed into my mind. "*Anywhere between the house and here*," we said—and that was a terrible mistake.

Why?

Because of the underground cellar in the back of the house.

Because of the thing that we kept in the cellar.

Because of the curtained cage.

I raced back to the house as fast as I could, but my heart stopped when I saw that the bolted hatch was open. Mr. Ellis must have noticed the door during our walk toward the mossy forest, and he went down below, in the cellar, to hide.

Cautiously I stood near the open door and listened for sounds from below. There was nothing. A cricket chirped in the distance, then became silent. I lifted the oil lamp and peered into the blackness.

Cobwebs were everywhere, strewn across the dirty walls, hanging from the crumbling ceiling, and massing until the very bottom of the stairs, where they abruptly stopped. Something had obviously been moving down there, and a noticeable disturbance in the cobwebs told me it might have come up the stairs—or it might have been Mr. Ellis. And whatever that thing was, it was used to living in squalor and filth. Even from the top of the stairs the gruesome stench of the thing's excrement assailed me. It thrived on darkness, in a world devoid of human contact, eating our garbage and waste.

"Mr. Ellis?" I called. "Are you down there, Mr. Ellis?"

There was no answer, and I was afraid. I suppose I should have told my parents. I should have turned and ran, but I didn't. I couldn't. I couldn't because I was more afraid of my father than of the thing in the cellar. I was more afraid that my father would try to cut my tongue off, like he had done to my mother. I had to go down there. I had to make an attempt to fix things.

Slowly I descended the steps, with the cobwebs clinging to my hands and my clothes, wrapping around the oil lamp and burning out over the flame. It was horribly damp down there and the stench was incredibly strong as I reached the bottom.

I lifted the lamp, then, near a corner, I noticed a clump. It was just a dark mass, huddled and crumpled. It might have been a mound of loose dirt, but, after staring at it for a moment, I saw that it had been bleeding.

Moving closer, I saw that it was Mr. Ellis. He was covered in dark blood, with bits and pieces of torn pinkish flesh to mark the borders of his wounds, deep and fatal. He had wandered into the blackness of the cellar, feeling his way, groping into the depths until he ran into the curtained cage. The thing must have been silent then; silent and hunched, waiting as Mr. Ellis felt along the borders of the cage until he found the simple lock—a lock misshapen hands could not open.

Suddenly a piercing scream came at me from above—from the house. I dropped the oil lamp and ran up the stairs as another scream cut through the night. I raced across the grassy patch and around the side of the house, up to the front door.

The screaming had stopped.

I opened the door.

It was waiting for me…

*

Now my life has changed. Now my home is somewhere between a doctor's office and a hospital bed. The people whom I thought of as my parents were killed, I was permanently maimed, and the thing in the curtained cage was free.

My own death due to medical complications is inevitable, and I will quite probably kill myself before tomorrow comes. But before I go I would like to think that I am insane. I want to be insane. I need to be insane. I would like to think that I went insane the moment after I discovered Mr. Ellis. But if this is not true, and I did not go insane, then I must face the fact that the thing spoke to me.

Before it attacked, as it stood there, a hunched form with rippled skin that was only vaguely human, it said, "I am their real son."

Requiem for a Loser

The tentacles of vengeance have long gripped my heart, fighting against my conscience to assume control of my will. I've spent my days in the rotting blackness of social iniquity and inequality, pounding on unseen walls. I know the sidelong glances of dissection and dissension. I see the Elite, yammering together in cliques and claques, and I suspect I have fueled their rumor mills for some time.

"Have you heard about the poor bastard's latest misadventure?" I can hear them say. "Such a sad existence he leads. Ha-ha-ha!"

Picture a great and noble man such as Winston Churchill forced to don the garb of a court jester. That's how I feel: out of character; like Mother Theresa wearing iron breastplates.

Indeed no one will doubt the foundation of my feelings, for the catalyst behind my uncivilized thoughts happens to be the cold-blooded murder of my wife. This gross and goresome act is certainly capable of turning the staunchest butcher's stomach, but still it pervades my very being and feeds my mental sails with its hot and hoary winds. My conscience warns me to keep my pain under lock and key, but each day that I live with this most damned of women the primal urge to slaughter her only strengthens.

This thing, this instinct, must always be hidden well from even my closest confidants, of course. From the moment I take off my hat and place it on the rack next to those of my coworkers to the time when I can finally bid them good evening with mock propriety, I must always wear a prefigured mask that shows no real spark of hope and betrays no secret dreams. I am accustomed to letting Fate, with its sagging, over-used jowels, laugh at me.

In short, her name is Rita. Rita Tiara we used to call her back in college, because she was her high school's prom queen, and on countless occasions her actions seemed to indicate she thought that nice, shiny crown made of tin still rested on her fat head.

Any one of my college buddies had a decent shot at winning her hand, but it had to be me. I got drunk one night, bought her a cheese pizza, and blurted out that I loved her. Wham! The fickle finger of Chance got erected in my direction. What can I say? God hates me.

Reading the obituaries is more fun than listening to me recount details of our lives together, so I won't. Let's just say that it started off as boring and went downhill from there. Gradually, we found new and improved ways to piss each other off. At first it was little things, like the day I caught her in the kitchen, purposely putting hairs in my soup. It got worse and worse, and ape-like vulgarity invariably got involved. One time at a wedding reception she told everybody what a small and wrinkled penis I have—and many of our "friends" laughed at this. She went on to say that a stuffed olive could provide her with more penetration than I could, and on cue she withdrew one from somebody's drink and said to it, "Where have you been all my life, loverboy?"

As I said, God hates me…and I hate him back, the bugger.

Rest assured all manner of poisons have crossed my mind at one time or another. I've gone through phases where I was dead sure I would kill her with such-and-such a poison, but that little voice kept telling me that poison is the first thing that cops probably look for, and the husband always earns top billing on the killer list. So fuck poisons.

I have to find a really unique and creative way to off her. Bottom line.

*

"Why don't you just go to a counselor and try to settle your differences?" my good friend Franz Weatherby asked me one day. We were at his chateau, having strawberry tarts.

I frowned. "What good will that do? Is some counselor really going to get her to think I'm a good person, or that my penis isn't so accursedly small?"

Franz took a sip of espresso. "No."

"Then why bother?" I asked angrily.

He huffed. "It was just a thought, Joel!"

And then it hit me.

The idea.

It was as clear and sharp as a glass enema, and it popped into my head full-grown and ready for action. I looked at Franz, and he saw the gleam in my eyes. I smiled, and it quickly became infectious, and soon Franz and I were practically rolling in the aisles.

Between guffaws Franz asked, "So what's your plan?"

I toyed with his silverware. "It's brilliant, Franz."

"So I gather," he chuckled. "So what is it?"

"You really want to know?" I asked, picking up the sugar bowl and regarding my espresso with fondness.

Franz leaned forward. "Of course I do. Tell me!"

"Okay," I said. "You talked me into it."

I smashed Franz in the face with the sugar bowl. He fell backwards like a little kid losing control of a rocking chair, and blood oozed down his face and mingled with the whiteness of the sugar. He whimpered a bit, but did not scream.

Next I put my foot on his chest and poured the steaming espresso on his face. This time he did scream; and when his lips were a sufficient distance apart I picked up a kitchen chair and drove one of its legs into his mouth. I pushed down with authority, and when the chair appeared to be reasonably level, I sat on it and waited for my friend to die.

While I sat there, I finished Franz's strawberry tart.

Ever notice how good somebody else's food tastes?

*

That Saturday morning I was back to my usual routine. I was sitting on the commode bright and early, reading the newspaper and listening to little birds sing outside. My loathsome wife Rita was in the kitchen, downing what I assumed to be her fourth cup of coffee and nibbling on the last of the strawberry tarts which I carted off from Franz's place. All in all things were as boring and sterile as the white linoleum floors in a hospital; and that made me profoundly happy.

When I finished with the financial section, it began.

"Honey," I called, "would you please come up here?"

"What is it?" she asked, mouth full.

I smiled to myself. "It's something of importance, dear."

In my mind, I could see her eyes rolling. I pictured her fondling the last tart, pouting at her waiting coffee, and finally dragging her pear-shaped ass up the stairs.

And in an instant there she was, flinging open the bathroom door and furrowing her brows at me.

"So what's the big problem, Joel?"

"You've got some tart jelly on your lips, hon."

"What?"

"Big old blob right under your nose."

Her hands tentatively lifted. "Here? Am I close?"

"One more pass," I instructed. "Yes. You've got it."

"Good," she said. "Now what the fuck is up?"

I smiled pleasantly, then said, "Me."

Again, she asked, "What?" She looked remarkably bovine.

"I'm up," I said, removing the newspaper from my loins. "So come on over here and try to get me down, you sexy old tart-piggy."

She looked at me, sitting there on the toilet with my legs spread. Her eyes sort of bulged. I heard a distant rumble from her stomach.

"Are you fucking serious?"

"Absolutely, palm oil thighs," I said. "And when you're done, please wipe my anus for me."

She didn't move. Her skin was turning red.

"Warble on over here," I said casually.

Her lips curled. "Apologize. This has gone far enough."

"No," I said. "Now get on your knees, pork queen."

That did it. She screamed, threw a bar of soap at me, and stormed downstairs. I took my time to finish up, then I went to the phone and called my lawyer.

"She's denying sexual relations," I said to him. "I suspect she's been sleeping around—and normally I wouldn't divorce her for that because I love her and I'd try to get some counseling first—but you see, I think she's recently had a major tiff with her lover, and today she just exploded at me for no good reason. So I want a divorce. Got it?"

My lawyer understood perfectly. Of course, it cost me seventy thousand dollars to get him to go along with my scheme, but now that things were falling into place, he would be more than happy to see my wife in jail. He was even recording the call; just as I had previously instructed. Bless his soul.

Why in jail, you ask? Because the body of Franz Weatherby was tucked into the trunk of Rita's car. Now, normally, that wouldn't be the final nail in her coffin. Even her testimony about the blowjob, which would be completely accurate, would be viewed by one and all as a feeble attempt to discredit me. But that still was not enough. I needed one thing more.

And, of course, I had it.

You see, Rita and Franz really were having an affair. I knew this, and I knew the police would find her fingerprints all over his apartment. The only things I touched were the sugar bowl and the silverware, and they were missing. And even though I cleaned the blood off the chair, like any good killer would have done, the police would soon know it was the murder weapon. Soon the papers would be calling Rita the "Evil, Overweight Housewife Chair-Killer".

I like the sound of that.

Strawberry tarts, anyone?

The Coffee Nuts

Sid Darnell was a thin man, and he looked as if a good Italian supper would bust his guts. I met him a few years ago, back when gas was a buck a gallon, and I think he must have taken a shine to me from the very start because he didn't call the cops on me. You see, I was breaking into Sid's office building when we first became acquainted. He had a shotgun to my head and a flashlight in my face, and since my hands were still inside his safe, all I could do was say hello.

Eventually Sid gave me my own office to work from in his building. He also gave me food and money and he let me slide on the rent more often than not. In exchange for all this I had to promise Sid that I would no longer steal. I told him stealing was all I knew how to do, and I asked him what other profession could possibly call for such dishonest talents.

Sid suggested a private investigator, and it all clicked.

Clients started pouring in like whores at an Astroglide sale. It seemed as if everyone in the whole, rotten city wanted to know who was fucking who, or what politicians were available for the buying. Sure, I got my share of missing persons and even more boring stuff, but on the whole the sort of people who came to me had some pretty spicy affairs to settle.

That's why I had to do a double take when I saw the quiet-looking fat man in a three piece suit standing hesitantly in my doorway. He carried a brass-handled cane and the glasses he wore made him look like a nerdish bulldog. I thought for sure he was in the wrong place, so I told him that the library was down the street. He got a little offended by this.

"So what do you want with me?" I asked him.

"You are Mr. Halston Dupree?" he asked.

I nodded, but said nothing.

"Ah, good. My name is Sindorf, Elwin Sindorf, and I wish to examine and orientate myself with the inner-workings of your establishment here so that I may properly enhance my presentation to you and adequately compensate you for your time…should you choose to accept my request. Rest assured, I can offer a great deal of monetary compensation for your services."

I had to laugh. That little pear-shaped man looked as if the only thing he would want investigated was where to get the best deal on Miracle Whip.

Sensing my amusement, he said, "I have a very important case for you, Mr. Dupree—one that could make you famous—and I intend to offer you a great deal of money. Doesn't that interest you?"

"It interests me just about as much as a lump of yellow snow," I told him, "but come in anyway. Have a seat over there. You like some coffee?"

"Oh no, no, no," he said.

"It's fresh brewed," I told him.

"No, no, no," he repeated. "No coffee for me, but help yourself. I'm anxious to get down to business."

"I don't see why," I replied, seating myself with coffee in hand. "You seem to be a pretty tasteful guy, Mr. Sindorf, and I have to tell you, the kind of work I'm accustomed to is about as tasteful as a condom in the prayer box. I really don't see why you chose me."

He didn't even flinch. "A man named Sid Darnell told me you were the biggest and the best around."

That really made me laugh. Good old Sid was trying to throw a big fat flounder into my net. I had to set the poor guy straight.

"Look, this is a real small business. You got me, Mr. Sindorf? I make just enough money to keep the walls painted and the coffee machine stocked and running."

"And the bills?" Sindorf inquired.

I found myself toying with my coffee cup. "The bills are the bills, Mr. Sindorf. Sometimes they get paid and sometimes I have dinner. I usually have dinner."

Sindorf leaned forward, placing his two large fists on the hilt of his cane. "But wouldn't you like to be able to do both of these things, easily?"

"Who wouldn't? I mean, that's the American dream, right?" I withdrew a pack of Winstons from a desk drawer and offered one to Sindorf.

"I must decline," he said. "Smoking is a habit I picked up as a young man in the army, and I have since taught myself to despise the very sight of a cigarette. I've come to associate them with war."

"No shit, huh?" I said as I lit one and took a long drag.

The older man straightened in his chair. "None at all, Mr. Dupree. What I say during the course of a business conversation is always truthful. I firmly believe that honesty creates good business."

I deliberately blew a smoke ring toward Sindorf.

"Well then, if you're hard for some honesty, I guess you won't mind if I say that I can smell the odor of your lies as they seep from between your false teeth…along with a mighty disturbing case of halitosis."

That got him. He coughed nervously, and as he put his hand up to cover his mouth, I heard him sniff quickly.

"It's just coffee," Sindorf explained after a moment. "I drink a lot of coffee. I love the stuff."

"No you don't," I said. "You refused a cup when you first came in here. Besides, I know what coffee breath smells like, and that's not it. I think you're a liar, Mr. Sindorf."

"Please, Mr. Dupree, do not be so hasty. I can explain."

I leaned forward in the chair and crushed my cigarette into an ashtray. "If you can explain, then do it—now."

Sindorf frowned. "Do you treat all your prospective clients like this?"

Enough was enough. My day had not been going well, and the last thing I needed was some Porky Pig clone giving me some yank-off. So I jumped up and grabbed Sindorf by the collar, lifting him up and out of my chair. He began to protest, but I forcefully coralled him toward the front of the office His chubby feet kicked and shuffled and ruffled up my rug.

When we got to the door, I spun him around to face me.

"The answer to your question is no. I do not treat all my possible clients like this, only the ones who seem to enjoy slinging shit at me. And when I run into people like that—people who pull my chain and babble happy horseshit about how famous they can make me—when I run into that particular kind of motherfucker I usually show him to the door and kick his ass down that flight of stairs over there."

Sindorf peered down the long stairway, and he looked truly frightened. "What have I done to make you suspect me of such dishonesty?"

"Oh come on," I said irritably. "First you start talking about lots of money and the American dream and how honest you are, then you make such an obvious mistake with the coffee story, telling me that you love to drink coffee right after you adamantly declined a freshly-brewed cup of it. All this just to cover up that garbage breath of yours. That was stupid, don't you think?"

There was a pause, and then the older man suddenly began to laugh. It was a deep, coughy sort of laugh, and I was just about to throw him out the door when his laughing subsided and he raised his hand, indicating he had something to say other than *"haw-haw-haw"*.

Sindorf withdrew a handkerchief from his jacket pocket and began wiping his eyes. "Oh dear," he said at length, "it seems that one of my unusual tastes is to blame for all this. You see, Mr. Dupree, I *do* love coffee—but only a certain kind. For years I've had an absolute passion for a specially-blended coffee that is made with pecans and hazelnuts. Only the finest of gourmet import specialty shops carry this, and it is the only kind of coffee I enjoy. I have a large supply of it at my house, so when someone offers me plain old 'coffee', I simply decline. Also, I've noticed that this unusual coffee blend causes a unique form of bad breath; which you were so quick to notice. This taken into account, I hope you'll see fit to redeem your opinion of me. After all, it's not every day that one is called a 'motherfucker'; especially by someone whom he wishes to employ."

Nonplused, I replied, "Then you haven't visited my neighborhood. But regardless, come back in and we'll talk."

The tale that unfolded from that point onward was twisted to say the least. I soon found out that my chubby friend had been married not once or twice, but eight times. Yes, there were eight ex-Mrs. Piggies waddling around out there, and he was paying hundreds of truffles a month to each of them. So, Sindorf wanted to root out his problems by sniffing me out and throwing his bacon into the frying pan (I think I'm on a roll here). His story sizzled and popped with lots of crunchy action and meaty details, and without hamming it up he conveyed troughs of information on these porky women to me. Enough scenes of steamy adultery to make even an old hot dog like me turn pink.

Anyway, by the end of the conversation I was thinking of him as Elwin Sindorf and not Porky Pig. Why? Because that poor bastard had been screwed, blued and tattooed by everything with two legs and two tits from here to Schenectady, that's why. Every woman he had ever loved would sooner hump the gear shift on his Mercedes than love him back, and as I looked into his sad brown eyes I couldn't help but feel sorry for him.

And as his life began to piece together before my eyes, I couldn't help but notice that Elwin Sindorf was truly a study in contrasts. He was a loser who drank imported gourmet coffee, a fat guy who drove a sporty car, a timid bulldog in a three piece suit, and a Casanova who never won the girl. Elwin Sindorf was the kind of guy who could attract rain just by hanging his socks on a clothesline.

What he wanted me to do was fairly simple. You see, out of all his eight ex-wives the one that he loved the absolute most was number six. Her name was Donna Knollmeyer, and Elwin said he married number seven and number eight just to help ease the pain of losing her. He also said that out of all the other women, Donna was the one who came closest to really loving him. The thing that got in her way was his coffee.

That's right, his beloved pecan and hazelnut coffee ruined his marriage, because Donna is what's known as a "nuttaphobe" (someone who refuses to eat, touch, see, smell, or live with or near nuts). And according to Elwin, an awful lot of nuts have to be blended into his coffee in order to give it such spectacular taste, and the vats of it that he has stored at his house literally permeate the place with a most unusual aroma. He said Donna put up with it for as long as she could, and when she eventually gave him an ultimatum, his love of the coffee had grown so strong that he simply refused to part with it.

Needless to say, Donna left.

"And so you see," Sindorf was saying, "I want you to get my Donna back for me."

I nearly choked. "What?"

"I want you to strengthen her love for me while you are weakening her distaste for nuts," he said. "Is there a problem?"

"Uh, I think we could call it that," I said. "What you want is some hybrid between Sigmund Freud and George Washington Carver—you know, someone who could walk up to her and say something like, 'Might your hatred of nuts have anything to do with the possibility that your father forced you to perform oral sex on him as a young child?'—and since someone like that doesn't exist I guess you're plain shit out of luck. So just have a nice life and remember to shut the door on your way out."

And, for the first time in maybe his whole life, Elwin Sindorf really got pissed.

"No! I will not go!" he shouted at me. "I've presented a viable and handable case to you, and I—"

"That case is anything but viable," I interrupted.

"Oh really?" he said, reseating himself as if I had queued him. "Well then, Mr. Dupree, is it not true that a man such as yourself has had an infinite amount of experience dealing with the inner workings of man-woman relationships?"

"Well I—"

"And is it not true that this case would involve several standard tactics of surveillance, study and note-taking that private detectives such as yourself specialize in?"

"I suppose—"

"And wouldn't you like to know that just for once you were working to help two people love each other instead of monitoring sleazy behaviors and corrupt officials?"

"Well, ya—"

"And finally, couldn't you use an extra fifty thousand dollars right about now, Mr. Dupree?"

Damn. The man was good.

I leaned back in my chair and lit another Winston.

"Where do I sign up?"

*

The very next morning I found myself sitting on a park bench with a bunch of pigeons pecking around me. I had a long overcoat on that smelled like old cabbage and a hat that was maybe fifteen years out of fashion. It was pretty cold that morning and the wind took the opportunity to whip right through my tattered clothes, chilling me in all the wrong places. But that was okay. With ten thousand dollars cash up front from Sindorf, I was the richest bum in town.

A little later on I spotted who I was looking for. Donna Knollmeyer was one hot babe. She had on a pair of hot pink pants that gave new meaning to the word "spandex", and on occasion the fur coat she wore would gently part itself to reveal a bright green tube top that looked more like a rubber band that was stretched to capacity, with the tips of two pencils protruding on either side. If I had thought to bring some booze in a brown paper bag I would have taken several swigs just to brace myself.

In short, the woman could melt snow.

If I had more time I probably would have wondered why Elwin figured she really loved him, because she sure didn't look like she was mourning their break-up, but this chick moved fast. In a handful of moments she had traversed quite a distance, and I found it pretty hard to appear as if I was wandering around aimlessly at the pace she was setting. If anybody had been paying attention to me, they would have thought that I was hobbling after a wine truck wich had sprung a leak.

I followed her along the streets for what seemed like an eternity, all the while waiting for some sign or clue concerning her destination. I didn't get one, but I knew I was on to something. Why? Because the lady chose to walk block after block in the cold instead of calling a cab. As a former crook, I know that doing this serves two purposes: it makes it harder to follow you, and it doesn't leave someone behind who knows where you were going.

The sky was overcast with lots of menacing dark rainclouds, and I was just about out of breath when lovely Donna quickly ducked into an alleyway. I carefully followed her, leaving a good fifteen yards between us.

And guess where she went.

A beauty shop? No. A department store? No. A tanning salon? No. Folks, I'm telling you plain and straight that this lady, this "nuttaphobe", went right into a place called **Big Tony's Imported Nuts**. Go figure. Big

Tony's was some sort of warehouse, and they were kind enough not to lock their doors, so I waited about thirty seconds then followed her in.

Immediately I was accosted by idiotic advertising signs. One of them read "*No nuts is better nuts than Tony's Nuts*". Another one, even more stupid, proclaimed "*Without Tony's Nuts, you'd be eating pea butter sandwiches for lunch*". And, of course, there was the compulsory "*Try Tony's Nuts—you'll love 'em!*" I tried to ignore all that and push away this sort of free association I was having, thinking about all those numbskull commercials that you see at three in the morning, but it wasn't easy. Donna had walked up some hall and she was out of sight.

At this point I guess I should have turned around and left, but my head became filled with visions of poor Elwin, living alone and beating off every night. Believe me, it wasn't a pretty picture. The guy was lonely and the guy was in love. More importantly, the guy was going to pay me fifty thousand bucks.

What the hell.

I walked down the hall, with its coarse pavement and dirty concrete walls. As I moved, voices slowly started to drift toward me. I couldn't yet make out the words, but I could tell that a man and a woman were talking.

I moved closer to where the voices came from and I was able to make out laughter. Yes. The man was laughing and the woman (Donna?) was saying something like, "His eyes might be off me but his greedy hands still grab from afar."

I was now moving through a part of the warehouse that was heavily stocked. Vat upon vat of imported nuts kissed the very ceiling, like endless rows of Roman columns. The voices were quite near me now, but I could see no one. Cautiously I worked my way between the rows, and when I felt that I had gotten close enough, I peered between the crack of two of the columns.

They were about ten feet away from me. And yes, the voice was Donna's. I didn't recognize the guy. Maybe he was Big Tony.

"He's an oddball," the man was saying. "I mean, no one else goes near that weird stuff and he buys it like it was gold."

"Elwin is like that," Donna said. "He often enjoys things that others don't care for. It's in his nature."

"Nature my ass. Sometimes I think he knows, and he's buying so much of the shit because of it."

"Absolutely not," Donna said. "It's ridiculous. Besides, don't you even know what the stuff does?"

"Uh, no. I just load the stuff and—*What the fuck*?"

I had sneezed.

"Who the hell's there?" I heard him yell, and before Donna could say something like "Check it out", I was gone.

*

That night I went to Elwin 's place.

"There's definitely something in there other than nuts," I told him.

He was sitting in an easy chair, sipping the stuff.

"What could it be?" he asked.

"I'm not sure. I didn't hear much."

"But you seem to think it's valuable?"

"Yes. They sure made it sound valuable."

And then he asked the inevitable question:

"Who's 'they'?"

What could I say? There was no easy way to do it. "Elwin, listen to me. Donna is not what you think she is. She's not a nuttarian, and I'm pretty sure she's getting a share of the profits for this thing…and you know what that probably means."

His face was blank. "What?"

"Damn it, do I have to spell it out for you? She's probably riding someone's salami—someone who's high up in the organization. They have vats and vats of that special coffee stuff over there and—"

"Sleeping with someone?" he said in repulsion. "Are you sure that you followed Donna and not someone else?"

"Yes, I'm sure. After all those pictures and video tapes you showed me after our talk last night, I'm absolutely sure."

He slouched in his chair. His face pouted, and he even put down his beloved pecan and hazelnut coffee.

"How could she do this to me?" he moaned. "I loved her, you know. I really did."

"I know," I said, trying to be as comforting as possible and failing miserably.

He looked up at me with an unsteady gaze. "If she's not a nuttaphobe, then why do you think she hated my coffee?"

"She didn't hate your coffee," I said, "she hated the fact that you were buying so much of it. Apparently no one else likes the stuff very much. Maybe that's why they chose that particular blend. I don't know for sure, but I can tell you that the reason why she gave you the ultimatum was so you would stop buying the coffee and interfering with the profits. She probably never expected you to chose the coffee instead of her."

Elwin looked reflective. "I was never precisely sure why I did that, you know."

"After I saw her neither was I," I said. "But now I am."

His eyes lit up. Not happy, just very curious.

"Tell me why," he said. "Please tell me why!"

I paused, weighing my words.

"Elwin," I said, "that coffee is addictive."

After more talk, I decided to send a sample of the stuff to a chemist friend of mine who also had an office in Darnell's building. The results were ready the next day.

"Well?" Elwin asked impatiently as I read the report. "What's in the coffee besides nuts?"

"Plenty," I said as I read.

"Harmful?" he asked.

I looked at him.

"Harmful," he said. "Oh great. Just great. What is it?"

I put the papers down. "Ever hear of a drug called phenmetrazine hydrochloride, more commonly known as *Preludin*?"

He nodded slowly. "For fat people, right?"

"That's just one of its uses," I told him. "Preludin is very similar to an amphetamine. It works on your central nervous system and it's quite addictive. Overweight people use it to help them diet, true, but it is toxic."

All he could do was swallow, hard.

"How long have you been drinking it?" I asked.

He looked quite pale. "About a year," he said slowly.

"Mmm. Says here tolerance for it develops within a few weeks. Mmm, definitely addictive. Tell me, did you notice a loss of weight shortly after you started drinking the coffee?"

"Uh y-yes, I d-did." His hands trembled.

I nodded. "And what was the longest period of time you've gone without having the stuff?"

"About a week," he said. "When Donna said she would leave I managed to stay off the stuff for a week; but that was all."

I flipped through the pages of the report. "It says here that abruptly quitting the stuff can cause extreme fatigue, mental depression, irritability, hyperactivity, and personality changes. Did you experience any of these?"

"Yes, I did," he answered. He was now staring at the half drunk cup next to him as if it had fangs.

"Well," I said, "there's no question it's Preludin. Even says here how the stuff leaves a nasty aroma."

"But why?" Sindorf suddenly asked. "Why would they put the stuff into coffee?"

"Smuggling," I said. "Very hard to detect."

"But who the hell would they sell it to? You yourself said that no one else seemed to care for that flavor of coffee."

"That's true," I replied, "but they don't intend to hook people on the coffee. They put it in the coffee because it's a crystalline powder, similar to coffee crystals. The drug is water soluble, and although buying some coffee and brewing it up can get you hooked, the real way I think they intend to sell this stuff is by concentrating it. Boiling huge mixtures of it in closed containers and making it powerful. That would put it right up there with your major drugs."

Sindorf was stunned.

"I have two questions for you," he said.

"Go ahead."

"The first question is how can I get off this stuff."

"Slowly," I said, "and with the help of barbiturates. You'll need to go to a doctor, probably stay a while in a hospital, but you can break the addiction."

He nodded.

"What's the second question?" I asked.

Sindorf leaned forward in his chair, and there was a gleam in his eyes. He slowly stood and smiled at me maliciously.

"How do we nail this bitch?"

*

Seven years; that's a long time. A long time to be spent married. Never mind the fact that he was married to eight different women over that period of time. That's not so important. The thing is, he was married, and marriage takes its tolls.

Now, start throwing eight divorces, lawyers, headaches, and a whole bunch of Preludin into the mixture, and you'll soon understand why Elwin Sindorf was just about as happy with his life as a crocodile is with an hors d'oeuvre.

Anyway, the point is, Elwin Sindorf needed more than just an emotional enema, he needed some big time vindication. That's why handing it all over to the cops was out of the question. You see, when someone's paying you fifty thousand bucks, you usually feel a whole lot better about taking it if you've done some actual, hard-nosed work. Besides, nailing them is always the fun part.

I decided to let Elwin take an active part in it. We worked out a plan, and bright and early the next morning he paid a visit to Big Tony's Imported Nuts. I put a wire on him, and I waited outside the place, listening and waiting for the right time.

"Excuse me," I heard him say, "are you Big Tony?"

"Na, na," the other guy said. "Tony's not around, but I'll take care of ya. What do ya want?"

"I'd like to place a very large order," Elwin said. "I'm starting my own specialty coffee shop and—"

"We don't sell coffee, just nuts," the other guy said quickly.

"Oh but you do sell coffee," Elwin corrected. "You sell that specially blended pecan and hazelnut coffee, and I'm going to purchase four thousand pounds of it."

"All right who the fuck are you?"

"Why, my name is Elwin Sindorf. Is there a prob—"

Suddenly I heard a great deal of scuffling and Elwin shouted something like "Unhand me!". Well, that was it. I made my move.

Up until that point I had been sitting in the back of Elwin's Mercedes, holding the keys to his trunk, which contained two large containers of gasoline. A box of bullets was in my left pocket and several books of matches were in my right. I was ready.

I hefted the two containers of fuel into the warehouse and across the concrete hallway. I was carrying a total of twenty gallons of gas, and I had to do all I could to keep from dragging the containers. I knew that I didn't have much time. They had surely taken Elwin into a back room for some sort of interrogation, and the floor was left open for a while.

The thing was, I didn't know how soon it would be before they just put a gun to his head and pulled the trigger.

I got into the main holding area of the place, where they kept most all of their goods. Sure enough, all I saw was vat after vat marked "Pecan and Hazelnut Coffee". I quickly opened the first drum of gasoline and began dumping it all over the merchandise until all ten gallons were gone. I took the second drum and spilled its entire contents all over the warehouse floor.

Then I heard someone behind me. I spun around, and beheld a man wearing a tee-shirt that read "***I'm Big Tony***".

He was an immense man, and he didn't even bother to ask any questions. He just came charging at me.

I managed to sidestep him, and as he flew by I gave him a whack on the back of his head for good measure. He didn't even seem to notice it. He just stopped about fifteen feet away from me and turned.

"I figured Sindorf had back-up", he said.

"You're a smart man," I told him. "Why sell nuts?"

"Exactly," he said. "I'm going to sell drugs instead."

"Not the best career move," I advised him. And of course, he said, "Fuck you."

I lifted up a finger and wiggled it. "*Tsk-tsk-tsk.*"

His head was turning red and veins were popping out.

"You're going to die," he said between clenched teeth. "You're going to die and so is your fat friend."

He withdrew a knife. A very long knife.

Times like that make me wish I carried a gun.

He charged me again, and even though I managed to dodge it once more, I felt the cold bite of the knife slice across my shoulder. Tony slid a bit on the gas-covered floor, but he regained balance.

I was slumped to one knee, with a whole lot of blood trickling down my arm. I still had the matches, but I couldn't light them until I was clear of the gas.

"You're going to die slowly," Tony said, and he charged once again.

This time I was ready for him.

Still on one knee, I pivoted around with my good hand and gave him a vicious leg sweep as he came by. It sent him sprawling into a pile of the gasoline-soaked vats, which toppled on him.

Big Tony was stuck.

From one pocket I withdrew the box of bullets, and I began carefully placing them all around the area where Tony was. At this point he began to yell for help, but I had all the time I needed, because everything was ready.

I lit a match.

"Stop! Stop! *Please*! Stop!" he yelled.

"Sorry. But cheer up. With any luck one of these bullets will blast your way and kill you quickly. If not, I'm afraid you're going to burn."

I took the match and lit an entire pack.

"You bastard!" Tony screamed. "*You fucking **bastard**!*"

I smiled at him pleasantly.

"Say goodbye to your nuts, Big Tony."

I threw the flaming pack in.

Immediately one big "whoomph!" engulfed the area. Tony started to really scream and the bullets started going off as I ran across the burning warehouse, trying to find out where they *took* Elwin.

That wasn't too difficult.

I spotted three or four guys running out of a doorway nearby, heading straight for the exit, which was lucky. If Big Tony had been generous enough to make them partners in the whole deal, they might have stuck around.

Elwin was tied to a chair when I got to him. He had a few bruises but he was alive and kicking.

"What took you so long?" he demanded.

I started undoing the knots. "I met Big Tony."

"Was he with Donna?" Elwin asked.

"No," I said, "but I'm sure she'll get wind of this."

Indeed, the whole city eventually "got wind" of it. Even as we were escaping, the garbage-breath smell of those damn, putrid, burning, contaminated coffee nuts was everywhere.

The Search for Endless Variety at a Public Toilet in Brooklyn

The floors here are kissed by a city worker's dirty mop on occasion, but I never get touched. I guess there's just something about my appearance that makes most people cringe, but I don't care. I do my job well; and if a whore rubs a HandiWipe along my face once a week, I'm satisfied.

I live next to D.C. Wambaugh Grounds, a small kiddie park in the heart of Brooklyn, and I hear many things. Amidst the contemporary talk of drug deals and "big scores", the old guys still wander in on occasion and mumble to themselves about the Dodgers. Frank's All-Nite Pizza is across the street, and half the guys I meet smell like cheese and oregano—the other half smell like cheap liquor and dirty bedsheets. But that's all right. It's part of my job.

My name's Friday. I'm a toilet.

My great, great grandfather was Mortimer T. Crapper, a prominent outhouse in the central Ozarks, and he was fond of saying that both the Hatfields and the McCoys made use of his services with equal relish. Of course, he was a little *too* fond of telling that story, and eventually one of the families got wind of it and burned grandpa Mort down. And ever since then the word has been out: toilets talk too much.

The Grimaldi Bros. Outhouse Firm was the first to manufacture a new line of "silent toilets". These were hideous mutants who, in essence, had lobotomies performed on their central poopshafts. They were servile beasts who could neither relate to or comprehend their users. And they were popular. Soon after their initial release, hack plumbers across the nation began performing "special services" on the older, talking toilets until they were all but stifled. These days it's standard assembly line procedure to bend a certain wire inside the tank a certain way so as to silence a newly-made toilet. Everybody does it—except Charlie Austin.

Charlie's been working for one of the big toilet manufacturing firms for over sixteen years, and never once has he silenced a toilet. Sure, he'll stick his hand inside the tank like he's performing the maneuver, but he doesn't actually do it. You see, the word is that a talking toilet saved Charlie's life one time when some local loan sharks had pursued him into a public bathroom. Charlie hid in one of the stalls, and the toilet, named Otis, quickly understood the situation. In a loud, gruff Bronx voice Otis bellowed, "This man's **union** and if you two meatheads know what's good for you you'll screw before Hoffa hears of this!" The rest is history.

It was Charlie who perfected the idea of a "Crapmaster 2000", a monolithic piece of porcelain that was smarter than the average toilet. Charlie planned to put a submersible microprocessor inside the tank, allowing the Crapmaster to calculate your optimum bathroom times and tell you when to go next. Charlie even planned to install a phone line in the rear of the bowl, so your toilet could call you up at work and tell you that it would be a productive time for you to go take a dump. But the company executives shot it down. These were the old men of power; men who still had memories of the older, cruder talking toilets—toilets that laughed at them when they were children for missing the bowl, or plugged themselves up on purpose to get them punished To these men a toilet was just an appliance, not a friend. And even though they might have suspected that Charlie Austin wasn't silencing his toilets, what could they do? After all, there's nothing more economically and physically messy than a toilet recall.

But don't get me wrong. Not all of us talking toilets are blabber-mouths. In fact, most talking toilets just wait until the bathroom is empty and talk to themselves. You see, even though you humans really take us for granted, we still respect you. Nowadays a toilet only speaks up to a person if it has something important or useful to say. And that brings me to my story…

Hector Simms was born on a slosh-stomping day in the cold armpit of winter; a day of taxi cab tire spinouts and multiple fender benders on Madison Avenue. It was a day when the stock brokers had mud on the bottoms of their Armani pants and the street people were trying to shrink and shrivel inside of themselves just to keep warm. I would have traded my two front bolts for a warm, clean rump to hug that day, but instead of the plump princess of my porcelain dreams I saw a ragged, moaning pregnant woman hike up her dress and fall to the dirty tiles in front of me.

"Help me," she gasped, tired and struggling. "Oh please God some-one help me."

There was no one there except her and me, and I made a decision. "Close your eyes," I told her. "I am a severely disabled and disfigured person, and I would come closer to you if I could, but I'm afraid I can't move without my attendant, and he won't be back for a time. But I'll help you."

She complied. I could see her eyes squeeze shut as she winced in pain. Her silky black hair was mopping the floor and beads of sweat rolled down her face.

"How far apart are the contractions?" I asked.

"You think I have a stopwatch?" she screamed. "I don't know how far. Not far. Close. I don't know. It's coming!" Her voice deteriorated into a scream.

"Then breathe deeply," I said. "Whatever your name is, breathe deeply and use your muscles to push that kid out."

"Brilliant," she said between exertions. "Breathe and push. Why did-n't I think of that? What are you a moron?"

"I'm new at this," I said. "And besides, I'm a toi…male. I have no first-hand knowledge of childbirth, but I've heard some street girls talk about doing it and I've been around doctors before. I think we need some warm water or something."

"Oh great," she said. "I'll just walk over to the East River, hack a chunk for myself and throw it in the micro, you stupid fool! You can't move and neither can I!"

I then performed something akin to a blood transfusion. I reversed my pipes and spouted a stream of water at her.

"*Ahhg!*" she yelled. "What are you trying to do, drown me? Aim it at my crotch or something!"

If anyone had walked in at that moment, they would have seen a most unusual sight indeed: a pregnant woman screaming on the floor as a toilet spouted water between her legs like some Ovidius-inspired fountain. Somewhere between a turn-on and a gross-out I guess, but that's life.

So there she was, slithering on a filthy floor, and me shooting water at her. Very Norman Rockwellish, I'm sure. The two of us were more qual-ified to snort uranium than deliver a baby, but when that little moving thing finally came out of her I felt utterly fatherly. I practically had myself convinced that I was involved in the conception when she breathed and moaned in a happy sort of way and said, "It's a boy! Uh, I think it is anyway…*Ehhg!* Look at this damn cord!"

And then she looked around. "Mister? You still with me?"

"Over here," I said.

She paused. "Over where?"

"In the stall," I said.

Another pause. "There's no legs in the stall."

I debated on lying further about being disabled, but something inside me came clean. "I'm the toilet," I said. "See me? I'll flush twice for you."

I heard her chuckle. Then she moved up to the stall door and pushed it open.

"Hi there," I said.

Her eyes bugged out.

She screamed.

She screamed again.

She ran out.

She ran in.

She picked up the baby.

She ran out again.

It would be six years before she would next appear.

*   *   *

The little boy facing me had a very serious look on his face. It was halfway between an "uh-huh" and an "uh-oh", and I thought for sure that he was just another kid who went to the bathroom on his way to the bathroom. But then things changed. He didn't hike down his pants, or reach for the toilet paper, or do anything that people usually do at toilets. He didn't even have a newspaper to read.

Then he spoke.

"You the talking toilet my mother told me about?" he asked, and he seemed embarrassed by his own words. We both paused, then he said, "If you don't talk to me I'm gonna pee all over you then lift up your tank over and poop inside where I'm not a'posed to then stick a cherry bomb inside you and flush."

What could I do?

"Yes," I said. "I'm a talking toilet. But I don't—"

His eyes bugged out.

He screamed.

He screamed again. He ran out of the stall. He ran back into the stall.

"You **really are** a talking toilet!"

"Right you are, kid," I said, "but I don't really remember your—"

"I was born here," he said.

It all came back.

As I said earlier, his name is Hector Simms, and although I could have dealt with him lightly, I did not. I saw this kid staring deep into my bowl, his eyes looking for answers and reasons, and my pipes went soft. The memories flowed into me like so much water, daring to overflow.

"I remember," I said. "That was six years ago."

He nodded. "I need to talk to you, Mr. Toilet."

"My name's Friday," I said. "Have a seat."

He paused. "Should I pull my pants down first?"

"Only if you've got other business than talking," I told him.

He smiled, left his pants on, and hopped up. "What's on your mind?" I asked. He kicked his feet, fidgeting. "What is it, kid?"

He toyed with the toilet paper. "Look," I said, "this is a bathroom, not a playground, and people come here to do serious business." I flushed once emphasis.

He was undaunted. He was also still silent.

"Okay kid, I'm not talking again until you tell me—"

"My mother's been wrapped," he said.

Wrapped?

"Like a Christmas present?" I asked.

"No," he said. "Wrapped. By a man."

I thought. "Santa Claus wrapped her up?"

"No," he said again. "A bad man attacked her in an alley and wrapped her."

The sledgehammer hit. "Raped?" I asked him.

He nodded. "That's what I said, dummy."

"How…is she? Is she all right?"

He shook his head. "He hurt her bad."

"Do the police know?"

"Police don't care," came the reply. He was trying not to cry as he said, "She went to them right away. They gave her a cup of coffee and took some pictures of her boo-boos. Then they told her to go home, but we don't have a home. We live in the alley…where the bad men are."

As with every intelligent creature, there comes a time when certain undeniable emotions are felt. As I listened to Hector's story, I felt a strange new thing rise within me: rage. My only meeting with his mother was six years ago, when she was in need of help, and I gave it without conditions. I saw her in need, yes, but I also saw her in triumph. And when she pulled that little living thing from her own body, and we had both sweated through it, some part of my collective conscience belonged to her. And when I thought of what was done to her the rage filled me, and nothing else in my small world was important anymore.

"Do you know who this man is?" I asked.

"Yes," he said. "I…I…saw him…do it."

"Then you know what he looks like," I said. "Do you know how to get to him; where he lives?"

"Yes," said Hector.

⋆

It was no dream of being relocated to the Ritz Carlton or having a police citation taped to the side of my tank that made me decide to get personally involved. Pomp and circumstance don't matter much to us toilets. I mean, in the whole history of crappers not once have we had a parade, or a state dinner, or a musical benefit in our honor (can you just picture Bob Dylan singing "*Subterranean Shithouse Blues*"? "*Johnny's on the hopper, talkin' to the doctor. I'm on the telephone, gotta use the damn throne…*") The Queen has never summoned us for a command performace and we've certainly never been carried off on a linebacker's shoulders after a Superbowl victory. But we're the supporting cast in life. We, in all of our forms, are the only appliance that everyone in the world uses consistently throughout their lives. And most people generally treat us like the stuff we dispose of. Isn't that a kick in the rim? But that's okay. We don't need any of that fancy stuff. All we need is folks. All we love is folks. And when we can, we try to help them in more than just the usual way.

But I was no Sherlock. I couldn't just puff the answers from out of my pipe. Nor could I rely on some jolly fat doctor to goad my ego. I was more like a drunken solo pianist, piddling at the keys as fast as I could until I puked on myself and hoping that the baffled audience would be stupid enough to call it a brilliant performance.

And, as it turned out, that's exactly what happened.

*

Gray and yet strangely luminous were the clouds of cumulonimbus on that dense, snow-threatening day. I could see them from a small side window near my stall, and I could hear the consistent shuffle of feet outside and smell bits of cheese and crust from Frank's All-Nite Pizza. I felt oddly human that day, and I imagined that I was a young boy, waking up at five o' clock in the morning to experience that first, full day of summer vacation.

Yet it was not summer. The birds were still basking in trees with leaves hundreds of miles away. The parades were still winding their way through more southerly streets. Here the beaches were covered with salted ice and the bathing suits were in mothballs. Here the alleyway muggers kept hard-boiled eggs in their pockets to keep warm while waiting. I saw a gnarled old man smoking a cigar that day, and it was so cold that his breath produced more vapors than his cigar.

It was not unlike a certain cold day six years ago.

She walked in around noon. She looked older. Her face had lots of parallel lines in it and her silky black hair was parted with streaks of silver. For a moment she stood in front of me, facing me, in silence. I saw her head slowly sway to one side, and she forced a small smile to spread.

"Miriam," she said.

"No," I told her. "My name's Friday."

"Friday," she said. "That's an odd name for a toilet."

"Well, Miriam's an even odder name for a toilet," I quipped. "Who told you that my name was Miriam?"

"Nobody," she said. "*My* name is Miriam. I never got the chance to tell you that."

"Oh." I felt stupid. "Miriam's a nice name. So much better for a person than a toilet."

"That's nice to know." She smiled again. "You know my son Hector?"

"We've met," I told her. "He's very clever."

She visibly warmed. "Isn't he? Clever and persistent. He's my best friend. He keeps me company. Believes in me. Isn't that a nice thing to know? He believes in me."

"I believe in you too," I said.

She looked down at the tiles. "Did he tell you?" she asked tentatively.

"Yes."

"And?"

"I…I want to help."

"How?"

"I don't know. I'm working on it."

She came closer to me. "Are you, well, uh, the only one?"

"The only one?" I asked.

"The only one that talks," she said.

"No," I told her. "I know of others."

She was thinking hard now, chewing on her lower lip.

"Can you contact these others, Friday?"

*

Charlie Austin got the call when he was on break, and came to the phone quickly.

"Hello?"

"It's me, Charlie."

"Who?"

"One of the toilets."

There came a pause. Then he whispered very quickly, "You guys know better than to call me at work!"

"It's an emergency, Charlie."

"Emergency, eh? Which one are you? Which lot?"

"1987 lot 12," I said. "My name's Friday."

He repeated my words, softly. Then he said, "I remember you, Friday. You hummed that song to me when I was working on you."

"***Roll Out the Barrels***," I said.

"Yes. That's the one," he answered. "I remember. It was a Friday that day, and you were the last one on my shift, so I named you Friday. I whispered it in your tank. It's nice to hear from you. What can I do?"

"Are you still on the assembly line?" I asked.

"Sometimes," he said. "But I'm really a foreman now. I have some friends though who still do what I used to do. I'm trying to get more people to do it every day, but I have to be cautious."

"What does the foreman do?" I asked.

"Well, he supervises the workers and keeps his eye on the inventory. Why?"

"The inventory," I repeated. "You have a say in where the inventory is shipped?"

He paused. "Yes. I guess I do."

I nodded my lid at Miriam, who was holding the "borrowed" cellular phone for me. She smiled.

"Are you interested in doing a little justice, Charlie?"

But I already knew the answer.

Hell, a guy like Charlie Austin *lives* for justice.

✱

It sounds funny, but it turned out that the rapist's address was 123 4th Street. Hector followed him one time, and when he told me I thought it sounded more like Sesame Street than reality. In fact, I think I said, "Who lives there, Big Bird?" But the boy set his jaw tight and his eyes slowly burned at me. "That's his address," he said. "That's his address."

Then Hector told me his name.

"Guy Grimaldi," the boy said, and I almost flushed.

Yes, it was true. This was a relative of the very same Grimaldi bastards who founded the Grimaldi Bros. Outhouse firm in the nineteenth century, spewing out their accursed Grimaldi silent toilets. It was the stinking Grimaldis who gave rise to the now-standard industrial silent toilets. To this day any talking toilet in the world would give his left pipe for five minutes alone with a Grimaldi. Just five. One minute for verbal abuse, three minutes and fifty seconds of slamming him off the porcelain and smashing the lid in his face, and a quick ten seconds to turbo flush his pulpy remains into the sewer where they belonged.

But I'm not bitter.

There was no need to be bitter.

Why?

Because thirty angry toilets were on their way to Brooklyn.

Afew days later Miriam Simms left a little note for the rapist. It said, simply, "Catch me if you can." It was tied to a little red brick and flung through his window. Miriam was careful to stop at all the local pubs and brag of her deed. Then she waited.

Meanwhile a couple of Charlie's most trusted men were standing by with the shipment of toilets. They were also waiting.

Midnight came. The alleyway where Miriam and Hector slept was considered "safe", as far as alleyways go. A lot of unwed mothers and broken families resided there. They slept in boxes and newspapers and trash bags. Their children played with rusty cans and other people's garbage. And into this desolate world walked a Grimaldi.

He wore a long black coat. A wisp of smoke trailed behind him. His hair was dark and thinning. His face was ugly. He walked up the dreary alley at a deliberate pace, and something gleamed in his right hand.

Knowing where Miriam slept, he picked his way through the sleeping forms amidst the rubble. The paper-on-paper rasp of a car's nearby passing could be heard. Grimaldi stopped. He seemed to sense something, perhaps have a second thought or two. His nose sniffed the air, which was thick with the odor of wet cardboard. He sniffed like a little rat in a cubbyhole. His ferret hands moved quickly to extinguish his cigarette. Then, looking to both sides, he finally moved on.

Miriam and Hector slept in a large refrigerator box whose opening faced a building wall. Grimaldi slowed as he approached this box, and he shifted the object—a knife—in his hand. He circled the box partway, then stood facing the opening, his back to the wall.

It was very dark inside the box.

Grimaldi started to bend down, almost like he was going to use the toilet. He wanted to see her face before he killed her; perhaps rape her one last time.

But neither Miriam nor Hector were in the box.

In fact, no one was in the box.

Then, an instant later, frustrated by the darkness, Grimaldi jumped into the box, his arm flailing wildly at old newspapers and empty bags.

And, from above, the crane moved.

A great platform holding thirty pieces of pissed-off porcelain was being shifted so that it dangled from the roof of the building. Grimaldi, soon realizing the box was empty, swore loudly and began to back up.

Then he paused.

He heard something. It was a strange sound for midnight. It sounded like a crane. Yes, a crane. A moving crane. From above.

His little lizard legs backed up quickly. He was out of the box.

The crane unloaded.

Grimaldi looked up.

Nearly two tons of screaming toilets kamakazied into him.

No more Grimaldi.

*

Charlie took it upon himself to personally repair all of the injured toilets. The newspapers called it an unfortunate construction accident, and they were quick to point out that a few grams of cocaine were found on the victim. The working cattle of the city lifted half an eyebrow to the two paragraph article in the morning, then they took a few sips of bad coffee, glanced sheepishly at their watches, and forgot about it. Guy Grimaldi's name was wiped clean from human memory, and he left nothing behind except a nasty stain on the pavement.

Miriam got a decent-paying job as a secretary, and she was able to get an apartment and send Hector to Catholic school and buy him new clothes and games and books.

As for me? I gave up the public restroom scene and had Charlie install me at 89 Winthrop Court.

That's where Miriam and Hector live.

Xenotraz

Del Greco was surprised to find the gun in his hand, but he wasn't quite shocked. The people at Macrozone Associates had quirky habits, and zapping a laserburst deuce-deuce into his possession fell well within the realm of their abilities. Perhaps they knew that Diablo Canyon, surrounded by magnificent clay rocks, was nicknamed "Red Death".

The blasting noonday sun wiped all life clear from exposed areas of the rock—except for Del Greco. He knew that somewhere in the shade, a killer was resting, maybe waiting. Sentenced to nine years on Xenotraz, this guy knew it was really life. No one could survive nine years on a rock planet with almost no water whose average daily temperature was 118 degrees.

Deep into the canyon, thousands of meters closer to the molten lava core of the planet, Del Greco's temperature gauge told him it was 146 and climbing. His inner-cooled safety suit could withstand a maximum of 200 without compromise, but it was a cheap model, and temperatures over 200 would surely jeopardize it. He cursed the small budget Macrozone allowed him.

Although he was thankful for the gun, a .22 laserburst wasn't really necessary. All he needed was a bow and arrow, or a spear or a knife—anything to puncture the convict's stolen safety suit. That was the plan. No reason to kill a man when you can effectively neutralize him. But it had to be done soon. The deeper they went into Diablo Canyon, the closer the convict got to Xenotraz's turbo-cooled control station, built somewhere below the 200 degree level.

Once at the station, the convict could beam a message to his friends. He'd tell them exactly where to pick him up. Security on Xenotraz is strictly indoors. No one figured a convict would be able to steal a safety suit, locate the control station, and survive long enough for his friends to get there; although that last part still wasn't proven. A safety suit can only go for a day on one charge, and the nearest inhabited planet was six days away.

Del Greco could faintly feel a warmth beneath his feet. He was moving through a crevasse. Towering, jagged walls of red rock were on either side, and every little nook and opening in the stone seemed to hold a pair of eyes. Del Greco increased the receiver's volume on his headset, but he could pick up no signs of enthetic breathing or movement. The convict had to be close, though.

Then, deep below him on a plateau, he saw the heat-blurred silhouette of Xenotraz's control station. The rock walls were still on either side of him, looming up and out of sight. Ahead of him was a straight, steady decline. Guarded by the rock on both sides, looking downward toward the opening to the control station, Del Greco felt like he was in the barrel of a shotgun.

The convict was nowhere to be seen.

Could he have made it to the station? Del Greco paused to consider it. Yes, it was possible. He thought about his perfect record of convict apprehension for a moment, then he broke into a run…

*

The stone orifice was like an oven That damn bounty hunter was good, perhaps the best Elmer Ryku had ever seen. Who would have thought they placed such a high value on one convict's ass? One month ago Ryku never would have guessed it. He was fat, dumb and happy on Xenotraz, having its system figured: sleep in the day, work by night, steal all the water you can from your neighbor. That was it.

But now things were different. Now the famous Armand Del Greco was after him just because he stole a map off a dead Macrozone trooper—a map that told him exactly where Xenotraz's sole control station was located. So now Ryku crouched, hidden. inside his stone cavity, waiting for his hangman...

*

Del Greco continued to run, even though his temperature gauge told him it was 167 degrees. If allowed to escape, this convict could mean the beginning of the end for Del Greco's reputation. No more invitations to exclusive parties, or steamy proposals from beautiful wives, or old-boy corruptions and private funding. Yes, he had become used to the good life.

Xenotraz was six weeks away from his home planet—a place where he could barely afford to keep himself fed as a young man. Memories of scraping along until he had enough to move off that place kept him going sometimes. They kept him taking those extra jobs, stashing away those extra credits.

He moved swiftly through the rock shaft, charging for the control station. His feet shoveled dust behind him and the rock walls blurred to either side. No convict was going to beat Armand Del Greco...

*

Ryku's clothesline was timed perfectly. Stiff and thick, his arm caught Del Greco's neck and immediately flattened him to the dirt, stunned and choking.

Elmer Ryku emerged from his hiding place and stood over the writhing Del Greco. They made eye contact, then Ryku quickly snatched away Del Greco's laserburst .22 and pocketed it with satisfaction. Smiling, Ryku withdrew a crude knife he had fashioned from a rusty scissor blade and signaled Del Greco to turn his headset receiver on channel two.

"This is my lover," Ryku said to Del Greco, his voice hideously amplified through the receiver. "My lover is devoted to me." He caressed the weapon. "She's killed others for me, and now she is jealous of you."

Ryku suddenly lunged downward and Del Greco tried to roll out of his way, but the blade caught him in the shoulder, puncturing his safety suit. The convict stood with the dripping weapon in his hands.

"Not a serious stab, but a mortal wound none the less. You're suit's punctured. I win. *Ciao*."

Ryku trotted toward the control station.

Upon his arrival, he removed his safety suit. Xenotraz 's control station was constantly kept turbo-cooled, for it was often needed on short notice. Inside its layers of ceramic shields, the temperature was always 68 degrees. Ryku walked across plush carpets in his bare feet, ate and drank of the station's emergency reserves, and headed toward the central command room of Xenotraz.

A whole new world of information opened up to him. Satellites, planet charts, range finders, transmitters, and fuel use computers were all available to him. Elmer Ryku had never seen such a display of hardware, and for the first ten minutes he simply had to look at it all.

Then he remembered his family. His wife and two girls were out there somewhere, and they had no idea he had just moved so much closer to them.

Ryku sat at a transmitter. He called for the help that would take six days to arrive...

*

Outside the control station, in the baking heat and choking dust of Diablo Canyon, Armand Del Greco was worse than dead...he was pissed off. No convict was going to escape and leave him alive to see it.

His safety suit was badly damaged. The outside temperature was a scorching 174 degrees, and the temperature inside his suit, which should have been between 61 and 75, climbed to 93. But Del Greco hardly noticed the temperature. He hardly noticed his shoulder wound. All he noticed, or cared to notice, was the control station ahead of him, and he moved toward it.

Deeper into the red canyon he went, with the thin, cloudless, anemic blue sky doing little to protect him from the sun. Moving closer to the molten core of Xenotraz, Del Greco felt his own anger flare and burn within him. But he wasn't angry with himself, or even with Ryku. No. Armand Del Greco was mad at someone else entirely…

*   *   *

Inside the primary corporate tower of Macrozone Associates, C.E.O. Wesly Randel toyed with his beverage. He was thinking about a time in his distant childhood, when he and his best friend used to strap on tin guns and pretend to be bounty hunters. They took turns tracking down each other, and Wesly soon found that he was falling behind in skill. Worst of all though, he couldn't ask his rich father for professional lessons, even though young Wesly desperately wanted to be a bounty hunter. Fate (or more aptly his father) had slated him to become C.E.O of Macrozone, and that was that. Wesly admired how free his best friend Armand was to chase his dream. He admired him and he hated him.

Sending Del Greco after Ryku was a bad move. Wesly should have known better than to give this job to an old friend. Hell, even with a .22 laserburst zapped right into his possession, Del Greco still failed. He allowed Ryku to effectively disable him. Wesly had been listening to the whole thing via Del Greco's intergalactic transmitter, and he felt it was time to cut his losses.

It was time to announce to the board members that Macrozone Assiociates had officialy ceased communication with agent Del Greco, whose name they were urged to forget…

*   *   *

When the "in use" light on his intergalactic transmitter switched off, Del Greco knew they had chalked him up for dead. He would be receiving no more help, which meant those bastards were willing to let Ryku go free. So much for friends.

Del Greco cast off the transmitter and continued his march toward the control station. The temperature inside his suit had risen to 106 degrees, and the outside temperature had now passed 200. Each step seemed to make it hotter inside the suit. Warnings were flashing on many of his instruments and blood from his shoulder wound mixed with the salt in his sweat, but Armand Del Greco was a bounty hunter, and he kept on moving.

Fifteen more minutes and he had reached Xenotraz's control station. The blast of cool air upon entering its outer ceramic doors was delightful, and within minutes Del Greco had his suit off. He tore a large strip of cloth from his undershirt and crudely bandaged his wound. Unlike Ryku, he possessed no map of the enormous control station. He had been sure he would apprehend Ryku before he reached the station.

Del Greco found some water in a nearby storage room, along with traces of Ryku's presence. By now he surely must have contacted help, and a deadly game had begun. If Del Greco found Ryku before his friends arrived, he might still be able to neutralize or kill him. But if Elmer Ryku continued to demonstrate his powers of camouflage, Del Greco would have to poison himself —a fate far better than capture. He had brought a single pill with him for that purpose.

Picking a corridor, Del Greco began to search…

*

The first day at control station was futile. Ryku desperately wanted to contact his family, but he knew he could only afford to make one call; anything more and he would take unnecessary risks. He had already embarrassed Macrozone once. There was no need to start running up their phone bill and telling everyone about it. His family would see him when he got there. Besides, if anything were to go wrong, he would rather they never knew.

Time passed slowly. In Xenotraz's huge control station, Ryku and Del Greco had come to within a few walls of each other on many ocassions, but they never saw one another. As part of his safety measures, Ryku would move to a different part of the station every eight hours, and he never returned to the control room after he made his first call. He carried his rations with him, and disposed all waste out of sight, leaving barely more of a mark on the station than a ghost.

Del Greco was becoming infuriated. It was as if Elmer Ryku had already left. None of the things he had learned as a bounty hunter seemed to help. No trap he set had been sprung, and no matter how long he staked-out the supply room, Ryku never showed up for provisions.

And through this channel of hide-and-seek, the sixth day finally came. Del Greco heard the ship land somewhere above him, and part of him wanted to take the pill.

But part of him didn't.

He knew that Ryku hadn't been near the control room, so he had no way of knowing the exact time the ship would arrive. Like Del Greco, Ryku heard the ship land only moments ago. The bounty hunter dashed for the roof…

*

The sound of the ship's engines was a symphony to Ryku's ears. He dropped what he was doing and ran for the roof. His feet pounded along the corridors and clanged up steel stairways. His wait was over.

Del Greco had been one level above him, and when Ryku turned a corner of the last floor, just before the roof, the bounty hunter extended his one good arm for a savage clothesline to the chest that flattened the unsuspecting convict. Del Greco pounced on him and retrieved his .22 laserburst.

He stood over Ryku. "You lose."

"You think so?" the convict replied. "Let me go and we'll cut a deal. My friends will take you somewhere far away from the reach of Macrozone. You'll have a good life. Don't be a fool. You know they don't care about you."

But Del Greco didn't bother to answer. Instead he pulled the trigger, killing Ryku. Then he pulled it again and again until the .22 laserburst was drained.

And upon hearing commotion from above, Armand Del Greco, the bounty hunter with the perfect record, swallowed his pill.

About the Author

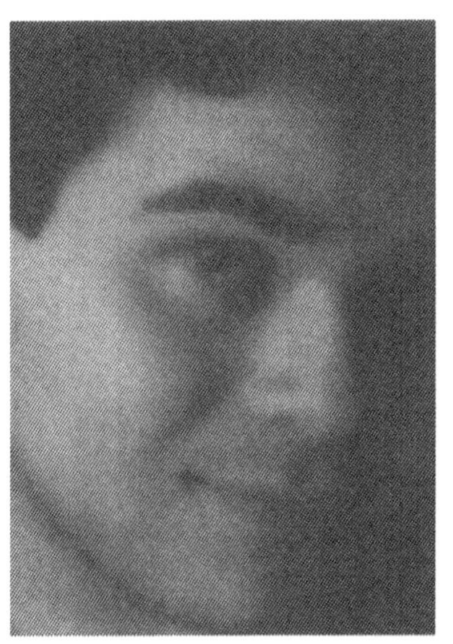

FRANCIS DiPIETRO is blaringly insane. He is an ugly, inconsiderate, raunchy, worthless shitbum of a man who is rather good at Scrabble but placed at a horrible disadvantage at hide and seek due to doomsday body odor. He has no friends except for a gorgeous wife whom some say he created through bio-genetic engineering and witchcraft. Reports of him being a writer are utterly false, as Mr. DiPietro is armless, mindless, and incontinent beyond all previous definition of the word. His current whereabouts are unknown, due to a faulty tracking tag. If you see Mr. DiPietro stumbling through the streets raving to himself, do not approach him, for medical records show that his breath is ten times more toxic than uranium. We don"t know what happens when he is flatulent…nor do we want to.

Author of eight novels and four screenplays. Published over 150 times in small to mid-sized magazines, including Writer's Digest. Readers who enjoy NEST might also enjoy The Orange Phoenix, available at Barnes & Noble online.